The Angel Tapes

By the same author

John Millington Synge: A Biography
A Night in the Catacombs

The Angel Tapes

A BLADE MACKEN MYSTERY

David M. Kiely

St. Martin's Press
New York

A THOMAS DUNNE BOOK.
An imprint of St. Martin's Press.

THE ANGEL TAPES. Copyright © 1997 by David M. Kiely.
All rights reserved. Printed in the United States of America. No part of this book may be used or reproduced in
any manner whatsoever without written permission except in the case of brief quotations embodied in critical
articles or reviews. For information, address St. Martin's
Press, 175 Fifth Avenue, New York, N.Y. 10010.

Library of Congress Cataloging-in-Publication Data

Kiely, David M.
    The angel tapes : a Blade Macken mystery /
David M. Kiely.—1st ed.
      p.   cm.
    "A Thomas Dunne book."
    ISBN 0-312-16772-5
    I. Title.
PR6061.I3297A8   1997
823'.914—dc21   97-16902
                                    CIP

First Edition: November 1997

10 9 8 7 6 5 4 3 2 1

To the men and women of the Garda Síochána,
the Guardians of the Peace

The author gratefully acknowledges the following,
whose kindness, assistance, and inspiration
made this book possible:
Paschal Anders, Neal Bascomb,
John Conlon, William Dillon, Derek Guildea,
Michael Kelleher, Vere Lenox-Conyngham,
Freeman and Geraldine Lynn, Paula Kane,
Mary McCarthy, Monika Riethmüller,
Rachel Serpico, and Jonathan Williams.

The Angel Tapes

One

The searing flash took the beggar-woman by surprise. She shut her eyes and clutched her baby hard to her breast. Then the shock wave rolled.

The bomb went off on O'Connell Street, a major thoroughfare at the heart of Dublin city. The street is broad enough to accommodate three lanes of traffic on either side and a very wide traffic island in the middle. Some of its buildings date from the eighteenth century. They are stately and imposing—when you can see them properly, when their neoclassic façades aren't hidden behind the bright lights and primary-colored signboards of fast-food outlets and movie theaters.

At eight in the morning on Friday, July 3, 1998, there was already much activity on the traffic island. A street cleaner was fishing empty beer cans and other jetsam out of the filthy waters of the Anna Livia Fountain; the early morning drunks had assembled around the reclining bronze nude, and they toasted one another and life in general with the cans that would shortly replace those dredged out by the cleaner.

Gatherings of sharply dressed commuters waited at the curb for the lights to change. The waiting was long, for this is not a pedestrian-friendly city. The traffic was building up; even now the haze of pollution, mingled with the heat haze of this sultry morning, was blurring the outlines of the statue of Daniel O'Connell at the southern end of the street.

The panhandlers were out in great numbers, too, knowing that Dublin's tourists like to make an early start. Most of those asking for handouts were women and children; if you thought to detect a family resemblance between the beggars and the drunks at the fountain, then you would not have been mistaken.

I

The beggars were of nomadic stock—Ireland's traveling people. Their grubby garments were carefully chosen to maximize the wearers' chances of separating both commuters and tourists from their small change. One of the beggar-women had an infant at her breast, swathed in a thick, plaid shawl, though the morning temperature had reached the high seventies by eight o'clock. She squatted on the paving stones of the traffic island, with her back to the fountain, facing south.

And so she'd a clear view of the explosion.

Eyewitnesses who were closer to the blast said later that it was as though the earth had suddenly opened, as though all hell had—"quite literally"—broken loose. Others described the detonation in the language of the cinema: they spoke of glass and other flying objects sailing past in slow motion; of human beings lifted off their feet as if by an invisible hand, and set down again—battered, bloodied, and incomplete— many yards distant. Of a roar like Krakatoa.

The comparison with an angry volcano was a valid one. The asphalted roadway erupted directly beneath a black taxi-cab traveling in the middle traffic lane. The vehicle disintegrated. The cabdriver's death took place in the time needed for flesh and bone and blood to atomize.

The other deaths—four in all—took a little longer.

But not much.

Blade Macken woke as his buzzer sounded a third time, more insistent than before. Whoever was at the front door was holding his finger on the button.

He sat up in bed—and wished he hadn't. Somebody was crushing his head in a vise; he could feel his brain being forced out through the sockets of his eyes. He could hardly breathe; his torturers appeared to have sealed off the route to his windpipe with a Velcro strip. There wasn't so much as a lungful of oxygen in the room; he'd left the windows shut and the curtains open. The light was blinding; even when he closed his eyes, it still burned pinkly through the lids.

"Oh shit, oh Christ, oh Jesus," Blade moaned, as the buzzer

buzzed once more. He shut his eyes again and cupped his palms in front of them. He didn't know what time it was, what day it was. He barely knew *who* he was. Hangovers, he reflected, used not to be like this.

Macken sat on the edge of the bed, and that made things worse. His vision grew faulty, his head pounded, his stomach started to heave. He was still wearing all his clothes, he saw now. Even his shoes. He staggered from the bed, stumbled to the window that faced the backyard, raised it to let in some air. Then he went to the other one, the one that looked out on the street, that allowed in the morning sunlight, and raised that as well. The draft caused the net curtains to flutter and Blade to shiver, though the air was warm and moist.

The buzzer sounded again.

"Oh, my fuck," he said with feeling, left the bedroom, shutting the door behind him, and went to the front door of the apartment. The judas gave him a fisheye-lens view of the back of a woman's head. There was dark brown hair, worn shoulder-length. Blade opened the door.

"God, you look terrible," Orla Sweetman said.

She didn't wait to be invited in but walked on past him. She was almost as tall as Macken, five feet and nine inches in her low-heeled shoes. He hadn't chosen her as his assistant for her striking looks, though that had been whispered throughout the department at the time of her appointment. She'd simply been the best damn detective sergeant the Special Branch could field.

"Did you stay on or what?" she asked.

"Stay on . . . stay on where?" What was she was talking about?

Sweetman didn't reply because her cellular phone, switched to silent mode, began to pulsate.

Macken waited awkwardly in his tiny hallway, smoothing his tousled hair, sick as a dog, throat dry as the Sahara, as she spoke quietly into the instrument, waited, listened, spoke again, broke the connection. Then she frowned and went to the place where Blade's house phone lay in disarray, under the little table in the hall. He heard faintly the busy signal before she replaced the receiver and returned the unit to its rightful place. He saw that his mother's painting, the one she'd done all those years ago for his twenty-first birthday, was hanging askew above the table—and wondered about that.

"God, I've only been trying to reach you for the past hour," Sweetman said. "They want us in O'Connell Street"—she looked at her watch—"in ten minutes."

He shook his head in incomprehension; a bad mistake—he swore he felt something drift loose.

"Duffy and the deputy commissioner. Ten minutes. Do you think we can make that—sir?"

He glanced at his own watch. It was a little before nine; he wasn't scheduled for duty until eleven today—that much he *could* remember.

Sweetman saw his troubled look.

"The bomb," she said.

"Bomb?"

"The car bomb." Something resembling pity crossed her face. "You really haven't heard, have you, sir?"

Blade hated it when she called him "sir" when there was no one else present. He knew she did it for the same reason others prefaced a scathing remark with the words, "With all due respect . . . " He knew very well that Detective Sergeant Sweetman's "sir" meant: "Macken, you're a slob, and if I outranked you or if I was a detective superintendent, too, I'd be only too pleased to tell you just what a clapped-out, drink-sodden slob I think you are." Sweetman's "sir" made him feel guilty, as if in some way he'd betrayed her trust, broken a promise he'd never made.

"Somebody's after putting a bomb under a taxi in O'Connell Street."

"Jesus."

"There's feck all left of the taxi—or the driver. We think there may be at least five people dead; God knows how many injured. The morning rush hour, Blade—in O'Connell Street.

4

Feeney says there were arms and legs and bits of bodies everywhere. Can you imagine?"

Macken could—all too clearly, and he wished then that he didn't have such a vivid imagination. His stomach heaved again; he tasted sour whiskey in his mouth and felt his face go white. Sweetman was at the door of the bathroom before him, had the handle turned as he came charging through. Tactfully, she shut the door as he headed for the toilet.

When he was finished, he brushed his teeth with a liberal worm of toothpaste and it tasted much sweeter than usual, in contrast with the acid bitterness of the bile that was still in his mouth. He swallowed cold water, threw some more in his face, and raised his eyes to the mirror.

Blade saw a stranger. Agreed, the retching had caused his eyes to turn even redder than they had been. Nevertheless, the face in the mirror belonged to a man fourteen or fifteen years his senior, someone pushing sixty. He was horrified by that image because it bore no relation to the one he carried within him. He was accustomed to thinking of himself as a young man—late twenties, say. A young man who was aging at a rate far slower than that which governed the rest of the human race. Small wonder, then, that he was always surprised to see himself in photographs; he'd to do a double take on recognizing himself, so at odds with reality was his self-image.

Did mirrors lie? He thought they did. For some reason the man in his shaving mirror never seemed to have so much gray at the temples; nor were his cheeks and chin so flabby as photographs claimed they were; the skin of the man in the shaving mirror possessed far fewer wrinkles about the eyes and mouth. And as for those dangerous-looking liver spots: surely they were caused by flaws in the photographic emulsion?

Blade Macken had begun thinking more and more about mortality ever since he'd turned forty-four. *Forty-four.* It was no longer middle age; thirty-five was middle age, halfway to three score years and ten. Maybe, just maybe, he would make seventy, if he cut down on his drinking and gave his throat a rest from the Hamlets. But ninety? No bloody way. His grandmother-in-law was all of ninety-two, and looked it. She also sounded it, smelled it, behaved it, and that was one road Blade didn't want to travel down.

He was aware that Orla Sweetman was pounding on the bathroom door.

"Are you dead or what?"

He wished to fuck she didn't have to be so damn noisy about it. Why is it, he wondered, that the sober always take a sadistic pleasure in exploiting the vulnerability of those suffering from a hangover? A perverse strain of Puritanism, that's what it was.

"Be right with you," he called out.

He squirted some aerosol lather on his cheeks and ran the razor over them. Only when he'd completed the cursory shave did he notice the seven digits scrawled in ballpoint on his left palm. A phone number, now practically illegible. Blade couldn't remember having written it down, or who it belonged to. He shrugged, and scrubbed his palm clean. It was probably not important.

Sweetman was sitting on the sofa in the tiny living room. She'd made two mugs of instant coffee and he accepted one gratefully. It was strong; the first mouthful caused him to shiver. He noticed she'd removed the battery from his cellular phone, lying on the table. She caught his glance.

"No wonder I couldn't raise you," she said in a tone you might use to reprove a child. "Do you have a spare?"

He gestured vaguely in the direction of his drinks cabinet. Sweetman went to it and rummaged among the whiskey, gin, vodka, and wine bottles, many depleted. Eventually she found the recharger and slotted the fresh battery into the phone. In the meantime Macken had retrieved his jacket from behind the sofa; he took the phone from her and thrust it in his pocket.

There was a slim, yellow cigar pack on the coffee table. Hamlet, the Mild Cigar. Blade picked it up, saw it was empty, and flung it in the fireplace in disgust. It joined more of its fellows lying crumpled and discarded amid the ash, cigar ends, orange peel, and miscellaneous debris that were already encroaching on the hearth. Sweetman did her best not to look. Blade looked at his watch and switched on the radio. He'd missed the main news item.

"*—in Downing Street, dismissed allegations made yesterday by the Liberal Democrats that no trace of explosives had been found on board the hijacked plane. He questioned whether the—*"

Macken had silenced the radio.

"What is it about the summer?" he asked. "Everybody goes mad. Imagine, Sweetman: being stuck on that runway for three days in this heat. Desperate altogether."

"We'd better be off," she said. "We can pick up a sandwich or something later."

She drove with all the car windows open. They traveled north from Ranelagh, crossed the canal that shimmered with a heat haze, and headed toward St. Patrick's Cathedral. Macken was grateful to be in the passenger seat because the sun on Sweetman's side was already strong and hot. Following on the heels of a cold, late spring, the July of 1998 was unexpectedly hot and humid; Blade couldn't remember a warmer summer. It altered Dublin in subtle ways, made it somehow more cosmopolitan, more foreign.

Now it must be said that Blade Macken didn't know many cities apart from this one. He'd been in London three times, once in New York, a few times in Stuttgart, and once in Barcelona. (He'd also visited Jerusalem, when assigned to the UN peacekeeping force in southern Lebanon. But that wasn't so much a visit; more a pilgrimage—when he still believed.)

He didn't know many cities. Yet, when they'd descended the steep hill that ran from ancient Christchurch Cathedral down to the river Liffey, and waited at the lights to allow the heavy traffic to thunder westward, he suddenly remembered a trivial thing. All the cities he'd known had *smelled* the same. Not everywhere, just in certain areas, the places that have always known heavy industry. If he shut his eyes, he could be in any of the cities he'd visited, and it was because of certain odors.

They were the odors you associate with diesel exhaust fumes, carbide, and old metal left to dry and disintegrate in the sun. There was nothing human about these smells; they were the smells of a technology that marched almost without human intervention, thumbing its nose at mankind.

The funny thing was, he liked them.

They crossed the Liffey, turned right, and headed into the sun, up along the quays toward the place where O'Connell Street began. Sweetman drove fast—she always did—but this time Macken made no comment; the rush of air from all sides was doing wonders for his head. He didn't flinch when she drove at speed through a gap between two double-decker buses, a maneuver that Blade would barely have attempted on a motorcycle. He sat back and considered the previous night.

His recollections were vague. *Vague?* Who was he codding? Half the bloody night was missing; whole chunks had been erased from his memory. Sweetman had asked if he'd "stayed on." For the life of him he couldn't remember where he'd been after, say, eleven o'clock. Evidently he *had* stayed on. He wondered about consciousness; if his mind was a blank now, as far as those missing hours were concerned, had it been blank *during* those hours? Had he done things, said things, while in a state of unconsciousness? Christ, it was a frightening thought and Blade dismissed it quickly. On days like this, he was beset by guilt, and by disgust with the man he'd become.

Sweetman had said something.

"Sorry?"

"I said: The cover story is that it was an accident. A gas main."

"I don't understand." He really didn't.

She turned to look at him, but had to swerve then to avoid colliding with a taxicab.

"Well, they had to make *some*thing up, with the state visit just around the corner."

"State visit?"

"Ah, Blade, I swear to God I'd do something about that

drinking if I was you. Your mind's gone. Sure it's *only* the president of the United States who's paying us a little visit on the fourteenth."

A cordon had been thrown across the roadway on either side of the devastation, between the O'Connell Monument and Abbey Street. Hundreds of curious onlookers lined the sidewalk, held in check by uniformed police officers and lengths of taut, plastic tape that read GARDA—NO ENTRY. Sweetman showed her ID and they were allowed to pass.

The crater was smaller than Blade had expected, yet the force of the explosion had utterly demolished the taxicab; twisted pieces of metal lay scattered over a wide area. What was left of the engine and gearbox had come to rest in a blackened heap on the traffic island, close under the statue of William Smith O'Brien, the nineteenth-century freedom fighter. One of his stone legs had been sheared from the knee down by the blast. The island's beeches were leafless and scorched, like trees on a battlefield. Other vehicles had taken some of the explosion; they stood abandoned at crazy angles in the roadway and on the traffic island, amid shards of windshield glass, many of them bloodied. Blade had seen bomb damage before and wasn't surprised that every store window within a wide radius had been shattered. The great arched doorway of a branch office of the Bank of Ireland had suffered most; nothing remained of its glass panes.

A camera crew from RTÉ television was filming from a helicopter that made crisscross passes above the rooftops. Newspaper reporters jostled for position behind the tape, battling for the attention of every patrolman who came within shouting distance. The air crackled with two-way radio broadcasts; garda squad cars with flashing lights came and went in quick succession, as if following choreographed instructions.

Yet it wasn't the police vehicles that drew Blade's attention, but five small trucks belonging to Bord Gáis, the gas utility company. They formed a semicircle around the bomb site, effectively blocking the onlookers' view of the activity. An inner cordon of red-and-white plastic traffic cones marked the lip of the crater; they were stenciled with the curious words DUB GAS. A dozen men in hard hats and Bord Gáis overalls were assessing the destruction; some communicated by walkie-talkie; others made notes on clipboards. To the bystander, all this might have appeared perfectly normal: the explosion had, for all intents and purposes, been caused by a leaking gas main. But Blade had recognized two of the men in hard hats. He'd last seen them near Tyre in Lebanon, wearing the blue beret of the United Nations. They were soldiers.

"Macken," a voice behind him called out, "where the Jayziz have you been? We've only been trying to reach you for over an hour, y'know."

Blade rounded on the man with whom he shared both the running of the department and an intense, mutual dislike.

"Asleep. What's it to you, Nolan, *where* I've been? And who's this 'we' when they're at home?"

Detective Superintendent Charles Nolan was unfazed.

"Duffy, the DC, everybody. Jayziz, Macken, you look like shit, y'know. What's the—"

But Blade and Orla Sweetman were already moving away toward a knot of men in business suits and a gray-haired police officer with braid on his uniform. Assistant Commissioner Duffy acknowledged them with a nod.

"Glad you could make it, Macken," he said without a trace of sarcasm. "Look, I'm putting you in charge of this investigation. By rights we should have Nolan on it, too, but it's—"

"Now hold on a minute, sir!" Nolan was not a happy man. "This is very high-handed altogether. I mean, who was doing all the donkey work this morning while Macken here was catching up on his bleeding beauty sleep? *And* it's me day off as well, y'know."

"I know, Charlie," Duffy said. "And I appreciate it, believe me. But you have your hands full with that Delahunt business. If you must know, I've had her bloody husband breathing down my neck again. He's out to make trouble, Charlie, and he can do it, too. To the both of us."

Nolan, sullen, looked up quickly.

"Leave this to Blade, Charlie. I'm relying on you to sort out what exactly went wrong in Delahunt's house. God, you'd think it was *our* fault, the way he carried on about his bloody alarms. Get your friend Roche in, if you want; but let's have some results soon or there'll be hell to pay."

Nolan nodded, cowed; he mumbled something and left.

Duffy looked relieved and turned to Macken. "I believe you know Captain Fitzpatrick."

A tall man wearing gas-utility overalls extended a hand. "How are you, Blade?"

"Never better, Tom," Macken lied. "I thought you were still in the Middle East."

"They pulled us out. Not before time either. I got transferred to the Engineering Corps in May."

Blade gestured toward the hard hats. "Are those your lads?"

"They are. But you'd never think it now, would you?"

"Tell them not to work too hard, or they'll blow their cover."

Captain Fitzpatrick smiled briefly, then was serious once more. He turned to the uniformed Guard.

"Perhaps the commissioner can explain the situation better than me."

"We actually know very little at this stage, Blade," Duffy said. "As you can see, we're attempting to keep the lid on things for the time being. I had the press office put out a statement a little while ago, blaming it on a gas leak."

"So I heard. But will the press fall for that one, sir?"

"I hope so, I hope so. But I don't see why they shouldn't. It wouldn't be the first time something like that has happened. I've known half a block of flats to be wrecked by some absentminded housewife with a lighted match. Gas is volatile stuff."

"I hope you're right, sir. Has anybody claimed responsibility for the bomb?"

"Not yet, no."

"Who do we think it is? The UVF? The UFF?"

The assistant commissioner shook his head grimly.

"It *could* be loyalist paramilitaries—and we're not ruling that out. It's just that this isn't the way they usually work." He pushed his peaked cap a fraction higher. "To be honest, it's not the way *anybody* usually works; that's the devilish part of it."

"I don't follow you, sir," Blade said.

"No. How could you? The fact of the matter is, Macken, it wasn't a car bomb."

Blade looked blank.

"Somebody," Duffy said, "planted a bomb under the surface of the street."

"How in Christ's name did they manage *that?*"

"That's what we're trying to find out, Blade," Fitzpatrick said. "But there's no doubt that it was a subterranean explosion. I'm telling you, if it'd been a surface blast, then half of these buildings would have been demolished. We're talking about a *very* big bomb here. I'd say it was about six or seven pounds of Semtex. Have a look at this."

He led the way to the pit in the road and Blade peered over the rim. The bomb had gouged out a hole at least fifteen feet deep. There was pulverized stone, shattered ancient bricks, lengths of fused metal, bent and twisted utility pipes. He took Fitzpatrick's point; had the bomb exploded above ground, the destruction would have been enormous. Seven pounds of Semtex could have taken out an entire city block.

Macken rubbed his chin. "Okay," he said, "let's say you're right and that somebody managed to plant a bomb down there. When could they have done that? They'd have had to break the street open." He looked about him at the broad thoroughfare: the traffic, the hundreds of Dubliners on foot, whose numbers, at this time of year, are swelled by a million tourists. "We're talking about the main street of Dublin!"

"If it wasn't broken open already," Sweetman said.

Duffy threw her a sharp look. "That's exactly the theory we're working on, Miss . . . er . . . ?"

"Sweetman, sir. Detective Sergeant Sweetman of the Special Detective Unit."

"Sweetman . . . Sweetman. Weren't you in Mapping at one stage?"

"I got promoted, sir. I'm assisting Superintendent Macken now, sir."

"I see. Well done, well done." He turned to Blade. "We thought at first they might've planted it in a culvert—like they did in 1971—but there wasn't any culvert there to begin with. We checked."

"So you're saying the bomb was planted when roadworks were being carried out?" Blade asked.

Fitzpatrick nodded.

"Now *you* know as well as I do that you can't dig a hole in O'Connell Street any old time you feel like it; there are all sorts of procedures to go through. You have to get permission from Dublin Corporation for a start. So we reckon the bombers may have slipped the device under the street the last time somebody carried out repairs."

"And when would that have been?"

"You won't believe this, Blade." Captain Fitzpatrick looked sheepish.

"Well?"

The soldier licked his lips. "Your people have checked and double-checked. They've spoken to everybody: the electricity board, the gas company, the phone company, Road Maintenance—everybody."

"And . . . ?"

"Telecom Éireann were the last to go near it, Blade. Five years ago, almost to the day."

Two

"If it's not the perfect crime," Blade declared, "then it comes pretty close. If it'd been a car bomb, we might have some chance of tracing who planted it. You know as well as I do that it's pretty hard to cover your tracks these days when you're handling high explosives."

He paused and sipped water from a tumbler; the thirst was getting to him.

"But this thing," he continued, "was planned so far in advance that the trail must be ice-cold by now. The bomber, or bombers—and I prefer to think of it as the work of a group; I can't see how one man could have carried it off—the bombers don't know who the victim is going to be. I mean, five years ago they could've had no idea. They plant a massive device under a section of roadway that'll be used by a visiting statesman eleven days from now—"

"Just a minute, Detective Superintendent," Duffy said. "Aren't we jumping to conclusions here? There's no evidence so far that the two are connected."

Blade leaned against the wall of the conference hall on the fourth floor of Block One at Harcourt Square, and shoved his fists deep in his trouser pockets. He hated when Duffy did this. Blade was fond of the assistant commissioner—he wouldn't be heading up the Special Detective Unit if it hadn't been for Duffy—but the man could not delegate responsibility. He put you in charge of an investigation, yet shoved his oar in at every turn; he couldn't let go. This was the fourth time he'd interrupted in as many minutes.

Blade sighed and looked around the big room. They'd called in every available Special Branch officer. Top priority; there were at least one hundred twenty people present.

"No sir, there's no evidence whatsoever," Macken said

wearily but patiently. "But I think we should assume that they *are* connected."

"Hmm. If that's the case, then we'll have to tell the Americans what we know."

Blade smiled thinly. "If they don't already know."

"What do you mean?"

"With all due respect, sir,"—he saw Sweetman look up and grin—"that business about the gas main might fool the ordinary joe in the street, but I can't see the White House falling for it. In fact, I'd be willing to bet that they know as much—if not more—about it than we do. Christ, the CIA are probably using one of their spy satellites right now to eavesdrop on this very conference."

"Don't be ridiculous."

"I'm serious, sir. I bet you anything the CIA will have every operative in the country swarming over O'Connell Street by now."

"The CIA? In *Ireland?*"

"Jesus, sir, you make us sound like the arsehole of nowhere. I'm bloody sure the CIA are here—ever since they found out about the Libyans and the IRA. Colonel Gadhafi and his crowd are still public enemy number one as far as the CIA are concerned, so I'd imagine any friends of theirs are very closely monitored. Besides, they'll be arriving in droves in time for the fourteenth."

Just then a telephone rang. It was answered by a young officer in uniform. She signaled for Duffy's attention.

"Sir, there's a Lawrence Redfern calling from the American embassy. He refuses to speak to anybody except the assistant commissioner."

Macken looked at Duffy, spread his palms wide, and shrugged in a gesture that spoke more loudly than words.

"Have it transferred to my office," Duffy told the young woman. "Macken, you come with me. I suppose you'd better come, too, Sweetman."

And Blade adjourned the conference.

Duffy had put the phone in hands-free mode for the benefit of the others. The voice that came from the speaker was distorted and uneven and Macken guessed that the caller was using a similar facility.

"Good afternoon, Commissioner. My name is Redfern." The American sounded confident and assured, a man used to both giving and taking orders.

"Yes, Mr. Redfern. What can I do for you?"

"I have the ambassador here with me, sir. He expresses his deepest concern regarding this morning's attack."

"And which *attack* might that be, Mr. Redfern?"

"The bomb, sir."

Duffy looked sharply at Blade.

"Bomb, Mr. Redfern?"

"Please, Commissioner, let's not beat around the bush here. The ambassador has already alerted the president and I can assure you that the White House is taking the matter extremely seriously."

"I see. Kindly put the ambassador on, Mr. Redfern."

"Yes, sir."

The American's voice was replaced by an older one: slow, with measured, New England vowels.

"Commissioner, may I apologize first for Mr. Redfern's overzealousness. The only justification is that we are all very much on edge here, as I'm sure you'll appreciate. The president is worried; I am worried."

"I understand, Your Excellency."

"Call me Seaborg. I've already spoken with the minister for foreign affairs. He recommended that I contact you directly. Now, was it the IRA?"

"I very much doubt it, Mr. Seaborg. It was more likely a loyalist attack."

"And I understand that nobody has claimed responsibility so far?"

Blade used a vibrating index finger to execute a wide

parabola above his head, while cupping the other hand behind his ear. The mime was of a spy satellite. Duffy glared.

"Not as yet," he told the ambassador. "I take it your people will be canceling the state visit?"

"We're working on it, Mr. Duffy. I'm unable to give you a yes or no answer at this time. On the one hand, Washington considers it imperative that the visit goes ahead. The president cannot be seen to be swayed by terrorist intimidation at this time."

"Of course not, no," Duffy said. He'd followed closely the events that had taken place in the Middle East in recent weeks and was well aware of the tough stance that the U.S. president had adopted toward the warring factions. This was no time for showing the white flag to terrorists—not in Dublin, not at the very start of his six-nations tour.

"On the other hand," the ambassador added, "it would be foolhardy to expose the president to clear and present danger."

"Quite so, Mr. Seaborg."

"I'm glad we understand each other, sir. Now, I'd like to propose the following. Because time is of the essence, I feel that we should be working together as closely as possible on this. There must be no more bombs, Mr. Duffy! Whoever is behind this has got to be stopped. That's why I want to place Mr. Redfern and his associates at your disposal. It's our belief that a team effort here will greatly enhance our chances of apprehending these people before they can strike again."

"I couldn't agree more, Mr. Seaborg. In fact, I have my chief investigator, Detective Superintendent Macken, here at this very moment, and he shares my opinion."

Blade opened his mouth to speak, but Duffy stilled him with an impatient gesture.

"Good, good," the ambassador said. "Might I suggest a meeting sometime today between your team and ours? Four o'clock, perhaps, here at the embassy?"

"I'm sure that can be arranged."

"Wonderful. Thank you, Commissioner."

"My pleasure, Mr. Seaborg." He hung up.

Duffy prided himself on his good manners; he never smoked in company without first deferring to any nonsmokers present. But now he was seething. Ignoring Sweetman, he lit a cigarette and flung the lighter on his desk.

"Bloody Americans," he said darkly. "I might have known they'd want to interfere. But don't you take any shagging nonsense from them, Blade, you hear me? They've no business at all sticking their noses in. I won't have it! If there's the slightest interference, you're to refer them back to me. Understood?"

"Yes, sir."

"It's foreign affairs," Duffy went on. "They're as thick as thieves with the embassy crowd. That's where our taxes go, Blade: on fucking champagne parties and junkets for that lot of wasters. Sorry about the language, Sweetman."

He drew sharply on his cigarette and blew the smoke at the ceiling.

"They have me over a fucking barrel, Blade," he fumed, the words of apology blithely forgotten. "I have it from all sides." He stabbed a finger. "Don't you ever *think* of going for this job, you hear me? You don't know what you'd be letting yourself in for. I'm telling you, it'd put bloody years on you."

The phone rang again. Duffy stabbed the hands-free button. It was one of the garda telephone operators.

"Sir, I have somebody on line six who claims he's the bomber."

Duffy sighed. "That's number twenty-seven so far, Mary. Put him through to someone at SDU and stop wasting my time, there's a good girl."

Macken saw Sweetman cringe.

"Emm, I think you ought to take this one, sir," the operator said.

"What!"

"Emm, it's a bit hard to explain, sir. It's kind of . . . kind of like—"

"Oh, for God's sake, girl! Put it through to me, then."

There was a loud click. Blade felt the hairs on the back of

his neck rise as an unearthly voice issued from the phone. It was a deep, bass rumble—so deep that the small speaker vibrated with every syllable. The voice was almost devoid of inflection. It sounded, Blade decided, not unlike those early computer-generated voices—or even that of Darth Vader. Blade was convinced that it was a recording. But when the assistant commissioner asked his first question, the caller identified himself without hesitation.

"YOU MAY CALL ME ANGEL."

Three

"Are you sure now you're playing it at the right speed?" Nolan asked.

Blade hit the PAUSE button.

"Yes," he answered with unconcealed irritation.

"It sounds so . . . deep, and echoey, y'know. Like he's lying at the bottom of a well."

"That's the whole bleeding point, Nolan. He wants to make sure he's totally unrecognizable. Now can we hear the rest of it?"

Blade pressed the PAUSE button and the tape spun further.

Sixteen men and women were crowded into Macken's tiny office, some spilling out into the corridor. They listened raptly as the mechanical voice—now it really *was* a recording—continued its eerie speech.

"THIS MORNING'S EXPLOSION," the man calling himself Angel said, "WAS A DEMONSTRATION OF WHAT I CAN DO IF AND WHEN I WANT TO. THERE ARE MORE BOMBS—I'M NOT SAYING HOW MANY. NOW, I DON'T HAVE TO REMIND YOU WHO'S ARRIVING ON THE FOURTEENTH, SO I HOPE WE CAN COME TO SOME ARRANGEMENT BEFORE THEN. I MEAN, HOW WOULD IT LOOK IF DUBLIN WAS TO TURN INTO ANOTHER DALLAS? OH, AND DON'T MISUNDERSTAND ME; I LIKE THE MAN. IT'S NOTHING PERSONAL."

"*These other bombs,*" Blade's voice was heard to say: "*are they planted the same way? Under the street?*"

"IS THAT BLADE MACKEN?"

A long pause. "*It is. How did you know my name?*"

The man called Angel chuckled. The sound was that of a jackhammer heard in the distance.

"OH, I KNOW A LOT ABOUT YOU, DETECTIVE SUPERINTENDENT MACKEN."

Nolan looked at Blade bemusedly, but said nothing.

"NOW, YIZ WANTED TO KNOW WHERE THE OTHER BOMBS ARE. YES, THEY'RE ALL BURIED UNDERGROUND. AND I'M NOT TELLING YIZ WHICH STREETS THEY'RE UNDER, EITHER. YOOZE'LL HAVE TO WORK THAT OUT FOR YOURSELVES."

"*What is it you want?*" Duffy asked.

"WHAT DO I WANT? MONEY, OF COURSE. WHAT ELSE WOULD I WANT?"

"*Then you're not political?*"

"NO."

"*How much money are we talking about?*"

"TWENTY-FIVE MILLION DOLLARS—IN EXCHANGE FOR THE PRESIDENT'S LIFE. I THINK THAT'S A BARGAIN, DON'T YOU? SURE HIS INAUGURATION ALONE COST MORE THAN THAT."

There was a pause.

"*American dollars?*"

"YES."

"*That's about fifteen million pounds.*"

"I DON'T GIVE A FIDDLER'S FUCK ABOUT THE EXCHANGE RATE, DUFFY! WHEN I SAY I WANT AMERICAN DOLLARS, I MEAN I WANT AMERICAN DOLLARS. ARE YE TAKING THIS DOWN?"

"*We record all incoming calls.*"

"YEAH, OF COURSE YIZ DO; COMPANY POLICY. OH, AND YOU NEEDN'T BOTHER TRYING TO TRACE THIS ONE, DUFFY. I'M CALLING ON A MOBILE, SO YOU CAN'T. BUT YOU'LL TRY, ALL THE SAME, WON'T YOU? AND WASTE MORE OF THE TAXPAYERS' MONEY. WELL, IF IT KEEPS YIZ OFF THE STREETS AND OUT OF MISCHIEF . . . ARE YOU READY?"

"*I'm ready.*"

"TWENTY MILLION DOLLARS IN USED ONE HUNDRED-DOLLAR BILLS; FOUR MILLION IN USED FIFTIES, AND ONE MILLION IN USED TENS."

There was another pause; then:

"*Who do you think is going to pay this? I mean, who is it you're threatening? Us? The Americans?*"

"AMN'T I ONLY JUST AFTER TELLING YOU, DUFFY? I'VE NOTHING AGAINST THE BLOODY AMERICANS—OR THEIR PRESIDENT. I DON'T GIVE A SHIT WHO PAYS THE MONEY AS LONG AS IT'S PAID.

BUT I'LL TELL YOU THIS MUCH FOR NOTHING: I'M DEADLY SERIOUS, AND I HOPE THIS MORNING'S DEMONSTRATION MADE THAT CRYSTAL CLEAR TO YOU. TWENTY-FIVE MILLION DOLLARS, DUFFY—OR BOOM."

Silence.

The listeners were convinced that the recording had ended. But the silence from the tape stemmed from Duffy's appreciation of the enormity of the crime that was so casually intimated by the caller. The assistant commissioner's voice sounded weak, awed, when at last he was heard to respond.

"I understand. How long do we have?"

"TODAY IS THE THIRD OF JULY. YIZ HAVE TILL NINE IN THE MORNING ON JULY THE FOURTEENTH. THAT SHOULD GIVE YIZ PLENTY OF TIME."

"Fair enough. And how do we pay the money?"

"NEVER MIND ABOUT THAT FOR NOW. I'LL BE IN TOUCH. ANGEL OUT."

There was a click. Macken switched off the tape recorder. He turned his attention to the police psychologist and sociolinguist, Dr. Patricia Earley.

"Well?"

It had become very warm and humid in the office. Earley took off her glasses and wiped them with a handkerchief, an action that reminded Blade suddenly of his mother; how she'd looked in her early sixties, before the creeping horror of the dementia had taken hold. In all the years that Earley and he had worked together, he'd never noticed until today the resemblance between Katharine Macken and the psychologist. It was odd that he should suddenly see it now.

"Look, strictly speaking this isn't my field," Earley said. "Is he correct about the mobile phone—that it can't be traced?"

"Near enough," Blade said. "If we had the number he's using we might be able to bisect the signal and home in on that. But we'd never be able to pinpoint his location if he's moving around."

Earley accepted this with a slow nod. "And the voice? How is he doing that?"

"It's some kind of distortion device. We've people working on it up in the Park, but so far nobody's been able to unscramble it—if that's the right word. You think we might get a voiceprint, is that it?"

"Well, it would be a start. At least it might tell us something about his background, his education, that sort of thing."

Macken shook his head.

"It's too early to say yet, but I think I'd rule that out if I was you, Doctor. From what I gather, he's using a computer program that scrambles his voice. It's going to be bloody hard to crack that."

"What the super means, Doctor," said an earnest young man in a white shirt, "is that the bomber is using a digital-sound encryption program—probably one he's written himself—that interfaces with the telephone he's using. If my guess is right, there's an almost infinite number of variables written into the code. Let me put it this way: there are about six billion people in the world and each of them has their own voiceprint, as individual as a fingerprint. We think this encryption program gives even more choice than that. The chances of us being able to decrypt it back to the original voice profile are probably nil."

"I think I liked Superintendent Macken's explanation better," Dr. Earley said. "But I believe I understand. We can never find out how this character really sounds—not even where he comes from."

"You think he could be a foreigner, Doctor?" Sweetman asked.

She shook her head. "I very much doubt it. The vocabulary and syntax are clearly Irish. Did you notice how he used the locution, 'Amn't I after telling you'? Very Irish, that. Not to mention that colorful bit about the fiddler. No, I'd stake my reputation on his being Irish."

Blade toyed with the controls of the small tape recorder.

"So what are we dealing with, Doctor?"

"Off the top of my head?"

"Off the top of your head."

"I should say somebody with a very large chip on his shoulder; somebody who bears a grudge against society in general." She paused. "And the Guards in particular."

Blade was immediately alert.

"Why do you say that?"

"It was something about the tone of voice—not the sound, you understand, but his general attitude towards the commissioner and yourself. He seemed, well, downright contemptuous. I should say, at a guess, that we are dealing with a man who's already been in trouble with the authorities, has more than likely served a term in prison, and consequently bears a deep resentment at the penal system and the police. For a start, he knows you and the commissioner by name Superintendent. He even recognized your voice. Now, *that* fact alone should give us some clue. Furthermore, he feels—"

"We might have him on the books, then?" Nolan said.

Dr. Earley ignored the interruption as though nobody had spoken.

"He feels," she went on, "that he's been gravely wronged, and is determined to take revenge. And," she added, almost as an afterthought, "the fact that he doesn't hesitate to blow innocent people to smithereens makes him very dangerous indeed."

"It makes sense," Blade said. Thoughtful, he fiddled with the volume control on the cassette player. "Talk about covering your tracks! I said earlier on that this is the nearest I've ever come to the perfect crime. I still believe that. We know what the murder weapon was and there's no way we can trace where it came from or who built it—not after five years. And there are *more* shagging bombs. This bastard is the only one who knows where they are. So, short of digging up every square foot of every mile of every route from the airport to Leinster House, we haven't a snowman's chance in hell of finding them."

"The perfect crime doesn't exist, Blade," Earley said. "You know better than that."

He was not convinced. "What about serial killers? A killing without a motive and without witnesses? Without a motive, we've nothing to go on. I'd call that the perfect crime."

"Yes, well thank God we haven't got any in this country— at least not as far as I'm aware. But this twisted monster *has* a motive: money—and revenge as well, though we don't know that for certain. He also appears to have an enormously inflated ego, and that ego is standing in the way of an unsolvable crime."

"I don't understand, Doctor," Orla Sweetman said.

"I do," Blade told her. "What Dr. Earley is saying is that as long as men are born with egos, there can never be a perfect crime. Look, if this bollocks was content with simply making his ransom demand, then he'd stand a damn good chance of getting away with it. But he isn't. His ego is getting in the way. He wants to show us how bloody clever he is. And that's how he's going to trip himself up. Sooner or later he'll let something slip—some personal detail that he'll think is too shagging trivial to be a clue. You mark my words: he'll do it. And we'll be on the lookout for it. That's how he'll hang himself in the end."

"His ego, his pride," Sweetman said. "Every dark angel's undoing."

Macken smiled thinly. "You could put it that way, yes."

They'd missed the one o'clock news on Channel One but managed to catch the 3 P.M. bulletin. In Duffy's office.

The camera crew and newscaster had been denied access to the bomb site. There was only aerial footage. It was enough: O'Connell Street had not seen such devastation since the British had shelled it during the Easter Rising in 1916.

"A report just in has confirmed that a sixth victim of the explosion, Mrs. Martina Dempsey of Rosemount Terrace, Booterstown, died less than an hour ago in the Mater hospital of extensive head injuries."

25

"Fuck," Blade said. Duffy waved him to silence.

"—*say that thirty-two of those injured in the blast have been detained at the Mater, nine in a critical condition. The Taoiseach has sent a message of sympathy to the bereaved, and a special mass will be offered this evening in the Pro-Cathedral, Dublin.*

"*It is not known for certain as yet what caused the blast but earlier, Assistant Commissioner Duffy of the Dublin Metropolitan Area had this to say.*"

Duffy's features filled the screen as he spoke of regrettable accidents, tragic loss of life, and full-scale investigations. Sweetman thought it a good performance and said so. Duffy grunted.

"*With me in the studio now is Paul Donnelly, a spokesman for Bord Gáis. Mr. Donnelly, how could a thing like this happen? And what's to prevent it from happening again?*"

"*I'm glad you asked me that, Vincent. . . .*"

"Jesus," Blade said, "how much are they paying this guy? And, more to the point, *who's* paying him? Us?"

"Don't you be worrying about that," Duffy said. "You've enough on your plate as it is. But I *can* tell you this much: the gas company will be getting away with murder over the next few months."

He shut his eyes and grimaced, put a hand over his mouth.

"Now what possessed me to go and say a thing like that?"

Macken showed tact. "I thought you were grand, sir. You almost had *me* believing it."

"Thanks, Blade."

He turned as somebody walked in through the open door. The seven people in the room stiffened as Detective Superintendent Nolan joined them; he was not liked.

"Did I miss anything?"

"Everything and nothing, Nolan," Duffy said. He was about to continue when the local news story was abruptly replaced by an image of the president of the United States standing behind a panoply of microphones on the lawn of the White House. He spoke.

"Three days ago, a Bulgarian commercial flight en route to Paris was hijacked by four armed Libyans and forced to land at Heathrow Airport in London. The terrorists threatened to blow up the plane and its two hundred eighty passengers unless two of their associates were released from custody by the British authorities."

"Sir, I wanted a word with you about—"

"Not now, Nolan, please!" Duffy was irritated. "I want to hear this. It's important."

"Sorry. I'll come back later." Nolan left.

"—to express our deep disappointment with the British government, and with the prime minister in particular, at the handling of the crisis. The United States has always—and I repeat always—maintained a firm policy with regard to terrorism. And that policy very clearly states that we will never give way to terrorist demands. This the British government has done, in contravention of a pact entered into by a former holder of this office and other Western administrations."

Duffy was white. "It's the bloody *time* difference."

"What, sir?"

"The time difference," Duffy repeated. He lit a cigarette with a tremor in his fingers. He threw down his lighter and it fell to the floor. One of Blade's team retrieved it; Duffy barely saw the man.

"This is yesterday's news in the States, Blade, even though we're only getting it now. And they'll have got ours too late. Christ, what a mess! Unbelievable. Talk about timing!"

"I don't follow you, sir."

"Ah, Blade, would you listen to me? Don't you see it? The man's just after putting his shagging head in a noose."

It had gone quiet in the office. Somebody had turned down the sound on the television.

"He's just," the assistant commissioner said, "accused the Brits of giving in to terrorism. They turned the two Libyans over yesterday. They shouldn't have—though, as God is my witness, I'd have done the same. But if Thatcher was still in power, she'd have had every available squad of the SAS swarming all over Heathrow. There'd a been an almighty bloodbath, so there would. But it's done now, and it can't be undone. So ask yourself, Blade: Where does that leave *us?*"

Duffy answered his own question.

"It leaves us with an American president who's just told the whole shagging world that the Brits are a crowd of wimps. Not only that, but they've gone back on a deal that Thatcher did with Reagan back in the '80s. That pair swore on their mothers' graves that neither country would ever give in to terrorist threats."

Duffy crushed the cigarette in his ashtray and spread his palms wide.

"He's snookered himself, that's what I'm saying. Don't you get it? As far as the outside world is concerned, there hasn't been a bomb in O'Connell Street. But the White House knows there *has* been, so they can call off the state visit on any pretext and there's no harm done. But Blade, if the news leaks out that it was a bomb and that there might be more, then the president *has* to come to Dublin, no matter what; otherwise he'd never be able to hold his head up in Congress. Not after what he's said. He's left himself no choice in the matter. None."

Four

Blade had always liked the look of the American embassy in Ballsbridge. Built in the '60s, it is only now, more than thirty years on, that it has begun to exhibit signs of age. But this aging is a physical deterioration: the embassy's circular design sets it apart from the staid and nondescript buildings that surround it, and even those erected within the present decade seem old-fashioned by comparison.

Sweetman and he arrived some minutes after four. There was a man—Blade guessed by his accent and bearing that he was a U.S. Marine—and a woman on duty in the lobby. Macken was given a brief but thorough frisking and Sweetman's purse was scanned for weaponry. Then a junior aide escorted them to the ambassador's office. He tapped lightly on the door, opened it a fraction and looked in.

"Umm, his Excellency is on a call right now."

"Sure we'll be like mice, so we will," Blade said, and pushed the door open, to allow Sweetman in ahead of him. The aide looked startled, then shook his head slowly and left.

The office was almost exactly as Macken had pictured it. Its walls were half-paneled with the greenish brown wood that he always associated with American offices. But the big desk was mahogany; likewise the chair behind it. Two flags hung limply at the rear of the desk: the Stars and Stripes and the Irish Tricolor. Immediately behind and above the ambassador's head was the obligatory photograph of the current president.

The ambassador was dressed in a beautifully tailored dark-blue suit. His hair looked dark blue, too, Blade decided, and incongruously youthful and full, in contrast to his deeply lined face. A white scar ran along one tanned cheek. Blade wondered about that. Then he noticed the other photographs in the room—scenes from combat zones, uniforms, and war ve-

29

hicles that spoke of service in Vietnam. There were military souvenirs, too, placed at random among the books on the shelves.

Blade approved. He liked dealing with men with military backgrounds—partly because he'd one himself, but mainly because such men, in his experience, were usually more forthright than others. He asked himself, though, how a former soldier could adjust to diplomatic life, where an unwise word or too limp a handshake could have dire consequences.

Yet this old soldier had made the transition well, Blade saw; whoever he was talking with on the phone could not fail to be reassured by the ambassador's gentle and persuasive manner. Death threats? Not here, not here, he heard him say. No, the whole thing had been blown out of all proportion.

Ambassador Seaborg gestured toward the three chairs in front of his desk and Macken and Sweetman sat down. There was a paperweight in the shape of an army jeep on the desk— a parting gift to one "Col. E. William Seaborg"; a sawed-off and highly polished 30-mm shell casing held a dozen unused and meticulously sharpened pencils.

The ambassador smiled warmly in their direction as he finished the conversation and hung up. Then he came from behind the desk and shook hands.

"Thank you both for coming. Mr. Redfern will be joining us shortly. Coffee? Tea?"

They declined. Then the ambassador surprised them both: he became another person. Gone was the suaveness of Seaborg's telephone manner; it was as though a weight had fallen abruptly from his shoulders; he seemed to pull himself up to his full height—and that height was considerable.

"I won't bullshit either of you," he said. "I prefer to leave that to the politicians. We've made inquiries about you, Detective Superintendent, and it gives me confidence to know that a man of your background is handling the investigation."

Macken raised a quizzical eyebrow.

"Our Mr. Redfern's work. It's his job to find out these things. You know he's with the agency, don't you?"

"I guessed as much."

"Ever been involved with terrorists, Blade? . . . I may call you Blade?"

"You may indeed. And yes and no."

Seaborg laughed loudly; it took Macken and Sweetman aback.

"You know, I've served in this country for close to five years and I still don't speak the goddamn language. What does 'yes and no' mean?"

"Well, sir," Blade said, "I need hardly tell *you*"—he nodded in the direction of Seaborg's combat photographs—"that terrorism is a relative term; one man's terrorist is another man's freedom fighter."

"True."

"So, to answer your question: yes, I've come into contact with terrorists: mainly the Hizbollah, Hamas, and the PLO in Lebanon. And no, as far as they themselves were concerned, they weren't terrorists; to them, the Israelis were the terrorists. But we were the UN, so we didn't take sides."

Seaborg seemed satisfied with this reply. He sat down at his desk and opened a manila folder. Blade saw that it contained sheets of computer printout.

" 'Sandhurst Royal Military Academy,' " the ambassador read out loud. " 'Third battalion of the Royal Tank Regiment.' Forgive me for asking, but isn't that a tad unusual for an Irishman?"

"The pay was better in the British Army."

Seaborg didn't know if Macken was serious.

"Well, you certainly had a distinguished career," he said, flipping through the dossier. "Germany, southern Lebanon, Cyprus. Decorated six times. Then in, let's see . . . 1981, it's all over. You resigned your commission. Why in hell did you do that?"

"Mind if I smoke?" Blade asked. He didn't wait for a reply but took a pack of Hamlets from his breast pocket, stripped one of its clear foil wrapping, and lit it.

Seaborg frowned. He stood up, went to a cabinet and returned with a cut-glass ashtray. It looked as though it had never before seen real service.

"I put somebody into hospital," Blade said. "He raped a woman—a girl, a tourist. I thought he deserved what I gave him. The army disagreed."

"Could be because the man you hospitalized was your commanding officer," the ambassador said. He grinned wryly. "I can understand them being a bit pissed about a thing like that. You were damn lucky they didn't press charges."

He went pointedly to the air-conditioning, turned it up a notch, and sat down again.

"Anyway, Blade," he continued, shutting the folder, "I don't give a damn, either way. I've just been talking with the White House—tenth time today, incidentally, and it's still only eleven in the morning over there. They want a full-scale operation. Army, police, every available man. They figure that the more manpower we throw at this, the sooner we get our bomber."

Macken glanced at Sweetman; her expression told him that she'd read this the same way. Without having heard the tape recording of Angel's demands, Seaborg had dropped the plural and was referring to the bomber as a single entity.

"But that," Seaborg continued, "is not the way I'd go about it, if I were running things."

The door opened and a fair-haired man in his late thirties entered. There'd been no knock. His appearance fitted uncannily well with the voice Blade had heard that morning in Duffy's office; he knew before introductions were made that the newcomer was Lawrence Redfern.

Like stags in the rutting season, Macken and he embarked on the ritual of sizing each other up. This, Blade thought, is a man you would not want as an enemy. Redfern looked with disgust at the cigar, then eased himself into the vacant chair with the fluidity of movement of a beast of prey.

At that moment Blade's mind played back an image he'd seen earlier, an image he'd not consciously registered: a picture on the wall. It showed a somewhat younger Seaborg standing, against a backdrop of desert, in the company of an army officer wearing the bars of a major. That officer was Lawrence Redfern.

Redfern placed a boxed audiocassette on the desk.

"You might as well know," he told Macken and Sweetman, "that we're abreast of developments in this affair. We know about this guy Angel; we know what he wants, and"—he paused—"we're damned if he's going to get it."

"May I ask where you got that tape?" Blade said.

"You may. Commissioner Duffy had it sent over by courier. I assumed you knew that."

Redfern's tone suggested that Macken was very much a fool if he'd *not* known.

"Well, I didn't." Blade was irritated. "He didn't say anything about it to *me.*"

"Gentlemen!" Seaborg raised a hand. "Let's not get off on the wrong foot here. I apologize, Blade; I thought you knew. Mr. Duffy promised us full cooperation, and that included letting us have the same information you're working on. He ought to have told you, I agree, but it's not my place to criticize. Now, can we press on?"

Blade shrugged.

"As I was about to say before Mr. Redfern joined us," the ambassador continued, "I believe that the best way of handling this is to maintain as low a profile as possible." He stood up. "Do nothing—or at least behave as though you're doing nothing. Lull the enemy into a false sense of security. That's how battles are won. Make him think you're powerless. Then *he* has to bring the fight to *you.* If he sees that you're making no move toward him, then he'll feel obliged to make one toward you."

"And he'll make the wrong move," Redfern said.

"Exactly. Blade?"

Macken leaned across the desk and squashed his cigar out in the ashtray. It continued to smolder slightly and Redfern waved a hand under his nose. Blade smiled to himself, then sat back in his chair. He linked his fingers, started to stroke his chin with both thumbs. He half closed his eyes and began speaking in a soft voice.

"I was in command of a Saracen unit in Cyprus, patrolling the Green Line, as they call it, between north and south. The animosity between those two peoples—the Greek Cypriots and the Turkish Cypriots—had to be seen to be believed. You saw the North and South Vietnamese in action, Colonel, so you'll understand."

Seaborg nodded. If he thought it unusual to be addressed by his military rank then he gave no sign.

"One night," Blade went on, "a group of Turks raided a village in my sector, killed two men, broke into the church, and made off with a number of icons and gold objects—worth a lot of money, but the desecration was worse. So the headman called a meeting and the men discussed what to do about it. Most of the younger ones wanted to cross over to the north and raid the first Turkish village they came to. Maybe plunder the mosque, too, if they could. An eye for an eye."

He paused, then said: "But the headman disagreed; he'd a better idea. 'Let's pretend,' says he, 'that nothing has happened. Let's make these jackals believe that they can have their way with our village unchallenged.'

"But every night he posted armed men in concealed positions at the approaches to the village; they were well hidden. Sure enough, ten days later the same band of Turks returned, suspecting nothing. They were massacred—all of them. We found the corpses the next morning on the road. They were riddled with bullets and so mutilated with knives and machetes that their own mothers wouldn't have recognized them."

Blade stopped and nodded slowly. Plainly, the tale was finished.

"So what's the point you're making, Macken?" Redfern asked.

"The point is: I agree with the colonel. We keep a low profile. We call off the hounds. We tell this Angel character that we're having a whip-round for the money."

"But in the meantime," Seaborg said, "we're laying in wait for him."

Blade nodded. "Our police psychologist, Dr. Earley, is putting together a picture of this man. I trust her judgment when she says we're dealing with a huge ego. The swine wants to see us running around like blue-arsed flies. He'd like nothing better than seeing half the Guards in the country searching high and low for him. But if he thinks we're doing nothing, he'll be frustrated. We won't be playing the game."

"I'm with you," Seaborg said.

Redfern grunted.

"Think of him," Blade said, "as a hermit crab. He's in there, in his shell, and it's like a fortress; he's thoroughly protected. He wants to see the little blue fishes swimming past him, and he can stretch out his pincers and grab one of them every now and then and give it a good shake, just for the sheer divilment of it. But if the fish refuse to play and don't come looking for him, then he'll be forced to show more and more of himself. Until he's out so far that there's no going back. And then we *have* the bastard."

Five

"I thought," Sweetman said, "it went grand, considering. What did you make of Redfern?"

"Oh, he's not the worst. A bit tight-arsed, but what did you expect? They probably issue their people with special underpants. Did you notice something funny though? There wasn't a mention of the CIA. I think Seaborg referred to 'the agency' at one stage, but that was the extent of it. Like he was talking about an *estate* agency. God, they're secretive so-and-sos."

"*I* thought Seaborg was very up-front."

"No, I mean Redfern's mob. Seaborg's a good man. The Yanks are lucky to have him here."

It was approaching six o'clock. The air was cooler now in the shade of the limes that line the avenue outside the embassy. On the other side of the intersection, commuting Dublin was making its tortuous way back to the southern suburbs. Starlings chattered in the trees.

Sweetman removed the parking ticket from her windshield and tossed it in among the others in the glove compartment. She opened the door on Blade's side. Then she saw he had his cellular phone in his hand and was extending the antenna.

"I want to have a word with Duffy before he leaves," he told her. "I didn't like the way he handled that tape business. Fuck him; he might have told me first and not have me making an eejit of myself in front of Redfern."

But Duffy was in a meeting and couldn't be disturbed. Blade harangued the operator at Garda Command and Control, to no avail. Fuming, he broke the connection.

No sooner had he done so than the phone rang.

"Yes?" he said gruffly.

"HELLO, BLADE! TELL ME, DID IT GO ALL RIGHT WITH THE AMERICANS?"

Macken blanched. Sweetman must have guessed the identity of the caller because her silent lips framed the single word: "Angel?" He nodded.

"How did you get this number?"

"AH NOW, BLADE," the deep, electronic voice mocked, "THAT WOULD BE TELLING YOU, WOULDN'T IT?"

Macken's mind raced, covering all the possibilities he could think of.

His home number: that was in the book. For his mother's benefit; she was continually mislaying her diary, where she kept the numbers of friends and family. But his cellular phone number: who knew that, apart from the garda switchboard operators? Sweetman, Nolan, a handful of the senior members of the force. No friends or relatives, other than his son Peter, whom Blade had warned against using the number without good reason. It was strictly for business use.

"I HOPE DETECTIVE SERGEANT SWEETMAN IS GOING TO PAY THAT PARKING FINE."

It took Macken several seconds to register the fact that his caller was referring to an action performed by Sweetman just minutes before. Christ, Blade thought, he's *here*. He looked around him in panic.

"I DON'T KNOW HOW YOU FEEL ABOUT IT, BLADE, BUT I THINK IT'S A FUCKING DISGRACE THAT ORDINARY PEOPLE LIKE MYSELF SHOULD HAVE TO PAY OUR PARKING FINES AND THE GUARDS CAN DO AS THEY DAMN WELL PLEASE. I MEAN, WHO'S PAYING YOUR BLOODY SALARIES, ANSWER ME THAT? I'LL TELL YOU WHO: WE ARE, THE POOR TAXPAYERS; THE POOR, UNFORTUNATE NINE-TO-FIVERS. THE WAGE SLAVES. DO YOU THINK THAT'S RIGHT? DO YOU?"

Keep him talking, Blade thought. Say anything—any old shite.

"Sweetman pays her taxes, too."

His assistant looked at him in bemusement. Blade wished there was some way she could listen in, make notes. He rummaged in a pocket for his notebook and pencil, clamped the phone between jaw and shoulder.

"WOULD THAT BY ANY CHANCE BE YOUR GROCERY LIST YOU'RE MAKING, BLADE?"

Jesus, he sees every bleeding thing!

"Where are you?"

He scribbled a note and passed it to Sweetman. Her eyes opened wide in astonishment.

"I'M RIGHT HERE, BLADE. YOU CAN'T SEE ME, BUT I CAN SEE YOU."

The flux of cars, buses, and cyclists from three northerly and easterly points still converged on the busy intersection, though the rush-hour traffic was beginning to thin out. White- and blue-collar workers were making their way home. Men with briefcases and women in office dress waited on the traffic island for the lights to change; the daring jaywalked, or took shortcuts across the parched grass and flowers on the island. Most of the available parking spaces were still occupied; the bistro across the way at the junction of Clyde Road and the main thoroughfare was opening its doors to the first of its evening customers.

Blade looked about wildly; it was futile to think he could spot his caller.

"I COULD BE ANYWHERE, EH, BLADE? MAYBE IN THAT FLAT ABOVE THE FLORIST'S. . . . "

He was forced to look in that direction.

"OR DO YOU SEE THAT PARKED VAN . . . THE RED ONE WITH THE BLACKED-OUT BACK WINDOWS? MAYBE I'M IN THERE. WHO'S TO SAY?"

"Stop playing games, you fucking bastard!"

"LANGUAGE, LANGUAGE! AND WHO'S PLAYING GAMES? YE'RE THE ONES DOING THE SUCKING UP TO THE AMERICANS, NOT ME. WHAT DID SEABORG SAY? CAN HE LAY HIS HANDS ON THE TWENTY-FIVE MILLION? IF NOT, THEN HE CAN ALWAYS ASK THE RUSSIANS."

"The *Russians?*"

"AH, YES. DID YOU KNOW THAT MOST OF THE DOLLAR BILLS IN CIRCULATION OUTSIDE OF AMERICA ARE IN RUSSIA? IT'S TRUE. THEY'VE BEEN HOARDING THEM FOR YEARS. SO IF YOU WANT TO

BUY ANYTHING DECENT IN RUSSIA THEN YOU HAVE TO PAY IN DOL-
LARS. MAKES YOU THINK, DOESN'T IT?"

Blade was silent. His sharp hearing had picked up something: a car horn had sounded behind Angel's words. It was
no ordinary horn, but one that played six or seven notes: a
snatch of the theme from the old war movie, *The Bridge on
the River Kwai*—a tune called "Colonel Bogey." Like Angel's
voice, the notes were greatly distorted, yet Blade had heard the
same klaxon "in reality," undistorted. He heard it again now,
close by, as a bright-red Mazda sports car turned onto Elgin
Road. He checked the direction from which the vehicle had
come, searching for some clue. But the intersection was
thronged with people; it was a Friday evening in high summer;
not everybody was in a hurry to go home just yet.

Sweetman was out of the car, too, scanning the buildings on
all sides for anything that might give the bomber away: a face
at a window, the reflection of sunlight on binoculars, anything.

"GIVE UP, MACKEN! ADMIT YOU'RE BEATEN. I COULD BE ANY-
BODY; I COULD BE ANYWHERE. D'YOU SEE THAT LAD AT THE RAIL-
INGS OF ROLY'S BISTRO: THE ONE SELLING T-SHIRTS? WITH THE
WALKMAN? HE'S SINGING ALONG TO THE MUSIC. OR IS HE? IS THAT
REALLY A WALKMAN, OR IS IT A RADIO TRANSMITTER? YOU DON'T
KNOW, DO YOU? FOR ALL YOU KNOW IT COULD BE ME."

Blade looked.

"OR THAT TAXI WAITING AT THE CORNER. HOW MANY AERIALS
ARE THERE ON THE ROOF? TWO? THREE? THAT COULD BE ME AS
WELL."

There was a pause.

"I'M TELLING YOU, BLADE, I MIGHT BE ANYBODY. I'M COM-
PLETELY INVISIBLE. LOOK: MAYBE I'M THAT LITTLE OLD GRANNY
GOO-GOOING TO HER GRANDCHILD IN THE PRAM. YOU NEVER
KNOW, BLADE."

The jackhammer laugh sounded again.

It was too much for Blade. He knew that he shouldn't have,
that it was perhaps the most stupid thing he could have done

in the circumstances, that perhaps in doing so he was putting more lives in danger. But he couldn't help it; he'd suppressed the symptoms of his hangover long enough to get through the working day. And what a working day it had been!

Blade lost it. He let go his self-control.

"Fuck *you,*" he said, and broke the connection.

Six

Peter Macken loathed Jim Roche. You can hate or despise or have contempt for a man, a woman—or even a child. But *loathing* is a word that you reserve for creepy, crawling things. When a man is loathed, then he must have done something pretty rotten to deserve it.

Yet most people who knew Jim Roche thought him the most genial of men. Blade Macken and he had been practically friends at one time, drinking buddies. They weren't quite enemies now, but Roche's relationship with Blade's wife, Joan, had soured matters. Blade resented Roche. He found it hard to continue liking the man who was sleeping with his wife, even though Blade and Joan had been estranged for close to nine years.

At nineteen, Peter Macken was growing into the twin of his father. He'd inherited Blade's black hair and blue eyes—and the permanent five o'clock shadow that you associated less with the Celtic races and more with the men of southern Europe.

"Is that you, Blade?"

"Peter?"

"We have to talk. I—"

"Jesus, Peter, how many times do I have to say it? *Don't* call me on this phone unless it's an emergency. It's strictly for work."

Rarely of late had Peter heard his father so irritated. He guessed he was under considerable strain. Blade had slept badly and was in a foul mood.

"I'm sorry. It was the only chance I had to phone you. I tried you at home but all I got was your answering machine. Everybody's away at the moment. I'm on my own."

"All right. Fair enough. Now what was it you wanted to talk to me about?"

Peter's voice held excitement.

"He left two cases behind. They're full of stuff."

"Who? Cock Roche?"

"Yeah. You should see what he's got, Blade. It's like James shagging Bond."

"Has he microphones?"

"That's what I'm saying. Him and Joan won't be back before five. If I nick one, would you be able to show me how to use it?"

Blade was doing his own driving. The big six-cylinder car could have brought him to O'Connell Street in five minutes but now, as ever, he was going at a leisurely pace. It was hotter than yesterday on this, the second day of Angel; he'd turned the air-conditioning up full. It was close to ten in the morning; Sweetman had been at the blast site since nine.

A biker cut across his bows and Macken honked angrily, smacking the cellular phone against the steering wheel in the process, having forgotten it was in his hand. He heard a faint and concerned "Blade?" coming from the instrument.

"Sorry, Peter. Yes, look, why don't you meet me in . . . What about Graham O'Sullivan's in Duke Street? About two?"

"Cool."

"D'you see that camera, Blade?" Sweetman said, standing under the smoke-blackened statue of William Smith O'Brien.

Blade looked. The surveillance camera was mounted high on a gable close by the southern entrance to O'Connell Street. It and its twin on the other side of the thoroughfare monitored the progress of the traffic—and its violators.

Recent years had seen an increasing number of the devices on Dublin's streets. They were the eyes of many public and private institutions. They watched people at all times of day and night: people on the street, people entering and leaving buildings, people withdrawing cash from the omnipresent ATMs.

When Dublin's muggers struck, the cameras watched. When Dublin's myriad drugs changed hands, the cameras monitored the transactions. They sometimes saw rape, violence, syringe attacks, and sudden death.

"How long would you say it's been there?" Sweetman asked.

Macken squinted. The camera's housing looked as though it had braved many rainy seasons.

"Long enough. Ten years?"

"That's what I'd say, too."

The scene of the outrage was still a shambles. What little remained of the bomb had been taken away and, at that moment, teams of forensic experts at Garda HQ in Phoenix Park were subjecting the fragments to exhaustive tests. Captain Fitzpatrick and his men were long gone; now there were genuine utility workers in their place, repairing the damaged underground structures. A single line of traffic trickled past the cordoned-off crater. Glaziers were fitting new panes to the shattered windows. It would be days before this end of Dublin's main street was functioning normally again.

Sweetman pulled her phone from her purse and called Harcourt Square. Within two minutes, she had the information she was looking for.

"It's one of Dublin Corporation's cameras," she told Blade. "Traffic control. And we're in luck; it's been there since 1991."

She looked up at the camera again, then back at the bomb site.

"If I'm right, Blade, it's aimed exactly at the part of the street we want."

Macken looked skeptical. "I don't know, Sweetman. It's an awful long shot, if you want my opinion. I mean, you're asking a lot if you think that that yoke picked up somebody planting a bomb five years ago."

"I think it's worth a try all the same."

"And what if he planted it at night? He probably did, too. Sure we'd never recognize the fucker on the tape. He'll just be a dark blur off in the distance."

"They can do amazing things with computers these days."

43

Blade threw her a curious look.

"Jesus, Sweetman, if I didn't know you better, I'd swear you were being sarcastic."

He turned and watched the traffic move slowly over O'Connell Bridge. In January, scores of paving bricks on the westside had been removed and replaced by transparent tiles of Plexiglas. Below the Plexiglas, their digital mechanism buried in the stone of the bridge, a set of giant numbers glowed greenly, and altered with each passing second. The Millennium Clock was counting down the time left until the end of the century. At that moment it read: 48,167,650 seconds.

"What!" Blade demanded. "Two *weeks?*"

"Well, what did yiz expect?" the technician said. "We can't hang on to these recordings forever, y'know. The tapes cost a mint, for a start, so we reuse them over and over again. If we didn't it'd cost a bleeding fortune."

Macken and Sweetman were at the headquarters of Dublin Corporation, in the control room that watched over the metropolis. Sweetman was fascinated. She counted more than five hundred monitors, screens the size of a portable television set—all seething with Dublin life at that very moment. Immediate: all this was happening *now;* these were no replays of yesterday's events.

Look there: there was the south end of Parnell Square where it met O'Connell Street. The camera showed the monument and statue of the great statesman Charles Stewart Parnell, his challenging words etched in shiny metal: *"Thus far shalt thou go, and no further. . . ."* It was a favorite Dublin gag.

And here was the stretch of riverside street that ran past the Four Courts, the place that had seen the trials of the lowly and the mighty of Ireland's tumultuous past. There was a police van stopped outside the gates and uniformed Guards were escorting a man with a blanket over his head into the building. Press photographers' flashguns flashed. Doubly wasteful: the sunshine was blinding and no flash could hope to penetrate the harsh wool of the Mountjoy Prison bed covering.

Another camera looked past the bronze statue of Oliver Goldsmith that flanked the entrance to Trinity College. Its lens took in a pedestrian crosswalk that was perhaps Ireland's liveliest. Even in black-and-white, it allowed Sweetman to observe every detail of the people waiting to cross. It was the time of year when young Spanish students were out in great numbers on Dublin's streets; she didn't need to hear the language; she recognized their animated, staccato gestures. Dubliners ignored them, or tolerated them as a necessary nuisance.

Yet another camera must have been mounted on a tall pole at the entrance to Grafton Street, the city's most fashionable shopping precinct, for it gave a crow's-nest view of a quartet of street musicians entertaining the well-dressed passersby. The strollers barely noticed them, being much more interested in seeing and being seen by their peers.

But Dublin harbored darker places. There were narrow streets of tall Victorian and Georgian buildings, some more alleys than streets. There were areas of massive blocks of tenements with names like Sheriff Street, Sean MacDermott Street, Fatima Mansions. They'd never been pretty; they were far from pretty now. You didn't want to visit these places unless you really *had* to. Here the hard-core crime of Dublin walked, fought, shot up, and—of late, in numbers that grew at a frightening rate—died.

A vehicle could not traverse the city center without its entire journey being followed by a relay of cameras, each of whose ambit knitted almost seamlessly with those of its companions. One day soon, the technician had assured the police officers in his colorful way, "a pair of flies couldn't shag each other on a wall without us knowing about it."

And recording the venial act.

But the recordings were erased after fourteen days. If Sweetman had thought to discover, in some dusty archive, video evidence of the man who called himself Angel planting a high-explosive device, she had to admit defeat now.

She looked ruefully at the moving, black-and-white images and thought: He's there; Angel's there. His image is still there, *somewhere* among all those swirling magnetized particles that make up the videotapes. It's there, but it's scrambled beyond retrievability—in much the same way as Angel's true voice.

Sweetman knew a dead end when she saw one.

There was a table on a landing halfway up the stairs of the coffee shop, and a sign on the wall above it that read BRENDAN KENNELLY'S CORNER. Brendan Kennelly the poet. (Who knew what stunning verses had been conceived at this table, over espresso and sweet pastries?) Blade found his son waiting there punctually at two o'clock. The shop was self-service, so he left Peter seated and returned shortly with two cups of coffee and a plate of doughnuts.

"Jesus, Blade, you can't smoke in here!"

"Oh. Sorry. I forgot."

Blade returned the pack of Hamlets to his pocket. He dumped three spoonfuls of sugar in his coffee and stirred it slowly. He was very tired and wished he wasn't. It was trivial, he knew, but he never liked to appear this way in Peter's company: Their meetings were fewer, far fewer, than Blade would have liked.

His son wolfed down a doughnut with a voraciousness that startled him. Christ, wasn't Joan *feeding* them these days? Peter and eighteen-year-old Sandra. Anne, Blade's eldest, had flown the nest some years before. She was happily married in London, expecting her second child, and saw her father as often as she could—which was more, Blade thought, than could be said of Sandra.

But Peter's hasty eating was simply a mask for his excitement. He brushed sugar granules from his lips and, with the same hand, reached into a plastic bag and hauled out a small, black fake-leather case. He opened it and passed something across the table.

"A plug?"

"Ehh, it's actually a socket."

"Yeah yeah, I know it's a socket." Blade had to suppress his irritation.

But it *was* a socket: a twin-power socket. The object he held in his hand was about eight inches long and three wide. It was made of tough, white plastic and had a double set of rectangular apertures that would accept three-pinned plugs. The manufacturer's logo—an MK within an oval—was embossed below each of the earth slots. It was the most ordinary thing in the world—or in Ireland and Britain, at any rate. You saw those outlets in every home, in every room.

You saw them, yet your conscious mind rarely *registered* them.

Blade knew without his son's saying so that the device he was holding was no ordinary power socket. He didn't need to read the small sticker affixed to it; it advertised the services of Centurion Security. He opened it up with the little screwdriver that Peter had handed him.

The outlet had the regular fittings. It also contained a tiny, cube-shaped black object with a narrow extension like the antenna of an insect. A microphone.

"It works, too. I tried it in my room."

"The socket?"

"Yeah. But I haven't a clue how to get the mike working. That's why I wanted to see you." Peter reached for another doughnut.

Blade screwed the cover back on the power outlet and laid it on the table.

"It's a microwave radio transmitter," he said. "You'll need a receiver tuned to the same wavelength. I don't know how far the range is, but I'd say at a guess it's roughly a hundred yards. And, of course, you'll need a tape deck connected up to the receiver if you want to do any recording."

Peter wiped his lips again.

"He's got all that stuff. But I don't know if I can swipe it without him missing it."

Blade took a nip of his coffee, now lukewarm.

"If he does miss it, he'll guess who took it. No, I think it's too risky, Peter, I really do. You don't know what you're up against. The man's made his living from acting the sneak. Christ, it'd be like trying to lift a pickpocket's wallet."

"Yeah, well, I'll see. But I'll be careful."

Blade cleared his throat. "Supposing you *do* manage it. Just what are you going to record?"

"Ah, Blade, we've been over this a million times! I'm going to put it in Joan's room."

Blade wished that the coffee shop had air-conditioning. He didn't blush easily; now he felt his face redden with embarrassment.

"No, Peter," he said quietly. "No, I don't want you doing that."

"Ah, cop *on,* Blade, will you? It's the only way. It's the only room in the house where they're ever in private together." He looked his father straight in the eye. "Look, I'm nineteen years of age. I know what people get up to in bedrooms. Don't be such a bloody prude."

"Don't you talk to me like that!"

"Sorry. I was out of order. Sorry."

"And I'm not a bloody prude. It's just . . . It's just that, well, I love your mother . . . still. Very much. Jesus, Peter, the idea of recording things she says in *bed* . . ." He was unable to finish the sentence.

Something happened then between Blade and his son: a thing so novel that Blade, recalling it later that day, was deeply moved. All at once the roles of parent and offspring were reversed. Peter touched his hand lightly and spoke to him as a father would.

"It's the only way, Blade. *You* know it and *I* know it. If we're ever going to prove that Joan and the cockroach are living together as man and wife, then we'll have to record them in bed. It's where people talk about things—things they wouldn't talk about anywhere else. And I'm speaking from experience."

Blade looked quickly down into his now-cold coffee.

"I love you . . . Dad. Look, I have eyes in my head; I can see how the maintenance money is bleeding you dry. Jesus, I haven't seen you in a new shirt in years! It's *Roche* who should be keeping Joan, not you. And you can take it from me he's got plenty. I've had a look at his bank statements. Joan wouldn't miss that money from you."

"Ah, don't I know it," Blade said with bitterness.

At that moment his phone throbbed. It was one of the investigation team, calling from Harcourt Square. He thought he'd a lead but didn't sound optimistic. Blade told the officer he was on his way. He stood up.

"You should be getting back, too, Peter. Didn't you say they'd be in about five?"

"Thereabouts."

He picked the tab off the tray and put it in his wallet. It wasn't much, but he could declare it as expenses. It made him feel cheap, and he knew his son was right. The sooner they could prove that Jim Roche was cohabiting with his wife, the sooner Blade could afford to live a decent life again.

He squeezed Peter's shoulder.

"Just be careful," he said. "The man's a snake."

"Right."

"And *don't* call me on my mobile again, okay?"

"Promise."

A promise, Blade knew, that Peter would never keep.

49

Seven

There was no weekend leave. The investigation was far, far too important and Blade's team had fewer than ten days to track down the bomber.

"If you don't mind me saying so, sir," one of the assembled detectives grumbled, "you're asking us to do the impossible. How can you expect us to do something—and not *appear* to be doing anything?"

Blade saw Lawrence Redfern, against a wall, arms folded, nod his head. The observer. Just let him open his fucking mouth . . . Nevertheless, Blade had been assured that the other agency men were "behaving themselves"; some of his detectives had gone so far as to praise the efficiency of the Americans. But a conference like this one was strictly a garda affair and protocol didn't tolerate outside interference.

"D'you think I like it, Liam?" Macken replied to the question. "But that's the way we have to work this. The media are driving the assistant commissioner spare. They're sure it's a bomb but they can't stick their necks out—yet. They've nothing but speculation to go on, and we have to keep it that way."

Blade paused to let his words sink in. Then he lowered his voice slightly.

"But that's not the key issue. What's really important is that we mustn't let the bomber himself find out what we're up to. We've no idea how much the bastard knows about us already. For all we know, he may have eyes and ears everywhere."

"What do you mean, sir? Accomplices?"

"It could be. It could also be that he's managed to tap a few phone lines here in the Square—impossible though that might sound."

"Christ almighty."

"In which case, I want you all to be extra careful—more careful than you've ever been up till now—about messages or instructions given over the phone. Work out new codes between you."

A hand was raised. "But what about our Tap Alerts, sir? Surely they'd—"

"We can't trust them anymore, Detective Sergeant," Blade cut in. "They've worked grand up till now, but we don't know what we're up against. Maybe the bomber's using something completely new—something undetectable. I wouldn't put it past him."

Redfern coughed loudly and pointedly, drawing all eyes to him.

"Umm, permission to speak, Superintendent. . . ."

Blade looked at Duffy; Duffy nodded slowly.

"Go ahead, Mr. Redfern," Blade said.

"Thank you. Fact is, I've ordered a number of scramblers from headquarters. They ought to be here by morning." He addressed the room. "Hook one up to a phone and you can talk in complete privacy."

"How many are we talking about?" Duffy asked.

"Fifty."

"Very good," the assistant commissioner said. "My thanks, Mr. Redfern."

Blade grunted. "But work out new codes, all the same," he told his people. "I'm putting you in charge of that, Liam."

"Fair enough, sir." The detective made a note on his pad. "What'll we be calling our man?"

More than one hundred pairs of eyebrows were raised as Blade Macken, instead of replying verbally, tore a sheet from his notebook and wrote down something. He folded the paper in two and passed it to the nearest detective. It went from hand to hand.

The ticking of the wall clock was the loudest sound in the incident room in Harcourt Square. All knew that a precedent had been set. The Square was perhaps Dublin's most secure building, always had been. A visitor was screened to the point where the maiden name of his *grand*mother was no longer a family affair. And the incident rooms were more secure than any other part of the building. Here Guards and Special Branch officers could talk freely.

Until now.

"Pluto?" Sweetman said a half hour later, as they strolled in the open air of nearby St. Stephen's Green. If the public park wasn't secure from buggers, then they were in serious trouble. "Mickey Mouse's dog?"

"No, not that Pluto." Macken caught himself scanning the other strollers in the park. Angel was getting to him.

"Oh, the planet then."

Blade stopped on the little bridge that spanned the pond. He took a clear plastic container from his pocket and pulled apart a cheese sandwich left over from a hasty office snack. He tossed the pieces in the water and watched with interest as a score of ducks converged on them.

"No, not the planet either. You mustn't have been paying attention to your Greek lessons, Sweetman."

"We didn't *have* any Greek in County Galway. *Some* of us couldn't afford to be sent to boarding school."

"Hmm. Well, Pluto was the Greek god of the underworld."

She turned to face him, smiling.

"Now that's very clever, Blade. Angel, devil, crime, under-world."

Macken dropped the sandwich container in a trash can.

"And under*ground,*" he said. "That's where this particular angel reigns supreme."

Sweetman squinted into the sun, now hanging low above the trees to the west.

"Tell me honestly, Blade," she said. "What are our chances? I mean *really.*"

"Slim." He lit a cigar.

"Hopeless, would you say?"

"Ah no, I didn't say that. It's never hopeless, Sweetman. He may be calling himself Angel, but we're not dealing with some sort of superhuman being. He's fallible, like the rest of us—with the exception of course of himself in the Vatican."

"Only when he's speaking *ex cathedra.*"

"Which is Latin for speaking out of your arse. I bet they didn't teach you that in County Galway either."

"I wish you wouldn't say things like that, sir. It's not right, so it's not."

"Ah, don't mind me, Sweetman. I'm always the same at a time like this. When I've nothing to go on. Fuck it anyway."

He started back slowly the way they'd come. Sweetman fell into step beside him.

"Why don't the Americans call off the visit? It's suicide."

"They can't, Sweetman. The president can't pull out now; he's painted himself into a corner—him and his big mouth. The media would tear him to bits."

"Better than having a bomb *blow* you to bits."

Blade wanted to smile but couldn't. "It's all the Brits' fault. They're the ones to blame. Still, Duffy says he'd have given in as well. Maybe he's right. Anything's better than having the deaths of two-hundred-odd people on your conscience."

Sweetman stopped.

"Now you've put your finger on it, Blade. Why don't we just pay the shagger his money and let him jet off to the Bahamas or wherever it is he wants to go? I know what *I* could do with twenty-five million dollars, but the government wouldn't miss it. Sure it's chicken feed compared with what we got last year from the European funds."

Blade shook his head.

"I've said it before and I'll say it again, Sweetman: You've a bloody good head on you. But sometimes you're a bit naive, d'you know that?" He put a hand on her shoulder. She looked up in surprise and he withdrew it hurriedly.

"Th-think of it this way," he said. "Our bomber's like a kidnapper—without the kid. Now you know as well as I do what kidnappers are like. They're mad bastards; they don't give a toss. Once they have the ransom money they kill their hostage anyway—ninety-nine percent of them at any rate. And that's what this fucker Angel'll do. The man's a looper; I know it. You'd *have* to be loopy to dream up something like this."

"So you reckon he'll set off the bombs anyway?"

"I do. It's the spectacle, Sweetman! Seeing your handiwork on television, having half the country talking about you in the pub. Having everyone scared out of their wits over you. He probably wanked himself silly watching the news."

"I wish you wouldn't be so crude, sir."

"Sorry. But you see my point? There's no way we can give in to him like the Brits did in Heathrow. He'd do the job anyway. *And* we'd leave ourselves wide open to some other mad bastard with a bomb and a funny voice."

"You're right, Blade."

"I know I'm right. And I wish to Christ I wasn't."

Eight

Three women had left messages on Blade's machine. One was his mother. The message was garbled, and that didn't surprise him in the least—he'd have been very surprised had Katharine's words been fully coherent. He made a mental note to call her.

The second message had been left by someone at the bank. Politely but firmly, Macken was invited to review the terms of his overdraft. He knew what *that* meant. He muttered a curse and decided to ignore the invitation for the time being.

The third caller was a stranger. Yet her voice, husky as that of a Gauloise smoker, awakened memories in Blade. He remembered a club on Leeson Street. He'd visited it on Thursday night in the company of Sweetman and a half-dozen other officers, the leftovers of Paddy O'Driscoll's farewell party. Much wine had been drunk, dances danced. There'd been a blonde woman in her late twenties who'd been dancing alone, shoeless. She'd brushed off every advance made to her—apart from Macken's.

Christ almighty tonight, how could he have forgotten! She'd been stunningly beautiful. The last time he'd dated a girl like that was the week a man walked for the first time on the moon. Blade had empathized with that walker. And she— Elaine, that was her name, the answering machine reminded him; Elaine de Rossa—she'd responded eagerly to his advances. Unbelievable. Now she was giving him her phone number, with a request that he call her.

The number seemed familiar. Then Macken recollected the seven digits he'd scrubbed off his palm the previous morning. Stupid, stupid. You didn't always get second chances with women like Elaine.

Blade picked up the receiver. He hesitated. He didn't have

55

time for this. He really didn't; not now. But more memories of Elaine de Rossa were starting to come, and Blade was a red-blooded man.

He rang the number.

"I'm not here," Ambassador Seaborg said. "I'm not in this room; I'm not hearing this conversation. Is that understood?"

He had his back turned to them, as though to add emphasis to his words. He didn't see the look that Lawrence Redfern tossed to the others.

Seventeen of them were gathered in the ambassador's office: burly men dressed eerily alike in dark, double-breasted suits. The fashion was outmoded but purposeful: The loose jackets concealed the bulges made by heavy-caliber handguns, when such weapons needed to be borne. For the moment, these and other tools of Redfern's trade were stored in the armory in the bowels of the embassy, behind a door marked ARCHIVES. The double electronic keycard that would open that door was in the custody of Seaborg's driver, Thomas Jones, who sat in a corner of the room, idly filing his nails. Seaborg wasn't privy to Jones's real name; that information was guarded by the men and women of a government facility in Langley, Virginia.

Two others present were on the embassy payroll: one an interpreter, the other a minor office functionary. Seaborg mused that they actually performed their "official" duties damn well. He didn't want to know about their other business.

The strangers had arrived at the embassy in pairs, at three- and four-hourly intervals. Their number had been complete twenty minutes ago, and Redfern had called the meeting at once.

"The room's clean, sir," he told the ambassador. "You can speak freely."

Seaborg turned.

"No, no, *you* do it. I'm too old for this kind of thing. They're your men, Major. You do it."

"Very well."

Redfern half sat, half leaned against the mahogany desk. Thomas Jones slipped his nail file back into his top pocket.

"You've all been briefed on Macken," Redfern reminded the assembly, "so you already know about his service record. It's impressive; I'd be the last person to say it wasn't. A good soldier, a good cop. Or *was*—once."

Seaborg glanced around sharply.

"The man's a walking ruin," Redfern continued. "He's past it, over the hill. My God, we had to fumigate this office yesterday when he left! If he doesn't die of lung cancer, then the booze will get him. He smelled like a distillery—at four in the goddamn afternoon."

Redfern picked up a folder.

"The man can't even go near his wife, for crying out loud. There's an exclusion order in operation; if he comes within a mile of her home they can arrest him."

"Did he beat up on her or what?"

Redfern opened the file and flipped through it, confirming what he already knew. He shook his head.

"No, Mr. Roe. He didn't go as far as that. 'Mental cruelty' is what it says here—whatever *that* means."

"Why don't they replace him? Get somebody else to head up the investigation?"

"*You* tell *me*, Mr. Roe. His superior insists he's the best they've got. All I can say is: If that's so, then God help this country."

"And God help the president," Roe said with feeling. "Can't we put pressure on their foreign-office people?"

"No!"

It was Seaborg. "Out of the question. This isn't Panama; we can't go upsetting these people. The White House would have my head on a platter."

"The colonel's right," Redfern said. "The last thing we want is to make enemies of the police. They're touchy enough already; they don't like foreigners on their patch. It's imperative we keep them on our side. We might need them before this thing is over."

"Sounds to me like you want us to do the job alone, Mr. Redfern."

"That's what I *do* mean, Mr. Coburn."

Good grief, Seaborg thought, weren't they polite mother-fuckers; weren't they just. *Mr.* Roe, *Mr.* Coburn, *Mr.* Jones. . . . Like a board meeting of merchant bankers—as opposed to merchants of death, a more fitting description for some of them—Coburn in particular. Seaborg knew the man's reputation. Why Larry Redfern had asked for that dangerous son of a bitch was something the ambassador couldn't fathom. Seaborg pulled a tiny silver case from his pocket and swallowed one of the pills it contained. The whole business wasn't doing much for his heart.

"Consider yourselves," Redfern went on, "the only game in town." He spread his hands. "Maybe the Irish cops *will* get this scumball before we do. Could be they've got resources we don't know about. But frankly, gentlemen, I doubt it."

"Having said that," he went on, "it's also obvious that Macken and his people can lay their hands on a lot more local information than we can. The police commissioner has given us authorization to operate from Harcourt Square, and that's just what we're going to do. We're to have complete access to their files. Use them. If you find something interesting, then *I* want to know what that something is before Macken does. Is that clear?"

He stood up.

"We'll keep the units intact, we'll operate in twos. Mr. Jones and I will work alone, for the most part. He has his job to do, I have mine. I'll be covering Macken, so I'll be closest to the top."

"What about the tape, Mr. Redfern?"

"It's in good hands, Mr. Sachs. We've two secure Unix mainframes in Langley working on it, plus the Crays in Canaveral and the Pentagon. I'm hopeful."

"One more thing, Mr. Redfern," Coburn said. "Are we carrying?"

Redfern laughed without humor.

"No, Mr. Coburn, we are not; not for the time being. The White House doesn't like it, and the Micks are paranoid about guns. But I promise you this: As soon as we've got something to shoot *at,* you'll be the first to know."

Nine

Jim Roche kissed Joan Macken on the cheek, dumped his briefcase in the hall and went straight to the drinks cabinet in the front room. It had been a long—but fruitful—Saturday. He poured himself three fingers of brandy, drank half quickly, and eased himself into the club chair. Joan squirted soda water into her own glass and lit a cigarette.

"You know Charlie Nolan?" Roche asked.

She nodded, although it was a rhetorical question. Roche swirled the gold liquid around in his glass, enjoying a child-like fascination with the way a shaft of evening sun caused the brandy to glow as if with an inner light.

"Well, there's something going on there. I can't quite put my finger on it, but it's bloody queer."

"What do you mean, 'queer'?"

"Well, I suppose you heard about the burglary at Don Delahunt's house?"

Joan tossed her mane of thick, heavy hair. It was prematurely gray but she'd never considered having anything done about that. Her friends assured her that it suited her, and she agreed with them.

"You mean her ladyship's jewels? Who hasn't heard about it? Sure didn't the papers pester us with nothing else for days on end."

She drained her glass and helped herself to another soda water. "Can I top you up?"

Roche passed her his brandy glass. "Apparently Duffy's put Nolan onto it and he isn't too pleased about that. I had him on the line today and he did nothing but moan for the best part of twenty minutes. Jesus, sometimes I wonder about that man."

"Oh, why's that?"

Roche studied his glass.

"Ah, I don't know. He's fifty-five if he's a day—due for retirement in a couple of years—but you'd swear sometimes you were dealing with a bleeding six-year-old."

"In what way?"

"Well, for a start, there's this thing with him and Macken."

"Sure that's been going on for years, Jim. Charlie Nolan'll go to his grave still giving out about Duffy."

"Yeah, well, it was bloody stupid of Duffy to put them both in charge of the one unit; they squabble like a pair of Kilkenny cats most of the time. If he'd done the sensible thing now and given Merrigan's job to Nolan—"

"Or Blade."

"Hmm, well I won't comment on *that*. Gerry Merrigan always thought that Nolan was the best man for the job. He told me so loads of times. He never trusted Macken; not after the accident."

Joan put her glass on the table and sat down opposite Roche.

"What really *did* happen, Jim? Do you know? Blade would never talk about it."

Roche laughed bitterly.

"I'm not surprised. Sure wasn't he the one partly responsible in the first place? If Macken'd had his shagging wits about him that day, instead of going out on the job half-sloshed, then it never would've happened."

"Are you sure? I mean about the half-sloshed? I know he was bad—Jesus, no one knows better than me—but in all the years I've known him, he never touched a drop when he was on duty. Before: sometimes. After: well, *all* the fecking time!"

"I'm just telling you what *I* was told. Merrigan and Macken were called out on that robbery . . . Where's this it was?"

"Donnybrook?"

"Yeah, Donnybrook . . . the Ulster Bank I think it was; the one on the corner of . . . Ah well, it doesn't matter. It wasn't strictly speaking, their case—they just happened to be in the vicinity when they got the call. So Merrigan told Macken to wait in the car. He reckoned he'd be only five minutes, because the Guards were there before him." Roche nipped at his drink. "But what Gerry Merrigan didn't know was that the gang were still in there."

"The gang? The bank robbers?"

"Yeah. It was sort of a freak thing really. One of the cashiers had set off the silent alarm the minute he saw the gang come in and the Guards were onto it right away. They wanted backup because they'd got another call at the same time from a fella who said he'd seen the gang going in and they were armed. But somebody on the switchboard in Harcourt Square got the message mixed up. She put the Branch onto it, because she thought it was meant for them. So poor old Gerry arrived at the place thinking that the local gardaí were there already. The trouble was, they weren't."

Joan looked puzzled. "Wouldn't he have seen a squad car if they were?"

"He did; that's just it. It was right outside. But it wasn't from Donnybrook. The gang were using a fake squad car. Looked just like the real McCoy—from a distance."

"*They* had guts."

Roche nodded. "Blade was parked right behind it, so he should have spotted the scam straight away. Only he didn't, fuck him, because he was half-asleep. When he brought Gerry to the hospital, the staff said he'd a breath on him like a brewery."

"I see. . . . "

"So Gerry'd walked in, flashing his ID, just as the gang were on their way out." Roche swirled his brandy again. "They were only kids—sixteen or seventeen. They must have been as surprised as he was. The gun probably went off by accident. He was lucky: a quarter of an inch to the left and he was a dead man."

"That's not what it said in the papers."

"No. But that's the way it happened, according to Nolan, and he was right in the thick of it. I thought you gave them things up last week?"

Joan looked at her cigarette, then crushed it out, half-smoked.

"Now don't be at me again," she said, but she was smiling. Roche was not. "I'd have kicked the fucker out of the force if it was up to me. Instead, Duffy gives him Merrigan's job—well, half of it anyway. *I* don't know," he said helplessly. "I don't know what Duffy sees in him, I really don't."

"I think you're biased, Jim. You just don't want to admit that Blade is the best they have. Always was."

"Yeah, well, he's done okay for himself, fair dues. But Jesus, poor old Gerry. They should have given him the full pension; no one deserved it more. Bloody bureaucrats! The wife killed herself—did you know that? This was before they murdered Gerry."

"Yes. Blade told me. The poor woman."

"She couldn't handle it. They'd had to sell the house to pay the nursing costs, and take the daughter out of the Tech. She was a bright kid, too. It was a bloody shame, so it was."

He clapped his hands on his knees and stood up.

"But let's not talk about it anymore. It depresses me. I've something to show you."

Roche left the room and returned with his briefcase, opened it, and pulled out a number of glossy brochures. He laid them in rows on the table. Such neatness, Joan Macken mused; she'd never known a man more obsessed with neatness and order; there was definitely something unhealthy about it. Each brochure lay absolutely parallel to its neighbor, all at exact right angles to the sides of the table. They advertised the attractions of faraway—and expensive—vacation destinations: Bermuda, the Bahamas, Acapulco, Rio, Hawaii. . . .

"Are you out of your mind, Jim? Sure we're just back from Kenya!"

He smiled. "Not a holiday, pet. I'm deciding on our retirement home, and I want you to help me."

Linda Doyle of forensics called Blade at his apartment a little before nine-thirty in the evening.

"It's jelly."

"Sorry?"

"Gelignite, Superintendent. We didn't have many samples to go on: less than four grams from under the street and about the same amount we recovered from three of the bodies."

Blade winced.

"So what does it tell us?"

"It tells us that the bomber isn't a pro, for a start. Nobody uses jelly anymore—"

"I wish you'd stop calling it that."

There was a long sigh at the other end of the line.

"Okay, gelignite. Nobody uses it for military purposes. Semtex is your only man if you want to do real damage."

"You're talking to an old soldier, Linda; I know all about it. Still, he didn't do too badly with the gelignite. . . . "

"No, but he had to use *masses* of it. And it's far more dangerous to handle than Semtex. Tricky stuff, gelignite."

"I know, I know. So where does that leave us?"

"You're the detective. I'm only giving you my findings."

Blade tried hard to keep the irritation out of his voice. He was exhausted, had been ready for bed when Doyle called.

"All right. Would we be able to trace where it came from?"

"Sorry. We'd need a better sample. This stuff's got all sorts of impurities mixed in with it."

"Right. I follow you."

"But it's very likely homegrown, Superintendent. You'd be mad to try and bring in large quantities of it, as much as the bomber needed. Unless you dumped it off the coast and picked it up later. Like they did with the heroin last week."

Blade was thoughtful. Physically tired though he was, his mind was still functioning as sharply as ever.

"Look, Linda, is gelignite standard? I mean, are there different types, or is it all made the same way?"

"Well, there are different grades of course, but gelignite is gelignite. It's composed of—"

"Let me just get a pen. Sorry, yes, go on."

"Okay. Gelignite is a modification of gelatin dynamite. In its semisolid state it's a jelly composed of about sixty-five percent nitroglycerin, varying proportions of nitrate of potash, collodion cotton—"

"Never heard of it."

"It's nitrated cellulose mixed with alcohol and ether. They use it to coat photographic film with. Anyhow, there's collodion cotton and wood pulp."

"That's it?"

"That's it."

"So if I wanted to, I could make it myself, could I? Boil up a potful of the stuff in the kitchen alongside the spuds?"

"If you'd enough nitro, yeah. That's the hardest ingredient to come by—but I'm sure you know that."

"You've been a big help, Linda. I appreciate it."

"All part of the job, Superintendent."

She'd arrived by bicycle. She wore her long, auburn hair loose, a sleeveless T-shirt and shorts, and she turned many heads in Phoenix Park as she rode by. It was close to nine in the evening on Saturday, July 4, when she passed Garda Headquarters and made a left turn.

The Furry Glen is near the park's southern extremity. For centuries, even before a wall had been built around the park, its leafy nooks and hideaways had been favored meeting places for courting couples. Jim Roche liked it; it suited him. It suited him because nobody in his circle of acquaintances would expect to find his car here; the people in his circle did their extramural trysting in luxury hotels.

She called him Daddy. He detested it but couldn't persuade her to drop the habit. It was a continual reminder—almost a taunt—that she was indeed young enough to be his daughter. But when he saw her approaching along the winding path, and the way the sunlight danced through the trees and dappled her long, suntanned legs, he wouldn't have cared if she'd called him Lucifer.

He opened the passenger door for her, but she shook her

head with a smile and slid in the back of the big Mercedes. They always did this; it was their little game.

Even before he could climb in back himself, she'd crossed her arms at the waist and yanked her T-shirt off with one smooth movement. She wore no brassiere—didn't have to: her breasts were tiny. But they were deliciously formed and Roche could take them one by one in his mouth, whole and entire, a thing that drove her to lofty heights of ecstasy. Today she wore no underwear at all. She kicked off her sneakers and was completely nude before he'd removed his tie.

"Lie down, will you," he growled. "Somebody'll see you. Jesus, it's broad daylight."

"So what? You're ashamed of me, Daddy; that's what it is. You think my tits are too small."

He hated it when she teased him like this and she knew it. Yet there was a part of him that delighted in her exhibitionism. It was she who'd chosen this spot and they kept returning to it. It wasn't the most secluded of places, not by a long shot. A car drove slowly by and Roche saw the driver's head swivel.

"I *adore* your tits," he said—and proved it to her in the manner she loved.

Later she lay, slick with sweat, on top of him, caressing his paunch with an index finger. The first time she'd seen him unclothed, he'd been ashamed of the beer gut, had attempted to hide it by walking tall. He thought her ideal would have been the taut belly of youth, but no: she genuinely liked his body; it was part of the "Daddy" package.

Her fingers moved down lower and he felt the first creepings of another erection. So soon. It was the heat, he was sure of that. It was suffocatingly hot in the car; he'd kept all the windows shut so as to profit from the concealing condensation.

"What *do* you see in Joan?" she asked suddenly.

Roche went limp at once.

"Ah now, let's not talk about Joan, all right?"

"I want to, Daddy. Whose boobs do you prefer, hers or mine?"

"Ah, Christ, don't start *that* again."

"Does she do the job better?"

"Puhl-ease!"

"A girl likes to know these things. Does she or doesn't she?"

"No. Yiz are both different, that's all I'm going to say."

"A woman is supposed to be in her prime—sexually, I mean—when she's in her forties. That means she fucks better than I do."

"You know I don't like you calling it that."

"Does Joan?"

"God almighty, will you drop it!"

"Okay, Daddy. Just tell me one thing. Does she ever talk about Blade when you're by yourselves?"

"No, and I don't blame her. The less said about that gobshite the better, as far as I'm concerned."

"But she *must* talk about him. It's not natural for her not to talk about him, so it isn't."

"Amn't I only just after telling you she doesn't? Now, for Christ's sake leave it be, will you?"

"Okay, Daddy."

But the damage had already been done: Roche's second hard-on refused to materialize that evening.

Ten

"Dogs," Blade said. "We'll use dogs."

The investigation was no respecter of the sabbath; all but two of Macken's team were present in the incident room on the third day of Angel. Redfern occupied his mute station in the wings; the other Americans rubbed shoulders with Blade's people. A camaraderie had grown between them. Duffy approved; Macken did not. He couldn't quite put his finger on it, but was certain that the CIA had their own agenda. He didn't trust Redfern an inch.

"Dogs. To do what exactly, sir?" inquired a white-haired detective. Blade didn't like the man's tone.

"We'll use them to sniff out the gelignite," he said slowly. "They do it all the time in the airport and down the docks."

"Yes sir, I know that. But they go after cargoes and things. They know where to look. You're not suggesting we send a pack of hounds traipsing around every street in Dublin?"

Give me *strength*, O Lord. Blade went to the big two-inch-scale map of the city. He took a fluorescent yellow highlighter, reached up to the top of the chart, and began to trace a route with the marker. It ended in Merrion Square, at the entrance to Leinster House, the seat of government.

"This," he said, "is the most likely route the president'll take from the airport. Am I right, Mr. Redfern?"

May as well throw the doggie a bone every so often; keep him happy and out of your hair.

The American shrugged. "I can't comment on that at the present time. That information remains classified right up until the day before the visit, when we get our orders."

"I see." Blade returned to the map and pointed. "So let's *assume* this is the route. We start here, right the way down from Collins Avenue. It's unlikely Pluto's planted anything that far

68

north, but let's do it anyway. Now, that's somewhere in the region of four miles of street, and I haven't a clue how many manholes and culverts there are. But sniffer dogs work fast, so we should be able to cover it in a day, maybe a day and a half. Then we can start on the alternative routes. Yes, Sweetman?"

"How many dogs are we talking about, sir?"

"I don't know. I haven't thought it out yet. Ten, maybe more—if we have that many. Somebody make a note to phone the kennels and find out."

"I'll requisition a few more of the brutes if needs be," Duffy said. "This thing is important enough. Top, top priority. If a couple of more kilos of heroin slip through while we're busy, then so be it." He sighed deeply. "Half the bloody stuff gets through anyway, dogs or no dogs. It makes me weep. Which reminds me . . . " He turned to a detective. "What's the story on Thursday's haul, Bill?"

The man reddened. "It's ehh, still missing, sir. We're working on it. Store Street think it might be—"

"Four million quid's worth," Duffy snarled. "Honest to God, how can that much smack disappear into thin air? You get onto Store Street and tell them to pull their finger out."

"Sir, if we could—"

"Sorry, Macken," Duffy said. "Go on."

Blade sighed. "So we can get the dogs. Grand. What I wanted to—"

"Just a second though, Macken."

"Sir . . . ?" Here we go again.

"Aren't we forgetting something? Didn't we agree at the beginning that we weren't going to show our hand? How does that square with your proposal?"

"As I said, sir, I still have to work on the details. It only occurred to me last night."

He saw Lawrence Redfern making notes.

"And it's a good plan, Macken," Duffy said. "Don't get me wrong. Full marks. But think about it for a second. We're not going to be entirely inconspicuous with a herd of Alsatians leaping in and out of manholes from here to Drumcondra."

Duffy was right, and Blade—though he hated to admit it to himself—knew that he hadn't taken into account what was in effect his own strategy. He could think of no response.

"Might I say something, sir?" It was Sweetman again.

"Fire away, Detective Sergeant."

"Well, sir, they're forever digging up the roads." Heads were nodded in resigned agreement. "Couldn't we just set up a MAJOR ROADWORKS sign—and a tent—at both ends of the route? Then we send the dogs down and keep on moving the roadworks as we progress."

She blushed slightly as she became aware of scores of eyes upon her. Redfern made another note.

"Pluto can't be in two places at the same time," Sweetman went on, "and, even if he's driving the route, he won't pay any attention to the roadworks and the tent. He won't suspect anything—not unless we happen to be in the very place where he's planted a bomb."

"But that's only two dogs, Detective Sergeant," Blade said. "It'll take a *week*."

"No, sir, it won't. I've worked with sniffer dogs before and they're very quick. They can get in and out of a culvert in no time: five minutes at the most. And at the same time we're using the other dogs on the other routes from the airport to Leinster House. We could have the job done in two days."

"She's right, Macken," Duffy said. He beamed at Sweetman. "You're talking about a half-a-dozen traffic cones, plastic tape, and a tent. Put them in a Corporation van, together with the dog and its handler, and you can move very quickly from manhole to manhole. Maybe Sergeant Sweetman's two days is a bit optimistic, but if we work around the clock, I don't see how it's going to take longer than three days at the outside."

Blade took a tissue from his pocket and mopped his brow. "Fair enough," he said. "We'll do it. Yes, Brendan . . . ?"

It was the white-haired detective again. "I don't mean to play the devil's advocate, sir," he said, "but we're not looking for drugs. We're looking for gelignite. What makes you think the dogs'll be able to sniff it out?"

Sweetman came to Macken's rescue.

"They can. I've worked with them, as I said. You can train them to sniff out almost anything. All they need is a whiff of a sample and they're off."

"Grand," the detective conceded. "But I think Sergeant Sweetman and yourself have overlooked an important point. If the bomb in O'Connell Street is anything to go by, then Pluto won't have buried the others in culverts. They'd be easily spotted for a start; those things are used all the time by the Corporation and the gas company."

"You're right," Blade said, "and I haven't overlooked it. I'm not for a moment suggesting that this is going to achieve results. But it might—and we've precious little to go on otherwise."

Somebody at the back had stuck up a hand. He was a big, athletic type. Blade knew him as the chief of the Emergency Response Unit, the elite squad that was expert in the use of firearms and antiterrorist tactics.

"Have we thought of metal detectors, sir? The gelignite won't show up but the detonators might."

Blade shook his head.

"It won't work. Have you any idea how much metal is buried under the streets of Dublin? They use plastic pipes now for water and such, and concrete, but you'll pick up anything from a Victorian farthing to a Viking helmet if you try using a metal detector. You'd have more luck finding the proverbial needle in a haystack. And what do you do if metal does show up? Start tearing up the street? You might as well send in an excavator and a bulldozer to clear every square inch of asphalt between here and the airport."

"What about our friends from the CIA?" Duffy said, casting a quick look at Redfern. "Can they help? They must have sophisticated equipment for this kind of thing. Or their army people; maybe we should contact the Pentagon."

Blade made a note. Redfern was scribbling furiously; it gave Blade a good feeling, knowing that protocol gagged the bastard as effectively as a dog muzzle.

71

"We'll certainly follow it up, sir," he said. "But let's not overestimate their capabilities. Ask yourself this: Why do even the Americans still have to clear a minefield with some guy crawling on his belly with a long stick in his hand? If there was a better way, they'd have found it by now."

Macken: one, Yanks: zero.

Duffy was somber. "Do we have *any*thing else, Macken? Good God, we're almost three days into the investigation and we've feck all to show for it!"

"Don't I know it, sir," Blade admitted grudgingly. "We have the tape and everybody's working on it—from the Park, to Washington, to Interpol. But so far nothing. Now we have a little bit of old gelignite that could have come from anywhere, maybe from somebody's garden shed; we don't know. And it's probably more than five years old—untraceable now."

"Hopeless, hopeless."

"I don't think so, sir. The first plan stands. I still believe that the bomber will show his hand soon. He *has* to. The suspense must be killing him: he's wondering what we're doing—if we have any leads on him. He'll want to know. It's my guess that we'll be hearing from him again very, very soon."

Eleven

She was even lovelier than Blade remembered: groomed to perfection, expensive clothes and accessories. Her legs were bare and suntanned.

He was glad she'd agreed to meet him in the bar on Purcell Street, his favorite. It was plain and honest, right down to the bare flagstoned floor. But, most important, it was affordable.

"You look great," he told her.

In reply she kissed him lightly on the cheek. He'd no idea what her perfume was called but suspected that a bottle would set him back a full week's salary.

"What are you drinking?"

To his great surprise she asked for a glass of stout. He wondered if Elaine de Rossa was slumming. Perhaps not; perhaps she was doing as the Romans did in Rome.

"Did you get home all right?" she asked. "I was a bit worried about you."

Shit. He hoped she wouldn't start on about Thursday night. Blade could remember parts of it now but most remained a blank. He used the excuse of getting up to order drinks, to call a halt to Elaine's line of inquiry.

The bar was already full, although it was only a little after eight. There was the usual Sunday-night crowd and Blade nodded to familiar faces. Old Sandy O'Rourke was tuning his fiddle at the far end of the counter. There were two full pints in front of him and Blade knew from experience that the tuning could take several hours yet: Sandy was a perfectionist; he usually got it right—by his lights—somewhere around eleven o'clock, when the cry came: "Time, ladies and gents now, please!"

The barkeep glanced up from pulling a Guinness.

73

"Blade! How's she cutting? Nice bit of frock you have there. Where did you pick *her* up?"

"Never you mind, Joe, never you mind. Give 's a pint and a glass, would you."

Joe's three young assistants sped from one end of the long counter to the other, taking orders, pulling pints, squirting shorts, and handling money with a speed that always astounded Blade. You wouldn't, he reflected, see this in any other country. They were probably earning half his bloody salary, too, among the three of them.

"Desperate altogether about Friday," Joe said.

"The pits."

"I hear there's thirty people still in hospital. And they're the *lucky* ones. They reckon the little toddler'll be blind for life."

"It's fucking awful."

The barkeeper slowly poured more stout into the glasses. A customer, a stranger with a broad, country accent, shouted for service.

"I'll be right with you!" Joe called back. "Jayziz, they don't give you a bleeding minute, Blade. Fucking boggers."

He leaned across the counter. "What's this I hear about a bomb?"

"Give 's five Hamlet as well, while you're at it. Who said anything about a bomb?"

"Fuck's sake, Blade, don't be acting the gom with *me*. Was it or wasn't it? Yeah, yeah, I'll be right with you!" The customer from the provinces was deciding whether to move to more accommodating licensed premises.

"It wasn't a bomb, Joe," Macken said softly.

"Ah, who are you codding, Blade? A gas main! Sure if I heard it from Mother Teresa's holy lips, I'd make her say three decades of the rosary for telling lies. If you think I'd be stupid enough to believe a story like that, then you might as well dream here as in bed."

He topped off Macken's order with a practiced flourish of froth and tossed a pack of Hamlets on the counter.

"I hear they put *you* on it."

"News travels fast."

The barman winked. "Listen, if I hear anything, I'll let you know."

"Thanks, Joe. Now you better serve that Kerryman before he wrecks the shagging place."

Blade returned with the drinks. Elaine was leafing through a tabloid newspaper that a customer had left behind.

"Gosh, you took your time."

"Just saying hello."

"Well, cheers." Elaine sipped her stout and wiped her lips with a brilliant white handkerchief. Blade saw no lipstick smear left on the fabric. He'd thought her makeup flawless; now he realized she wasn't wearing any; she'd no need to.

"Listen," she said, "there's something I've been wanting to ask you. Did you mean that: what you said on Thursday night?"

Fuck. He'd hoped she wouldn't start on about that night. He prayed it wasn't anything embarrassing.

"Er, what's that, Elaine?" Blade tried to sound as casual as he could. He took a long swig of stout.

"Oh, you know: about your being a Special Branch man. It's not true is it? You were just trying to impress me?"

Macken breathed a sigh of relief; Elaine interpreted it as a Guinness drinker's sigh of pleasure on sampling the first pint of the evening.

"No, no. It's true."

"Golly! Is it dangerous?"

"It can be."

Her eyes were shining; Blade relaxed.

"You're not on the Drug Squad, are you?"

"No. Serious crime: murder and stuff."

"Gosh." She took another nip of Guinness. Blade nodded to a newcomer of his acquaintance and lit a Hamlet. "Is that how you got those scars?" she asked then.

"Scars?"

"The ones you showed me."

Blade almost choked on a mouthful of cigar smoke. He went red in the face, his eyes began to water, and he had to swallow a third of his drink before his throat returned to normal.

Had he heard her correctly? His scars. Jesus, had they *done the job* on Thursday night? He studied his companion. Had he actually been to bed with this beautiful creature? And he didn't remember a thing.

The waste, the bloody waste! He cursed himself, cursed his drinking, swore to cut down—or maybe cut it out altogether. This was what came of overdoing it. She'd probably been like a demon in the sack, too. And he couldn't remember a blessed thing.

He decided to feel his way.

"Er, I wasn't much use to you, was I, Elaine? I mean . . . er, on Thursday night. The drink. . . . "

Her eyes opened wide and he saw her hand go to her breast.

"You must be joking. You were fantastic!" She slipped a hand onto his thigh and whispered in his ear. "I *told* you that night that I'd never come before. At least, not that way—and never with a man. You were brilliant." She squeezed his knee.

He didn't know what to say. He was flattered—over the moon, in fact—that this young woman could say such things about him. But Christ and his blessed mother in a handcart, she could have told him he'd screwed her till dawn and he'd no way of knowing if it was the truth. He was definitely going to give up the booze.

But not right this minute. Blade went to the bar again for more stout. When he returned, Elaine was nowhere to be seen. But she reappeared five minutes later from the direction of the restroom. He saw Joe sizing her up.

"There were two girls in the ladies talking about Friday," Elaine said. "One of them knew somebody who's still in the Mater. On life support."

"It's terrible."

"They're saying it wasn't a gas leak. They're saying it was a bomb."

"Who is?"

"Everybody. It was in the paper again today."

"Oh? Which paper's that?"

"The *News of the World*."

"That's not a paper, Elaine. Jesus, I wouldn't have thought you'd be caught dead reading a rag like that."

"I don't. I only saw the headline when I went to get my own paper." She was peeved and Blade could have kicked himself.

She reached for her drink.

"Is it true, though? Was it a bomb and is someone covering up?"

"No one's covering anything up, Elaine. And even if they were, I wouldn't be allowed to talk about it."

She cast him a strange look; he couldn't read it.

"I saw something odd, too, today. In D'Olier Street."

"Mmm?"

"Yeah. There was this Alsatian with some Corporation men. If you ask me they were sending him down a manhole. Isn't that funny? On a Sunday."

"Probably sniffing for a gas leak."

"I've never seen *that* before. Don't they use detectors for that?"

"I wouldn't know, Elaine." He didn't like where the talk was going.

"You may be great in the hay, Blade Macken," she said with a grin, "but you don't seem much of a detective to me." She squeezed his thigh again, higher up. "I'm only kidding. It's funny though."

"It's a funny old world, yeah," Blade said, for want of anything better.

Just then his cellular phone rang.

"BLADE! DID I CATCH YOU AT A BAD TIME? YOU WEREN'T WASHING YOUR SMALLS OR ANYTHING LIKE THAT, WERE YOU?"

He stiffened and put his hand over the mouthpiece.

"Ehh, it's business," he told Elaine. "I'll have to take it outside."

"Work away. Don't mind me."

But Elaine de Rossa had minded Blade Macken, had caught his startled expression, and had wondered about the identity of a caller who could have that much effect on a man she'd regarded as being tough as nails.

She hadn't seen Blade's scars. It had been a hunch: men like Macken usually had scars. He'd told her that Thursday night that he'd been a soldier, and soldiers have scars. He hadn't told her much else, hadn't been able to. When she'd helped him into the cab she'd ordered to bring him home from the club on Leeson Street, he'd gone to sleep almost before she'd shut the door.

Same street, different nightclub. Blade had tried to make it clear to her in the pub that he'd planned on having an early night; the investigation took priority over carousing. Elaine hadn't listened. Now here they were again on Leeson Street, sharing overpriced wine at a wall table in the semidarkness of a club that could have been the one where they'd met. Only the brash, blue neon at street level had distinguished it from the others on "The Strip."

She was irresistible, that was the trouble. She sat with her head against Blade's shoulder and a hand brushing his thigh with soft motions. Her perfume made him lightheaded.

An invisible disc jockey was playing the Carpenters, music Blade detested, but he hardly noticed it. He was mesmerized by a pattern of tiny, rainbow-colored squares of light that winked on and off in two pillars that flanked the dance floor. If there were other Sunday-night patrons, then Blade didn't see them in the darkened club. There was no indication, apart from the miniskirted waitress, that Elaine and he were not completely alone.

"You were great that night," she said softly into his ear. "It's true what they say: older men are better."

Oh God, not again. He couldn't keep up the pretense forever.

78

"Hmm. Look, I know hardly anything about you, Elaine."
He took a shot in the dark. "Tell me about the horses again."
"My father's horses?"
Bull's-eye. "Yes, how many did you say he owns?"
"Oh, heaps. But he's never had a horse win the Derby and that kills him. It's not the prize money, Blade; it's the prestige he's after. But somebody else always pips him at the post. It drives him batty."
Blade saw two figures huddled together in the shadows on the far side. There was the flare of a cigarette lighter. Not alone after all. Dead, rake-thin Karen Carpenter still dispensed the saccharin.
"Do you still ride yourself?" he asked.
She giggled. "Now what's *that* supposed to mean?" He felt her fingers undo two buttons of his shirt and slide inside. Her fingertips were cool against his chest. "But if you mean do I still hunt: yes, now and then. You can't beat that sensation of the wind in your hair and a big stallion between your legs."
He laughed; Elaine giggled again. "Now you have *me* at it."
The waitress glided past and Blade ordered another bottle of wine, though he couldn't afford it. Twenty pounds! He'd have to economize on something else this week. Food, maybe. He was suddenly conscious of the luminous face of his watch glowing in the dark. He stole a surreptitious look at it.
Two A.M.
"Elaine, listen. I can't stay much longer. I've a busy day to-morrow. Today."
"Criminals to catch."
"Yeah."
"What a pity, now. I'm as randy as hell tonight." She poked her tongue into his ear and breathed. Elaine de Rossa was driving him crazy.
Blade allowed his hand to slide from her waist down to the curve of her hip. He felt no contour of underwear through the shiny, thin material of her dress. Jesus, when had she taken her panties off? She wriggled against him sensuously. Blade felt his blood pumping.

79

"Another time then," she whispered in her Gauloise smoker's voice. "I'll ring you, darling. We can have an early meal somewhere, and then . . . "

They finished the second bottle of exorbitantly marked-up cooking wine without speaking, listening to Barry Manilow's greatest hits while the other couple shuffled as one entity around the dance floor.

Later, as they were stepping into the cab that would bring them to their respective apartments, a police car raced past, siren screaming. Blade was reminded of the work ahead of him.

It struck him now why the distorted voice he'd listened to outside the bar had disturbed him more than ever. An old drinker like himself should have known straight away: The bomber had been far from sober.

His quarry was even more dangerous and unpredictable than he'd intimated to Sweetman. Angel could lose control just as easily as the next man.

But the next man hadn't got his finger on the detonator.

Twelve

Blade woke in a sweat on Monday, the fourth day of Angel. "Sweet mother of holy divine fuck," he groaned. On a scale of one to ten, he'd have accorded this particular hangover a six: less severe than that of Friday, but blinding and distressing nonetheless.

His doorbell was ringing, a playback of that morning. But this time it wasn't Sweetman. Groggily, blearily, Blade tried to come to terms with the fact that his visitor was Lawrence Redfern, soberly dressed as before, bright of eye and sharp of wit.

"Jesus . . . you!" was all Blade could think to say.

"Might I come in? It's important."

Redfern didn't even try to hide his disgust on seeing the condition of the apartment. He set his attaché case down carefully on a relatively clean portion of carpet.

"I've got a little something for you. Compliments of the agency."

Redfern looked around, saw a copy of Saturday's *Irish Independent* on the sofa. He folded it open—and stopped what he was doing when his attention was drawn to the five large photographs that dominated the front page. They showed the shocking harvest of Angel's deadly work. One was of a smiling young woman wearing a lace bridal veil; it was probably the only shot of the deceased that the picture desk could find at short notice. Redfern bit his lip when he saw the chubby, round face of the youngest victim of the atrocity: Little two-year-old Hughie Power had died in his baby buggy.

Redfern had a daughter that age.

With brisk, angry movements he spread the newspaper on the sticky surface of the coffee table and placed his attaché case flat upon it.

The insult wasn't lost on Macken.

Redfern flipped open the case and took out a smart, leather pouch about seven inches long. It contained a matte black cellular phone.

"I already *have* a mobile," Blade said sourly.

"Sure you have, but not like this baby."

Redfern extended the antenna and punched in four numbers. He held the instrument to his ear, listened for a few moments, then said, "Thank you very much. Have a nice day."

"Who was that?"

Redfern grinned. "A lady with a lovely voice."

Then he pressed a button on the back of the phone and held it a little way from Blade's ear.

"At the signal, it will be seven, forty-two, and twenty seconds."

An electronic blip sounded.

"Thank you very much. Have a nice day."

"A memophone," Blade said dismissively. "Big deal."

"It's more than that," Redfern said, retracting the antenna and shutting off the power. "This is different. Won't be on the market until the fall. This is *strictly* a limited edition."

He flipped up a semitransparent cover on the back of the unit and extracted a tiny audiocassette.

"Digital audio technology. A thirty-minute tape. Anything you or your caller says is recorded in high quality, twenty-four-bit digital sound. Oh, and there's even a built-in fax, too, if you need it." He replaced the little cassette and handed the phone to Blade.

Despite himself, Blade was impressed.

"I don't suppose it'll do my laundry though, will it?"

Redfern remained impassive. "We programmed it to the same number as your present unit. When Angel calls you, he's got no way of knowing that the switch has been made."

He reached into his attaché case again.

"Here. There's a pack of twenty tapes in there. Best to carry a couple with you at all times. It's unlikely he'll stay on the line that long but we can't be certain."

In spite of his dislike of Redfern, despite his reluctance to accept a "gift" from the CIA, Blade had to admire the ingenuity of the device. It was moreover a beautifully designed machine: its smooth, black contours fitted his hand to perfection.

"Is there a manual to go with it?"

Redfern shook his head with a thin smile.

"You shouldn't even be *handling* the goddamn thing. If the company who built it knew we'd loaned it to you, they'd hit the agency with a multimillion-dollar lawsuit."

Blade scratched the stubble on his chin. Something had just occurred to him.

"Who gave you my number anyway?"

Redfern smiled then in such a cocksure way that it was all Macken could do to stop himself from punching him in the mouth.

"Your chief. Duffy. Do you have a problem with that?"

Jesus, he was going to give Duffy the roasting of his life. The man ought to have had more sense. Wasn't he the very one who'd warned Blade about American interference? And now this.

Redfern shut his attaché case and picked it up, his mission completed. He barely looked at Blade as he made for the hall. He opened the front door, then turned on the step.

"I think it's worth remembering, Macken," he told Blade, "that we're on the same side. Seems to me you have a tendency to forget that."

The supercilious bastard! Blade had had *enough*. It wasn't the hangover—that was clearing. It went far and away beyond that.

"I don't think I like you, Redfern," he said slowly. "In fact, now that I think about it, I'm *positive* I don't like you. But it's nothing personal, you understand. It's your country's general attitude that pisses me off. You waltz in here and think it's fucking Grenada, and that you can lord it over us and throw your weight around to your heart's content."

He prodded the American in the chest.

"Well you're wrong, pal. This isn't some little banana republic. We already had a great civilization here when your country was nothing but a wilderness with tribes of savages living in their own shite and scalping you if you so much as looked crooked at them."

Redfern bristled. "I happen to be third-generation English."

"That's exactly what I mean," Blade said, and shut the door in the American's face.

Thirteen

Orla Sweetman was looking morose when Macken got to Harcourt Square. She leafed listlessly through a morning tabloid, taking nothing in—not even the front-page story that read: GARDA COVER-UP? A plastic beaker of coffee with a film of congealed milk on top stood on her desk.

"What's the matter, Sweetman? Did the budgie pass away in the night?"

"Ah, it's John, Blade. He keeps ringing me here, after I begged him not to. He's put *years* on you, that man."

Macken helped himself to coffee from the percolator, sat down at his desk, and cleared a space for the beaker between the untidy accumulation of papers.

"Why do you put up with him then?"

"Because he's my fecking fiancé!"

Blade grinned. "God almighty, Sweetman, if you're like this *before* you're married, I hate to think how it'll be when you do get round to it."

Sweetman turned more pages.

"How long are you two engaged, anyway?"

"Five-and-a-half years."

Blade whistled and tossed three sugar cubes in his coffee.

"Is that normal in your part of the country? I knew you were a bit traditional in County Galway, but I thought that sort of thing went out with the matchmakers and pigs in the parlor."

"It's not funny, Blade!" she retorted angrily. "You'd be depressed as well if you hadn't worked in four years." She folded the newspaper and laid it aside.

"There's no sign of a job then?"

"Ah, get real, Blade. In the printing industry? Sure they're

85

letting people go every day of the week. John is sick writing job applications."

"Jesus, it must be rough all the same, the pair of you living on your salary. Is he signing on?"

"He's too fecking proud. Anyway, it'd hardly be worth his while for what he'd get on benefit."

Macken's phone rang. It was Duffy, wanting to see him.

"The very man," Blade told his assistant. He picked up his coffee and pulled on his jacket. "I've a bone to pick with *him*."

He almost bumped into two men on rounding the corner. They were the last people he wanted to see that morning. Some of his coffee splashed onto his hand and he swore mightily.

"Hello, Macken," Superintendent Nolan said with a snide grin. "Rough night again?"

Blade grunted. "What's *he* doing here?"

Jim Roche, briefcase in one hand and beaker of coffee in the other, shifted uncomfortably. He couldn't meet Macken's eye, and walked on.

"Now, now," said Nolan, "a bit a common courtesy wouldn't go astray. Jim's here with Duffy's blessing, y'know."

"Oh? Is he helping us with our inquiries?"

Nolan smiled at Macken's little insult; the garda euphemism for the interrogation of a suspect was a running joke at the Square.

"If you must know, Jim's helping us look into the break-in at Don Delahunt's house."

"The family jewels? Yeah, I heard all about it. The wife's up in arms, isn't she?"

"That's right," Nolan said. "Old Don may be retired but he's still got enough political clout to make it warm for everybody. Look, Macken, I know we don't see eye to eye but surely to God you can appreciate that Duffy's on the spot. He won't have a minute's peace until this is cleared up. And you know what *that* means."

Blade knew. An unhappy assistant commissioner meant an

unhappy department; Duffy's moods had a habit of sucking you into them.

"Jim's the best man for the job, y'know," Nolan continued. "He's the only one in the country who understands the system that Delahunt's got up there. *I* thought microwaves were cookers until Jim explained it to me. Bloody amazing."

"Until they go wrong," Blade said. "Who installed the system anyway?"

"A Swiss firm. They went bust last year."

"Hmm. So Cock's the fireman, is he?"

"Yeah. Jim reckons he can rebuild it from scratch."

"Well, good luck to him." Blade went on his way.

Yet just before he stepped into the assistant commissioner's office, he pondered over the encounter with Nolan. Brief though it was, the exchange had been the longest conversation Macken and Nolan had had in a long time. They avoided each other whenever possible.

Nolan, Blade decided, was up to something.

The sniffer dogs had covered almost half the route to Leinster House by noon on Tuesday, the fifth day of Angel. They'd found nothing, as Blade had feared. It had been a very long shot.

The rest of Macken's investigation team had likewise drawn a blank. Several of the detectives had questioned IRA men incarcerated in Mountjoy Prison and Portlaoise, the country's most secure jail. Nothing. Pardons and reduction of sentences had been hinted at as rewards for information on the bomber. "Freelance" had been the term most used by the prisoners they'd questioned. Angel's modus operandi put him outside the working of a terrorist cell, the three-man IRA unit that was the bane of Britain's security forces.

Macken's team had had to tread carefully. The bomb on O'Connell Street remained hypothetical; the gas-leak story still held—tenuously, but it still held—and any allusion to devices buried underground had been couched in the vaguest language. Yet the detectives had come away from the prisons convinced that Angel was indeed a freelance. And all the more dangerous for that.

Blade's team had pulled the files on every known terrorist who'd operated in Ireland, Britain, and mainland Europe since the Northern Ireland "troubles" had begun almost thirty years before. Redfern's men had gone through their own lists. They'd scrutinized every bombing, searching for some detail that could provide a link with Angel. Again, nothing. The man seemed not to have existed before July 3, 1998.

Yet he must have had a past, and that was why Macken and Sweetman were visiting Dr. Patricia Earley at her rooms in Trinity College.

Sweetman ran a red light at the junction of Clare Street and South Leinster Street and blithely ignored the angry honking of horns.

"We're not in *that* big of a hurry," Blade muttered.

"Sorry. Force of habit."

She showed her ID at the rear gate of the college and they were directed to the visitors' parking lot in the shadow of the eighteenth-century buildings. The campus was thronged with tourists; the boundary of the cricket green had become a picnic area, as well as a mecca for sunbathers and groups of idle youths. Blade caught a whiff of an illegal substance and shook his head with a smile.

Dr. Earley was a gracious hostess. She served them Earl Grey tea in fragile cups and saucers of bone china. Seated in a club chair in her sitting room, among her books and antique furniture, the psychologist reminded Blade more than ever of his mother.

"I've been through the tape I don't know how many times, Blade," she said, "and I know most of it by heart now. What intrigued me in the beginning is how his language continually changes. At times it's almost as though we're dealing with two people. He can be extremely erudite one minute; the next he's using the language of the gutter."

She paused to sip her tea.

"But not only that," she went on. "It's his use of the second-person plural that had me baffled. He uses 'you,' 'ye,' 'yiz' and 'yooze' almost indiscriminately. Very few people do; they will tend to choose one pair and adhere to that pair, whatever the context."

Blade nodded.

"What, I kept asking myself, could account for this shift?" Earley said. "Background? No; we tend to adopt the speech patterns of our peers. Of course, we will change the patterns at times—for example when we are in conversation with someone either higher up or lower down the social ladder. We do this either to impress, or when we are engaged in what linguists call social bonding. In other words, we tailor our language in order that we might identify with a certain group."

"So how does Angel fit in?" Blade asked. Sweetman was making notes.

"Angel, I believe, is otherwise. It is my opinion that we are dealing with a working-class man who is largely self-educated. In the normal run of things, formal schooling eradicates much of the speech characteristics of one's roots. A self-educated man, on the other hand, would retain a good many of these speech characteristics, while adopting the patterns of better-educated speakers. This, I think, accounts for the fluctuations."

Blade put his cup and saucer on a low table.

"That's very interesting, Doctor. So you're saying he's a self-made man?"

"I believe so. I also believe him to be from the northside of Dublin."

"Oh, why's that?"

"It's a little complicated, Blade, so I won't bore you with the details. Suffice to say that his vocabulary points in that direction. I also believe him to be extremely disturbed mentally. Possibly schizophrenic."

"Split personality, doctor?" Sweetman said. She continued writing without looking up.

"No, the two illnesses should never be confused. Technically speaking, schizophrenia is not really an illness at all, but rather a set of symptoms that can differ widely. But it is not split personality. It is, rather, an almost total *lack* of personality. The schizophrenic cannot distinguish right from wrong; he cannot distinguish reality from delusion. To the schizophrenic, the world is a frightening place, Detective Sergeant. He must rebuild it each day of his life, according to his own perception of how the world *ought* to be. I believe that this man Angel is such a one."

Blade breathed hard. "So he *is* a nutter. I thought as much."

Earley frowned. "If you must use that word, yes."

"Hmm. How do we handle him then, Doctor?"

"With extreme caution, Blade. The next time he rings you, say nothing that might upset him. One word of criticism from you could set off a chain reaction of psychotic behavior. Make him believe that you're on his side, that you understand. No matter what he says, no matter how confused it may be, try to assure him that you are in full agreement with him. That he has a friend."

"I'll certainly try, Doctor. Thanks for the warning."

Blade stood up a half hour later. Dr. Earley's cautionary words had made a deep impression on him. Sweetman laid her teacup and saucer aside and shut her notebook.

"One more thing, Doctor," Blade said. "How do you actually recognize a schizophrenic? I mean, is there any pattern of behavior you should look for?"

Earley shook her head.

"I wish there were. Forget any preconceived notions you may have had about a schizophrenic being a raving lunatic. Outwardly he's normal—most of the time. You could be living with a schizophrenic for years without knowing it. Oh, there are little signs: compulsive behavior, obsessive neatness perhaps, overattention to trivialities. But generally speaking he'll appear to be as normal as you or I."

"I was afraid you'd say that, Doctor."

* * *

90

They left the car parked in the grounds of Trinity College, walked out into the milling lunchtime throng on Lincoln Place, and headed for a sandwich shop on Nassau Street.

They passed a street vendor selling small American flags and presidential paraphernalia: buttons, stickers, and T-shirts bearing the smiling face of the statesman whose visit loomed nearer. The sight of the souvenirs made Blade uneasy.

"Can you spare some small change for a bit o' food for the child?" a voice sang out.

It was a beggar-woman, squatting on the lowest step of an office building. She wore a plaid shawl in which an infant was swaddled. Blade ignored her.

"Is it my imagination," he said to Sweetman, "or are there more of them around than this time last year?"

"More what?"

"The beggars. You'd break your neck over them."

"Hmm, I hadn't noticed." Sweetman cast a glance behind at the beggar. "I'd give her a pound," she said, "but you know as well as I do, Blade, that she'd only spend it on drink anyway."

Dodging the traffic, they crossed the street, and managed to find a table in the crowded lunchroom. Blade had an egg mayonnaise sandwich, the cheapest item on the menu.

His phone rang just as he took his first bite. The sound attracted no attention; there was another cellular phone being used in the sandwich shop and he heard the ring of yet another two tables along. This was cellular-phone territory.

"HELLO, BLADE! ALL QUIET ON THE WESTERN FRONT?"

Macken swallowed, and quietly pressed the RECORD button at the back of the unit.

"Hello, Angel. I was expecting you sooner or later."

"YOU SOUND IN GOOD FORM, SO YOU DO. ARE YOU IN THE PUB AGAIN?"

"No, just having a sandwich."

He stood up and moved out to the doorway. The reception was marginally better.

"THAT'S GOOD. YOU SHOULDN'T DRINK ON AN EMPTY STOM-
ACH, BLADE. IT'S BAD FOR THE LITTLE GRAY CELLS. THAT'S WHAT
POIROT ALWAYS SAYS."

"I'll remember that."

"YOU KNOW WHY I'M CALLING, DON'T YOU?"

"I can guess."

"HOW'S EVERYTHING AT THE SQUARE? IS NOLAN BEHAVING
HIMSELF? HE ALWAYS WAS A BIT OF A BACK-STABBING CUNT, WASN'T
HE? AM I RIGHT?"

"You know Nolan as well?"

"I KNOW EVERYBODY, BLADE. LISTEN, A WORD OF ADVICE: KEEP
AN EYE ON CHARLIE NOLAN, OKAY? HE'S NOT TO BE TRUSTED, ES-
PECIALLY WHERE YOU'RE CONCERNED."

Macken felt his skin crawl. How could the bomber know
such things? It was eerie. He said: "I'll bear it in mind, Angel.
Thanks."

"THINK NOTHING OF IT. NOW LET'S GET DOWN TO BUSINESS. I'M
SURE I DON'T HAVE TO REMIND YOU THAT THERE'S LESS THAN
SEVEN DAYS TO GO. WHAT'S HAPPENING, BLADE? WHAT'S THE
STORY ON MY MONEY?"

"It's coming."

"I MEANT EVERYTHING I SAID ON FRIDAY, BLADE. I DON'T GIVE
A SHITE WHO COMES UP WITH THE MONEY, BUT IF IT ISN'T THERE
ON THE FOURTEENTH, THEN IT'S BOOM TIME."

Careful, careful. Kid gloves.

"Look, I understand perfectly, Angel, and I can imagine
what it's like being kept in suspense, but I can assure—"

"DON'T PATRONIZE ME!"

Fuck.

"I'm not, I'm not. I only wanted to make clear to you that
you've nothing to worry about. The money'll be paid. It's just
a question of cutting through a lot of red tape, that's all."

"GOOD. ENJOY YOUR SANDWICH, BLADE."

Blade heaved a sigh and partially rewound the tape. It had
worked.

Angel's voice had gone on record.

* * *

"Have you got a minute, Charlie?"

"Not really," Superintendent Nolan said. "I'm up to me bleeding eyes at the moment. What's up?"

"Is Roche still with you?"

"No, he left ten minutes ago. Look, what is it, Paddy? I really am up to me tonsils here."

He was, too. His desk was every police officer's tribulation: the stack of papers on the left was supposed to decrease as the stack on the right rose, but for some inexplicable reason the process appeared to be working in reverse. Then there was the pile of security-alarm manuals Jim Roche had left behind for his attention. Nolan had opened one at random—and had shut it again immediately. The diagram had resembled a map of the London Underground redrawn by a chimpanzee.

"Well, if I was you, I'd drop everything and get down here right away. I want you to be the first to see this."

"Fuck's sake, Paddy, what is it?"

"Not over the phone. . . . "

"Right. I'm on my way."

He found Detective Sergeant Paddy Flynn in a corner of the big incident room, shielded from the rest of Blade's investigation team by a shoulder-high dividing partition. Nolan's friend and golf partner was seated in front of a computer terminal, one of many identical units linked to the giant server in the basement.

"You better sit down, Charlie."

Nolan sat. "And this better be good."

"That's not exactly the word I'd use." Flynn gestured toward a neat pile of folded printout. "Macken asked us to go back nine or ten years. 'Solved and unsolved cases,' he said; 'leave no stone unturned.' Well, I did, Charlie, and would you look what I found."

Nolan froze, and was glad the other detective couldn't see the expression on his face. The chickens had come home to roost. He stared at the screen with a rapidly beating heart.

"Call it coincidence if you like," Flynn went on, unaware of his colleague's distress, "but this particular investigation is *exactly* nine years old. You should know: it was one of yours."

The roosting chickens were pecking viciously at Nolan's vitals. He was back in the summer of '89—the night of Saturday, July 1, to be precise.

The message had come into Harcourt Square at around eleven at night. Somebody at Centurion hadn't received the call-in from two of their security guards. It was probably nothing, the man had said; the guards had most likely forgotten to call headquarters at the routine time. Probably in the middle of a hand of poker. . . . But could they send a car to check all the same?

Nolan wouldn't have known about it had he not been drinking coffee with a friend at the dispatch desk at Garda Command and Control. The squad car had reported a break-in at Kildare House, a building shared by a number of government departments: Industry and Commerce, the Department of Finance, others. It was considered "low risk" by Centurion Security and consequently the company had it manned by their more elderly guards, retired policemen in the main.

The uniformed gardaí had found signs of forced entry at Kildare House, the desk unattended. It hadn't taken them long to discover the whereabouts of the two security guards; they lay on the third floor of the building, bludgeoned to death. One of them was Gerry Merrigan, Nolan's old superior. The patrolmen had recognized him and had called the Square.

Nolan had alerted Blade Macken and the two had covered the short distance to Kildare Street in under three minutes. Both men had wept that night. Gerry Merrigan had been more than simply their chief.

But if the Saturday night had been unsettling for Nolan, the following morning had brought even more surprises. Jim Roche had summoned him to his office at Centurion and told him facts that had made Nolan's hair stand on end. He'd known that Roche had his finger in many pies, but when Roche had passed the file across to him and informed him of its contents, Nolan had been taken aback.

The papers were fake, Roche had assured him; the genuine articles were now in safe hands. Were that not the case, then the following morning they'd have been scrutinized by an employee of the Department of Industry and Commerce and a scam, involving a multimillion-pound tax swindle, would have come to light. Heads would have rolled, including that of Jim Roche. Roche was on the board of the offending company: Banba Meat Marketing.

But there'd been more. Roche, panic-stricken, had confessed his part in the break-in that had led to the retrieval of the file. Calling on his contacts in the underworld, he'd hired the two burglars to ransack the office where the file had been kept. The security guards had surprised them. Roche had blood on his hands.

Nolan remembered the conversation in Roche's office as if it had taken place yesterday.

"I'll hang, Charlie," he'd said. "I'm up to me fucking neck in it."

"So what do you want *me* to do about it?"

Nolan should have guessed. Roche had patted the fake file.

"I want you to slip that in the safe where they kept the real one. Room forty-seven. The boys left the safe open. It'll be a piece of cake, Charlie. There'll be a garda seal on the building; all you have to do is rough up another office, so it'll look like they were after something in *there*."

"For fuck's sake, Jim!"

"You have to do it, Charlie. There's no one else."

"What do you take me for? That's tampering with evidence. I'd lose me job over it—and probably end up behind bars. No, no, find some other mug. I won't do it, and that's that."

Roche's eyes had narrowed. "You *will*, Charlie. 'Cause if I go down, then by Jesus I'll take you with me."

Then Roche had produced the tapes.

Nolan hadn't known how the fucker had done it—but it shouldn't have been too difficult for Roche, given his occupation. Roche had it all: every single "business" conversation they'd had together over the years. Each time Nolan had put

95

work Roche's way, he'd incriminated himself. What, he'd asked himself, was worse? Being found out tampering with evidence or being caught taking "commission"? Talk about a shagging rock and a hard place.

He'd been unable to contact Macken the morning after the slayings. Nolan had guessed that Blade was drowning his sorrows somewhere, and for once Blade's excessive drinking had worked to his partner's advantage.

It had gone according to plan. Nolan had been the investigating officer and so had had priority access to every square inch of the building.

He'd done it, and more. He'd even been able to convince poor Gerry Merrigan's widow that Macken was somehow involved in dirty dealings related to the case. The murderers had evaded capture; Nolan had seen to that. The case was closed.

Until this moment.

Detective Superintendent Nolan watched with mounting dread as his colleague summoned up a list of names on the computer screen. They meant nothing to Nolan.

"I didn't know anything about the case," Flynn said. "I'd just come on. But I did some cross-referencing. These are companies that were due to be examined the following Monday— the one right after the murder—by the auditors from Industry and Commerce."

Nolan scanned the list. An abbreviation, BMM, sprang to his attention. Banba Meat Marketing, exporter to the developing countries of the world.

"Where did you get this?" he asked in what he hoped was a neutral voice.

"Ah, that's the beauty of it, Charlie." Flynn patted the keyboard. "We didn't have these little boyos nine years ago. It was all paperwork then. But Duffy had a bunch of lads in last year—computer men—who transferred half the archive down below onto the system. It took them months, I believe. But it was well worth it. Watch."

Flynn called up another file, also containing a list of companies. Nolan's palms began to sweat.

"This is a year later—1990—shortly before the Beef Tribunal, when the bold boys in the meat industry were shitting themselves." He pointed at the screen. "These are firms that had 'convenient' burglaries just before the state auditors got round to them. Now watch this."

He hit a series of keys. Two names were highlighted on the screen; one of them was BMM. Nolan loosened his collar.

"Here's the good part," Flynn said. "Look who was involved, right up to his red neck."

There they were: the members of the board of Banba Meat Marketing. Jim Roche's name was near the bottom—and highlighted. Flynn then brought up another file; a bar across the top of the screen identified it as the property of the Dublin chamber of commerce. It listed the commercial interests of a certain James P. Roche.

"BMM," Flynn crowed triumphantly. "*And*"—he moved the cursor up the list—"Centurion Security." He turned around to face Nolan. "Who just happened to be guarding both Kildare House and BMM offices when they were burgled. How do you like *that*, Charlie?"

Charlie would have liked the tundra of Siberia better at that moment; it was safer. His mind was a ferment.

"Listen, Paddy," he said urgently, "let's keep this between ourselves for the time being, all right? What I mean is: Don't let on to Macken."

Flynn raised an eyebrow.

"What I'm saying, Paddy, is if anyone's going to nail Roche, then I want it to be me. Good fuck! I'm *working* with the hoor at the moment and you'd swear butter wouldn't melt in his mouth. The cunt!"

"D'you reckon he'd something to do with Merrigan's murder then?"

"I don't know, Paddy; I don't know. But that particular investigation gave me a few more gray hairs than I was due. *Plus*

97

the fact that Gerry was a good friend. The best. I owe it to him as well."

He looked at the screen again.

"So will you keep it under your hat, Paddy? For the time being? Blade has enough to keep him busy anyway. More than enough. He wouldn't be able to handle this along with the rest."

"Fair enough. So what are you going to do?"

"I don't know. I'll have to think about it." He gestured toward the computer terminal. "Is that it? Is there anything else I should see?"

"I don't think so."

"Can you give me printouts of those files you showed me?"

"Sure."

And Nolan carefully followed each and every move Flynn made, as he brought up and printed out the pieces of the nightmare.

Fourteen

Macken allowed Elaine de Rossa to do the ordering. She was doing the paying, too, and that suited him. He'd last dined in a restaurant like this on his fifth wedding anniversary. But it was Elaine's treat; she'd insisted on it and Blade, having first gone through the motions of protesting, had given in graciously.

He looked around the L-shaped room. There was nobody he knew.

"What I like most about this place," Elaine said, "is that they let you take your time. I simply can't *bear* it when you've a gaggle of impatient waiters buzzing around your table like bluebottles as soon as you've drained your coffee cup."

"Don't I know it. And you have to *tip* the buggers as well 'cause you never know if you'll be back. A friend of mine didn't once, only to be invited to the same restaurant by a client of his a week later. I don't know what the bastards did with his grub, but he was as sick as a dog for two whole days."

"Gosh!"

Blade liked her saying that; it sounded so quaint and little-girlish.

"But Gregory," Elaine went on, sweeping her hand to take in the room, "is super. Once you're drinking, he'll let you stay till closing time—or longer, if he knows you well enough. Ah, hi, John."

"Good evening, madam. Nice to have you with us again. Good evening, sir."

He handed them menus. Blade's had no prices marked.

"I shall send the wine waiter over directly."

Elaine looked a little flustered. "Umm, not for me, John. Wine doesn't agree with me."

99

The waiter raised one eyebrow, an almost imperceptible action.

"Perhaps for you, Blade?" she asked.

He didn't relish the thought of having a bottle of expensive plonk uncorked for him alone. Besides, he wasn't, strictly speaking, a wine drinker either. A pint would go down well now, he thought. But it wasn't the time—and certainly not the place.

"I'll have a large Irish, I think."

"And make mine a double vodka and bitter lemon," Elaine said. "The *good* stuff, mind," she added. "Gregory'll know."

They turned their attention to the menu and were not long in choosing: It was almost entirely à la carte. Evidently Gregory didn't believe in having his patrons stray far from his chef's recommendations.

"I think I'll just have the lamb," Elaine said. "I'm not that hungry."

Shit. He'd been deciding between the marinated quail and the salmon mousse as a starter. Thoughts of both had set his mouth watering.

"Hmm, me too."

But the rack of Carlingford lamb was delicious—if far from filling—and Blade finished every morsel. He resisted the urge to mop up the sauce with a hunk of bread.

They had more drinks: he whiskey, she vodka. The order had been repeated five times even before the meal ended. Elaine de Rossa, he mused, could sure put away her drink.

"Would it be all right if I smoked a cigar in here?"

"Of course. Shall I order one for you? John!"

"No, no. I have my own." He produced his yellow pack.

She giggled.

"A *Ham*let? That's not an after-dinner cigar, Blade. Are you trying to embarrass me or what?"

The waiter was already at their table.

"Yes, madam?"

"Bring the gentleman a brace of Romeo y Julietas."

"Certainly, madam. Will there be anything else?"

Elaine downed the contents of her glass with one, swift motion.

"Yes. I think the same again please, John."

Jesus, she could hold her liquor well. Blade was already feeling very tipsy, and Elaine had matched him drink for drink.

The big, hand-rolled cigar was an experience. He blew a small, blue smoke ring at the ceiling, and felt like a prince.

There was a sudden touch of smooth skin on his hand; Elaine slipped her fingers into his. She leaned across the table, her dress falling open to reveal high, round breasts held in place by a tiny, black lace brassiere. Her perfume vied with his cigar smoke, and won. She kissed him: just a peck on the lips.

"We can't go back to my place tonight, Blade darling," she said softly. "I have a cousin up from Kildare."

"That's all right." Fuck it.

"But we can go back to yours if you like."

Oh, *Christ.* He thought of a week's accumulation of dirty dishes in his kitchen, the living room a pigpen, and bed linen that he hadn't changed since . . . since whenever.

Blade's mind raced. He toyed briefly with the idea of checking them into a hotel—but a girl like Elaine wouldn't be caught *dead* in the only sort of hotel he could afford. He thought of calling one of his bachelor friends and "borrowing" a room for the night. But that was just as bad, if not worse.

"Okay," was all he said, stroking Elaine's hand.

Macken had lost count—as a clock struck midnight somewhere in the city of Dublin—of the number of large whiskeys he'd consumed at Gregory's. Seven? More? And the bould Elaine had downed an equal number of double vodkas. He'd known she was into horses in a big way but had never imagined she'd the constitution of one.

He rose unsteadily from the table, put an arm around her waist, nodded his thanks to the maître d'—and nearly tripped down the stairs.

As soon as they were settled in the back of the cab, Elaine flung her arms around his neck, cocked a bare leg over his, and kissed him passionately. Her tongue teased his tonsils. He felt a hand slide down the front of his trousers and wrap itself around his erection. She didn't squeeze, just ran her fingers and thumb lightly up and down the shaft. Jesus, but he wanted her.

They half walked, half fell into his apartment, Blade slamming the door behind them with a foot. *Fuck* the neighbors. He began to undo his tie.

"What are you doing?"

"Undressing. Hurry up and get them things off you or I swear I'll take you as you are on the kitchen table."

"Gosh, what's the mad rush?" She stood with folded arms. "We've all *night,* darling."

She stalked into the living room, found the light switch, and made straight for Macken's drinks cabinet. He followed her sheepishly into the room, as she sought among the depleted bottles for a relatively full one. While her back was turned, he kicked various discarded items of clothing and other jetsam behind the sofa and arranged its cushions. The rest of the room she'd have to take as she found it.

"Ah, gin!" Elaine said, studying a label. "That'll do me nicely. *And* there's a half-full bottle of whiskey as well. We're in luck."

She poured their drinks and sat down on the sofa. He joined her and put an arm around her shoulder, cupping a breast in his hand. Elaine leaned her head against his cheek.

"Who's that?" she asked lazily, pointing with a now-bare foot to a framed photograph on the wall. "Your mother?"

"Er, no; it's Joan, my wife. Well, *ex*-wife, I suppose. We're separated."

She giggled. "Sorry. It's the hair."

"I know. And you needn't say you're sorry. It's all right."

"She has an interesting face."

"Look, can we *not* talk about her?"

He squeezed her breast harder and leaned across to kiss her. She pushed him away, gently but firmly.

"Gosh, you're like a kid in some ways, do you know that, Blade? Just drink your drink."

She placed a hand on his groin and kept it there. "Plenty of time to show me again how good you are." She caressed his crotch slowly. "Now, tell me *all* about yourself."

Two hours later, Elaine extricated herself from Blade's limp arm and stood up.

"Where's the bathroom? I want to freshen myself up."

Blade saw two Elaine de Rossas.

"S-second on the right . . . no, I mean *left.*"

"Thanks. Here, let me top you up."

She filled his whiskey glass again.

Elaine returned fifteen minutes later, to find him sprawled full out on the sofa, snoring noisily.

"Blade!" she called. And again, more loudly. He didn't stir.

Elaine had no idea what she was looking for, so it was going to be a haphazard search. Yet she'd time on her side: Blade, she was certain, wouldn't wake for hours.

There was nothing of importance in his kitchen. Most people have a habit of "filing" things in kitchen drawers, with the intention of sorting them out at a later date. Blade was no exception: Elaine found invoices, old letters, bank statements; a final demand from an installment-plan company, long out of date. There was a lot of junk, and photographs of Macken's three children at various ages. Elaine lingered over a black-and-white shot of a younger and trimmer Blade wearing a United Nations uniform.

Nor did the rest of the apartment yield anything of value to her in her quest. She was about to give up and call a cab, when her eye was caught by the cellular phone Blade had tossed carelessly on the coffee table. It was lying face down, and there was something about it that set it outside of the ordinary. Elaine picked it up.

She'd never seen a phone like it before. A complete, built-

103

in tape recorder. Unbelievable; what would they think of next? Throwing a quick, cautious glance at the comatose Blade, she pressed the PLAY button.

"—DAYS TO GO. WHAT'S HAPPENING, BLADE? WHAT'S THE STORY ON MY MONEY?"

"It's coming."

"I MEANT EVERYTHING I SAID ON FRIDAY, BLADE. I DON'T GIVE A SHITE WHO COMES UP WITH THE MONEY, BUT IF IT ISN'T THERE ON THE FOURTEENTH, THEN IT'S BOOM TIME."

Elaine shut it off. She stood there quietly in the small living room for perhaps two minutes, musing and bemused. Then she wound the tape back to the beginning, took a notebook from her purse, and switched on a standing lamp.

She hesitated. No, it was too risky. Elaine turned off the lamp again and went back to Blade's minuscule bathroom, bringing telephone and notebook with her. She sat down on the side of the bath, laid the instrument on the toilet-seat cover and hit the playback button again. As the sound began to emerge from the phone speaker, she kept pace with the words in fluent, Pitman shorthand.

In the kitchen of a restaurant in the center of town, a chubby little man named Gregory picked up a half-empty Stolichnaya vodka bottle, and poured the water it contained down the sink.

Fifteen

Elaine de Rossa took a cab to work on the sixth day of Angel. Her head was reasonably clear, yet she never trusted herself to drive well enough after a late night.

Her secretary looked up from her terminal when Elaine entered the big, open-plan office.

"Coffee?"

"A gallon please, Margaret. And two fried Alka-Seltzers."

There were three E-mails for her: one from her father's trainer, informing her of the forthcoming sale of two thoroughbreds that "the old man" would probably be interested in. He himself could not be reached; he didn't wish to be. The other messages were junk.

Elaine opened a fresh file and called it simply BLADE. Then she pulled her notebook from her purse and consulted the lines of hieroglyphs she'd jotted down in haste the night before. It took her no more than two minutes to translate the shorthand into words on the screen. When that was done, she read them over and over, sipping from her mug of coffee, scrolling up and down through the document, trying to make some sense of it.

She printed the file.

The editor of the *Sunday Courier* didn't suffer fools gladly; he was also a snob of the worst kind. You might think that a tabloid newspaper would draw its reporters from the same demographic sector as its readership. Not Brian Cusack's. What he liked to call his "stable" was recruited from Ireland's ruling classes and elite: the sons and daughters of bankers, lawyers, politicians, businessman, academics, and gentlemen of leisure.

Elaine's father combined all the qualities of the last three.

Intensely rich, he owned a considerable swath of County Kildare—some of the finest horse country in Europe. Elaine had grown up in the saddle; knew her mounts, knew her racing, and knew her racing men. With such credentials, she was an asset to a paper that boasted the country's best-informed steeplechase pages. Yet it wasn't the horses themselves Elaine reported on, but the sleaze that attached itself with newsworthy regularity to the racing fraternity, and to their wealthy friends and business partners. It was fodder that appealed to a broad cross section of Irish society.

Cusack frowned when Elaine swept into his inner office and dropped the sheet of paper on his desk with a flourish.

"What's this?" he growled.

"You tell *me*, Brian."

Cusack scanned the lines and scratched his red goatee. A name had caught his eye.

"Blade? Blade Macken?"

"The same."

"I don't understand, Elaine. Who's the other character? This 'Anon' chap."

She went and shut the door.

"I won't stake my career on it but I'm almost certain it's Friday's bomber."

"Fuck *me*."

"No thank you."

Cusack was deadly serious now.

"Get him, Elaine," he said. "I want him." He studied her intently. "How well do you know Macken?"

"Well enough to have been able to get that transcript. There may be more, Brian; I don't know. Are we on then?"

One of Cusack's desk phones rang.

"Who?!" he roared into the mouthpiece. "Not *now*, Sammy, for Chrissake; I'll call you back!" He replaced the receiver.

"Bloody sure we're on," he told Elaine. "I want you to stick to Blade Macken like a poultice to a boil. Damn it, I *knew* Duffy was having us on—fuck him. A gas main: Did you ever hear the likes of it?"

He pointed. "You stick to Macken, my girl. I don't care what it takes, but whatever he has, I want it. And when you get it, we'll talk about reviewing your salary."

"I'll need expenses."

"You have a bloody expense account already."

"I mean," she said coolly, "a more expensive one."

While cycling past Leopardstown race track on Wednesday afternoon, Peter Macken had considered the worth of the tape recording he'd made two nights before. He'd blushed a second time when recalling the intimate things his mother had said in the heat of passion; he couldn't imagine what his father would think of them. Again and again Peter had to convince himself that his eavesdropping was justified, that it was to the benefit of his father and him—and maybe even to Joan herself in the long run.

Yet Roche had let little slip that offered concrete evidence that Joan Macken and he were doing more than sharing a bed. There'd been talk of Roche's cleaning out the garage "one of these days" and he'd given Joan permission to open a letter from London, which was due to arrive the following day (he needed to know its contents before he got back from the office). There was something, too, about "the deal-to-end-all-deals," and vague talk of early retirement. But that was all. Peter doubted if it were enough.

He had, however, bought a small Jiffy bag for the purpose of mailing the tape to his father. He hadn't sealed it. Peter had yet to hear what last night's recording had yielded; perhaps it would be better. If so, he could send both tapes in the one pack.

Joan was out when he got home. A thudding bass line and the soaring voice of Dolores O'Riordan told him that Sandra was in her room. That was good: The Cranberries at full volume would drown out any sounds from Peter's bedroom.

The audiocassette was full. They must have been going at it hammer and tongs, he thought grimly. He didn't regret having spent the night at his friend Stephen's house; his absence had spared him the real-time noises of Joan and Roche's coupling. And wasn't that the beauty of the setup? Peter didn't even have to be in the house.

He rewound the tape and hit the PLAY button.

"No, leave the light on."

"Are you sure now? Supposing someone sees it. . . ."

"Well, so what? Sure they'll think it's Joan."

"Mm, yeah. I hadn't thought of that. Hey listen, you're sure now she'll be away till three? I'd be afraid she'd—"

"That's what she said, but you can take it from me it'll be five at the earliest. The last hen party she was at, she stayed out till seven the next morning."

"Even so, I'd be—"

"Listen, Finola and her were best mates at school. Finola won't let her go before the hotel throws the whole shower of them out on their ear."

"Maybe you're right."

" 'Course I am. Now, take my little titties in your mouth, Daddy, and suck them till they hurt!"

Peter listened despite himself. He'd wanted to turn the damn thing off after thirty seconds. But a masochistic—or was it a voyeuristic?—side of his personality induced him to sit through the entire sordid recording.

And hear his sister commit what constituted the ultimate sin in Peter's eyes: that of sleeping with the enemy.

He'd completely forgotten about the party, even though his mother had reminded them of it only days before. Of *course* Joan would have stayed away until the small hours. Sandra was right about that: Finola wouldn't hear of Joan's leaving before she and the other women had overstayed their welcome. Divorcées, Peter reflected, were ten times worse than the young brides-to-be.

The recording ended with a barely audible click. Peter ejected the audiocassette and stared at it long and hard. There were tears in his eyes, tears of hurt and anger. Roche was, in his opinion, capable of anything. But *Sandra*. Good Christ. Had the fucker seduced her or had it been her idea? He desperately wanted to believe the former, yet some part of him guessed that his sister had made the first, tentative move. Peter was no psychologist—but you didn't need to be to notice how Sandra looked to Roche as a father: the abstemious, hardworking, caring father she'd never had.

He didn't know what to do with the tape. Allowing Blade or Joan to hear it was out of the question; he couldn't do it to Sandra, betray her like that. One betrayal was enough. And he didn't want to *think* about what Blade would do to Cock Roche if he were to find out.

But again: What to do with the incriminating evidence? Someday, he decided, he could maybe put it to good use. He'd use it to make the fucker *bleed!* For the moment, though, he would hide it where it wouldn't be noticed—in the most logical place, among the rest of his cassettes, anonymous.

Peter reached for a felt-tip pen and wrote the word BLANK on the tape's label. Then he put it in the box along with the others.

In his consternation, however, he'd failed to note two ostensibly unimportant things.

One: He'd forgotten to rewind the tape.

Two: He'd marked the label on the B side.

Sixteen

If it was unusually hot in Dublin in that July of 1998, then the temperature was almost unbearable in Langley, Virginia. Yet in the room that housed the three giant Unix mainframe computers, deep within the warren that was the headquarters of the CIA, the climate was maintained at a pleasant fifty-three degrees Fahrenheit the whole year round. For the benefit of the machines, not their custodians; in this room technology took precedence over human beings.

The room's temperature altered by a minute fraction of a degree when Jesse Murdock entered. The chief of the western hemisphere division in the Directorate of Plans was mopping his brow, and was grateful for the coolness. The air-conditioning in his own office was on the blink again.

He nodded a greeting to the computer team and went directly to the most senior member of the Unix staff.

"Anything?"

"Zilch, Jesse. We're throwing twelve hundred gigaflops from one machine at it, and almost a thousand from another, but it's like trying to find two snowflake patterns that match."

"Hmm. What does that mean in American: twenty-two hundred jiggy-what's-its-name?"

"It means more computing power than you can ever imagine. Look at it this way. *One* gigaflops is a billion floating-point operations. And that's roughly one thousand times more powerful than the computer they put on board *Voyager Two* in seventy-six. You know: the spacecraft that's headed out of the solar system, searching for other life-forms?"

"I'm impressed. But we're looking for only one life-form here, Nick. The lowest kind."

He handed the technician a small, padded bag.

"Here. Try this for size. It just came in from Larry Redfern."

"Another tape? Same voice?"

"Uh huh. Might be better, though. I'll let you people be the judge of that."

The technician opened the bag.

"A DAT. It's promising, I guess. But sound quality isn't the issue here, Jesse. It's calculating the algorithm that'll convert the voice back to its original state."

Murdock looked at the towering bulks of the number crunchers that were going soundlessly about their work. He didn't understand a damn thing about the infernal monsters—nor did he think he ever wanted to. Life was complicated enough.

"How long will it take," he asked, "to find this *algorithm?*"

The technician smiled ruefully. "Who can say? Maybe two weeks—"

"Too long. *Way* too long. We don't have that kind of time, Nick. I have the White House breathing down my goddamn neck. They want results right this minute."

"Can I finish? It *could* take up to two weeks—if we're lucky. If we're not lucky, we're talking maybe ten years."

"That's impossible!"

"I kid you not. Look, I won't hit you with the math involved here, Jesse, because it almost goes over my head, too." He jerked a thumb at the computers. "That's why we have these little fellers to help us. But I'll give you an analogy, if it'll help."

"I'm listening."

"You're not colorblind, by any chance?"

"No."

"Just checking. Okay, let's take the most common form of colorblindness: red-green blindness. Somebody who's RG blind can't distinguish between reds and greens, no matter what shades they are. And believe me, Jesse, there are a hell of a lot more than forty shades of green, in spite of what my old Irish grandmother used to say. I've a daughter doing art studies at Moore College. She reckons there are *millions.* Maybe she's right. Try talking to somebody in a body shop about getting colors to match if your car's scratched."

"I've been there."

The technician placed his fingers on his temples and pulled a face. "So here's our colorblind friend. Those millions of shades of green and red—they're all *brown* to him. You've seen the color tests, I guess: little dots of red, green and brown that make up a pattern? Say, the number forty-five in green and red on a field of brown dots?"

"I think so. Yes, I know them. Had 'em in the army—and in the tests the agency runs."

"They're pretty much standard. So this RG-blind guy can't read the number; everything looks brown to him. Now, ever been to the Guggenheim in New York?"

"A couple of times, yes."

"How many paintings have they got? Take a guess. Only the ones on show."

"Umm, two thousand? Three?"

The technician laughed.

"Try *ten* thousand; you might be closer. It's a very big gallery. But let's say there's half that number. Now: We give our colorblind friend a swatch of red and a swatch of green, like the color samples the paint companies put out. Then we set him loose in the Guggenheim and his mission is to find a portion of any painting that matches those samples *exactly.*"

"Mission Impossible."

"Right in one. It could take him years, maybe the rest of his life. That's what we're dealing with here, Jesse: Mission goddamn Impossible."

Murdock was sweating again. The Unix machines hummed to one another across the unseen, unimaginable tracts of cyberspace. Murdock had a sudden, wild fancy that their electronic songs sounded sad and frustrated.

Later the two men walked together through the long corridors of the Langley labyrinth. Murdock was a troubled man.

They rounded a corner—and the computer technician stopped dead in his tracks. He almost saluted, as a young woman wearing a CIA identity tag and a man whose ID dubbed him VISITOR approached from the opposite direction. The technician stood, slack of jaw, as the pair strolled past.

"That wasn't . . . *was* it, Jesse?"

Murdock smiled. He needed cheering up. "Nope. But I'll tell you something, Nick. I'd be mighty happy if I made *half* as much as that guy earns. Not that I'd trade places with him. I'm too fond of living."

The technician continued to stare after the retreating pair. "I'll be damned," he said.

Seventeen

There were few things Jim Roche enjoyed more than new gizmos. Give him a fresh piece of electronic wizardry and he was like a kid again.

The unit that he now held in his hand was no bigger than a television's remote control. It also worked in a similar way, using infrared technology. The difference was that this device didn't emit signals but was built to receive them. In the trade it was known as a countersurveillance sweeper.

Because buggers could be bugged, too.

He'd the house to himself that Thursday afternoon: Joan was at the tennis club, Peter was cycling in Wicklow, and Sandra would be staying overnight with a girlfriend. Roche could put his gadget through its paces at his leisure, undisturbed.

He decided on a multiple trial, in order to test whether the device was capable of isolating a number of signals simultaneously. First he fitted a microphone into a table lamp and married the transmitter's signal to a tape recorder in the garage. Next he placed in the hall an attaché case containing a built-in, voice-activated recorder. He rigged the third bug to the telephone; as soon as the receiver was lifted, a tape recorder would kick in.

It worked a treat. He experienced a little difficulty with the attaché case but soon had the glitch fixed. The countersurveillance sweeper scanned the house, registered, and homed in on the three bugs.

And found a fourth.

Roche stared with disbelief at the red light flashing on the dial. He went to audio and, sure enough, heard a faint zooming sound. He redirected the device. The zooming grew. Roche walked toward the rear wall, but the signal didn't increase significantly in strength.

Then he pointed it at the ceiling.

Many thoughts went through Roche's head as he climbed the stairs. There was always the possibility that he'd left a piece of equipment in the bedroom he shared with Joan. But that was nonsense: He never brought anything up there, let alone switched it on accidentally. Joan? That was crazy, too. Why would she? Why should she?

It didn't take him long to find the rogue power outlet: His sweeper led him straight to it. He didn't even need to disassemble it to confirm that it contained the bug; the device in his hand fairly hummed with excitement when it drew close.

It was one of Roche's own samples; he could see the rectangular trace of adhesive left by the removal of the Centurion Security sticker. He'd dozens of the things, yet kept account of each one of them, knew its exact location at all times. It was a matter of pride with him. He'd no idea how this one had gotten here—but by God he could find out easily enough!

He thumbed the dial on the sweeper that changed the mode from SOURCE to RECEIVER and let the device execute a slow arc. A zooming note sounded when he aimed it in the direction of the door. Peter's room lay beyond that door, on the other side of the corridor.

Goose bumps formed on Jim Roche's neck. Throughout his entire career he'd never—to his knowledge—been bugged. It was an unsettling feeling: as a soldier must feel when, having spent many months on the firing range, he's suddenly confronted in combat with targets that shoot back.

Peter's room was locked, a situation that Roche briskly remedied with the aid of one of Joan's hairpins.

The room was unusually tidy for that of a nineteen-year-old. Spartan almost. Besides the bed, a chair, a bedside locker, and a home trainer, there was little else apart from a bookshelf, a stereo, and a work desk. The sweeper homed in inexorably on a radio receiver. It was hooked up to a small tape machine on the desk, one of Roche's own.

The recorder was empty, and Roche quickly saw the reason why. Beside it lay a small padded bag, and an oblong-shaped bulge betrayed the nature of its contents. When Roche saw the name of the addressee, he swore loudly. He snatched up the bag and dumped the tape out on the desk, inserted it in the machine, and allowed it run for a few seconds. It was enough; Roche reddened to the roots of his hair.

Jesus, but he'd fix the little bastard! He ejected the tape and pocketed it. He needed another.

There was a box of cassettes on a corner of Peter's desk and Roche reached for it. BLANK read the first one that came to hand. Thank you, Peter, he thought: considerate of you to help old Jim like that; saves him a lot of time.

But Roche's years in the surveillance business had taught him that you didn't take even such minor details for granted. Blank tapes sometimes had a nasty habit of turning out to be the exact opposite. He slotted the tape into the recorder—and was rewarded with a satisfying, low hiss of white noise. Empty. Like Peter, he didn't notice that the machine was playing the B side.

He found a black felt-tip pen, used it to obliterate the handwritten word BLANK, and slipped the tape into the Jiffy bag addressed to "Mr. Blade Macken."

Eighteen

"I know it's not my investigation, sir," Superintendent Nolan said as he entered Duffy's office, "but I feel like a spare dick on a honeymoon, so I do, when I know there's a bomber on the loose and I'm just waiting on the sidelines."

"You're right, Charlie," Duffy said. "It's not your case. And I wish to God you'd let Blade get on with it. The pair of ye have me driven to distraction as it is."

Nolan sat down, uninvited, in front of Duffy's desk. The phone rang.

"Excuse me a minute, Charlie." Duffy listened to what the caller had to say. "Good, good. Have Brendan O'Sullivan question him. Oh, and make sure there's a woman garda present, okay?" He hung up. "They may have got the Dalkey rapist," he told Nolan. "That's a piece of good news at least. He's only fifteen, too, would you credit it? Now, what can I do for you?"

"I've come for a word of advice, sir."

Duffy sighed. "Fire away. You know that's what I'm here for."

"Well sir, it's like this." He paused. "I don't know how to put it, sir."

"Plain English is usually your best man, Charlie."

Nolan looked over both shoulders in quick succession, a move that had Duffy wishing that his phone would ring again. He hated histrionics.

"It's about Jim Roche," Nolan said at last.

"Right. What about him? Is it the Delahunt business?"

"It is and it isn't, sir. You see, I've brought him in on the case—as you know. But now I'm having me doubts, so I am."

"Oh? In what way?" Ring, phone, ring!

Nolan studied the front cover of the *Garda Review*, lying—

117

for him—upside down on the desk. The police rowing team was being tipped to carry off the trophy.

"I think he's bent, sir."

"Roche? Gay?"

"No sir. Criminal."

"Explain."

"Well, sir, I don't want to go sticking me neck out. . . . "

"Of course not."

"But I've reason to believe that Jim Roche may be involved in more than he lets on to be."

"Go on."

"He's been a great help so far with the Delahunt investigation, y'know. I'd be lost without him, to tell you the truth. I really knew next to nothing about high-tech security systems before Roche explained some of the stuff to me. He also gave me these to look through."

Nolan laid a small pile of glossy brochures on the desk. Duffy picked up the topmost one. It was entitled "Movement Sensor Systems." Duffy leafed through it.

"I can understand, sir," Nolan went on, "why that and things like"—he held up a second brochure—" 'passive infrared sensors' would be relevant to Delahunt's alarm installation."

Duffy nodded sagely. It was Greek to him.

Nolan pulled out a folder from the bottom of the pile.

"But what in the name of God," he said, "would Roche be wanting with something called 'Military and Civil Applications of Voice Encryption Software'? It doesn't make sense."

The assistant commissioner lit a cigarette. He said nothing for about a minute, continuing to stare at the text and diagrams contained in the folder. He shut it.

"Does Blade know about this?"

"No, sir. Should he?"

"I don't know, Charlie." He stabbed a finger at Nolan. "But don't *you* go bothering him with it, is that clear? Leave it with me for the moment."

Nolan's grin was broad as he turned out of Duffy's office.

The rank of detective superintendent in the Special Branch had its privileges, he mused. It opened doors that were closed to others. Folders that were out of reach to members of the general public could be acquired by the mere flashing of a badge of rank, if you knew the right buttons to push.

He could just about fit in one more interview before lunch. On returning to his office, he gathered up the rest of Roche's brochures, slipped them into a document wallet, and set off to Dr. Patricia Earley's rooms in Trinity College.

The assistant commissioner lit a new cigarette from the old one. He glanced through the folder again. Then he picked up the phone.

"Sweetman, is Macken there?"

"Ehh, no sir, he isn't. He went up to the canteen. Will I have him call you, sir?"

"No, Sweetman, don't bother. It's nothing important."

"Hello?"

"Hello, is that Sandra?"

"Yes. . . . Who is this, please?"

"It's *Blade*, love." She didn't even recognize her own father's voice anymore. Or pretended not to. Unbelievable.

"Oh. . . . Do you want to speak to Joan? She isn't here."

"That's all right. How are you, love? Are you well?"

"I'm okay. Is there anything else?"

Jesus *wept*.

"No, Sandra, there isn't. If Peter's there, will you put him on?"

"I'll call him. Bye."

"Ehh . . . bye."

There was a long interval before his son came on the line. Blade lit a Hamlet and puffed lightly on it while he turned the audiocassette over and over in his hand.

"Blade?"

"Peter. What's the matter with Sandra? You'd think I was the bloody Antichrist the way she behaves."

"Ah, she's just in one of her moods. You know how she gets."

"Mmm. Listen, Peter, can you slip down to the corner for me?"

"I'm on my way."

They'd developed the code together as a precaution against Jim Roche and his electronic ears. Blade thought it unlikely that Roche would bug his own home—but you never knew with someone like him. The coded message sent Peter jumping on his bicycle and riding almost a mile to a certain telephone booth; not only had this booth the advantage of being out of sight and earshot of Jim Roche, but it was rarely in use whenever Peter and Blade needed to communicate urgently.

"Peter?"

"Yep. Is it about the tape?"

"Yes." Blade drew on his cigar and chuckled. "It's *blank,* Peter."

A pause.

"Are you sure? But it can't be. I checked it before I posted it to you."

"Well, I'm just after playing it, and I can assure you there's feck all on it."

A longer pause.

"Are you sure you played the right side?"

Blade stopped his turning of the cassette and looked more closely at the clear plastic casing. Only then did he see the small, blind-embossed B in the corner. Stupid of him; Peter had scribbled over whatever it was that had been written on the label. He ought to have guessed that that was the wrong side.

"Er, sorry, Peter. My mistake. Look, I'll be in touch."

"You won't like what you hear, Dad. . . . "

"It's all right."

"But if it helps at all . . . "

"Yeah. Listen, I appreciate it; I really do."

"They didn't say anything about Roche living here, so it

isn't much use on that score. But Roche was talking about something I didn't follow."

"Oh . . . ?"

"Yeah. Something about him doing the deal-to-end-all-deals in a couple of days' time, and making enough to retire to the Bahamas on."

Blade looked at the tape in his hand. His mind was a helter-skelter. Jesus, what was it Duffy had said?

Duffy had approached Macken in the canteen.

"Charlie's on to something, Blade. Just thought I'd mention it. It may be nothing at all to do with the investigation, so I won't bother you with it for the moment. . . . "

"I wish you wouldn't do that, sir: half tell me something and get my curiosity aroused."

Duffy's next words had indeed aroused Blade's curiosity. More than that.

Christ, he thought now, had Nolan got it by the right end for once? He couldn't believe it. He unwrapped another Hamlet and lit it from the still-smoldering end of the first cigar.

"It's probably meaningless," he told his son, as calmly as he could. "Cock is always going on about his shagging deal-to-end-all-deals. Ever since I've known him. But I'll have a listen anyway. You never know."

"I'll keep trying, Blade. I'll ring you."

"Thanks, Peter. Bye."

Blade turned over the tape, inserted it in his machine, and sat back to listen.

Nineteen

Dr. Patricia Earley was in the conference room in Harcourt Square when Macken and Sweetman got there a little after seven in the evening of Friday, the eighth day of Angel. Duffy and Nolan were also present, as were Lawrence Redfern and several of his dark-suited associates. Blade nodded to Dr. Barry Keogh and Linda Doyle of forensics before he took a seat.

The center of attention was the long, white "blackboard" on the south wall of the room, on whose shiny surface Earley was adding some last-minute data with an erasable felt-tip pen. There was a sheaf of papers in her left hand. She turned and smiled on noting the new arrivals.

"The very pair," Earley said. "I think you'll like what I have to say, Detective Superintendent."

He was offered a chair, but remained standing. Outwardly, he was calm; only those who knew him well would have seen that, inside, Blade was burning up. Sweetman, having seated herself across the room from him, observed that his knuckles were white.

"We have reached," Earley said, returning the cap to her pen and addressing the gathering, "what I believe to be a watershed in the investigation—at least as far as profiling is concerned. I think I can say with confidence that we've been able to put together a pretty good picture of our suspect." She paused and threw Blade a smile. "This is largely due to the information gleaned over the past few days by Superintendent Macken."

Blade folded his arms and looked down at the floor. Earley went to the right of the blackboard and picked up a long pointer. She tapped a column of data. Diagonal lines ran from it to groups of words.

"First, we have established beyond all doubt that the bomber is a Dubliner. *This* . . . *this* . . . and *this* are all expressions native to the city." She turned around. "Yes, I know what some of you are thinking: that more than half the so-called Dubliners in this town are actually culchies."

There were sniggers around the room; it was a well-known fact that a large proportion of the gardaí were recruited from rural Ireland.

She tapped the column again.

"But locutions such as 'I don't give a tuppenny ticket,' 'If it was raining soup, you'd have a fork' and 'You've made a right haimes of that' are so typical of Dublin that their use is confined strictly to native citizens. Moreover, these are slang expressions which are not part of a young person's vocabulary but are found chiefly among members of the immediate postwar generation, say, forty- to fifty-year-olds. Which leads us to the second column . . . *here.*"

Dr. Earley continued in this vein for some fifteen minutes, displaying a profound knowledge of demographics and sociolinguistics. Blade listened with only half an ear. He was already familiar with most of what Earley was presenting, having worked closely with her on the study of the Angel tapes. He found it hard not to be distracted, as she went over ground they'd covered together, appending dry and long-winded glosses to keywords on the blackboard. Only when she suddenly referred to another high-ranking officer by name did Blade prick up his ears.

"I'm grateful to Superintendent Nolan," Earley was saying, "for his suggestions pertaining to certain electronic devices, not being familiar enough myself with such highly technical matters."

Where the fuck does Nolan get off, Blade thought angrily, sticking his nose into the investigation?

"The superintendent explained to me that the devices used by the bomber are not available on the consumer market—and will not be available for perhaps years to come. He suggested that our man must have either great personal wealth, in order to afford such hypermodern equipment, *or* that he has ready access to such things, possibly because he's employed by an electronics research company."

Nolan flung Blade a self-satisfied smirk. Bastard, Blade thought.

"So," Dr. Earley said, in a tone of voice she usually reserved for her summing-up speech, "what do we have so far? A great deal, I believe. He's probably in his forties, perhaps older; he has a working-class background, most likely to have grown up in the Phibsborough area. He is largely self-educated and has a brilliant mind. He's enormously conceited; he despises the guards and the government. He is not a terrorist in the sense that his crimes are motivated by nationalistic fervor or the like. Greed and revenge are his motives, probably as a result of some perceived wrong at the hands of the authorities."

She looked steadily at Blade, was about to say something to him directly, but then changed her mind.

"The evidence suggests," Earley continued, "that he is not a nine-to-five employee, because of the times at which his telephone calls were made." She pointed to a column of figures. "As you can see, they display a great variation; yet most of the calls were made at times when most employees are at their desks. This suggests that he is self-employed or has a private income."

"Or that he's on his hollyers," Sweetman said. There was a small ripple of laughter.

"The detective sergeant has a point," Earley acknowledged, "and we must not rule out the possibility that the suspect has indeed simply taken leave of absence from his job. Yet I ask you: Is it likely, given the circumstances? The amount of planning and preparation that must have gone into this operation would seem to rule out that possibility." She smiled. "But thank you all the same, Detective Sergeant."

Earley was once more in summing-up mode. "Superintendent Macken and I have looked time and again at our suspect's ability to work with high explosives. We've concluded that the handling of the explosives and detonators does not, in itself, require a specialist background—though we must not entirely dismiss this line of inquiry. The remote-control receivers and transmitters do, however, demand specialist knowledge. Which is why we should look for someone engaged in this line of work."

She took off her glasses, breathed on the lenses, and wiped them carefully with a tissue.

Blade recognized the ritual. Had she been a pipe smoker, then she might likewise have kept her audience in suspense, while going through the motions of tamping and lighting up. Earley stood poised to deliver the *coup de grâce*.

"Finally," she said, "it is my considered opinion—an opinion, I may say, shared by Superintendent Nolan—that the gardaí may well be up against one of their own, or possibly an outside expert."

The room broke up in disorder. Duffy had to call for quiet.

"He knows too much," Dr. Earley continued unperturbed, "about what goes on here in Harcourt Square."

She picked up the sheaf of papers and held them high.

"He knows more intimate details about Mr. Duffy, Superintendent Macken, and others in the Branch, than would be known by an outsider. He knows too much about police procedure, current and past investigations, and numerous other matters to which an ordinary member of the public would not be privy. That is why I am recommending that you embark upon a careful examination of your own personnel. Yes, Detective Sergeant?"

It was Sweetman again. "Past or present, Doctor?"

"Both. Perhaps we must go back many years. Let us not forget that the bomb was planted five years ago."

She was done. Duffy thanked her formally, then addressed the conference.

But Blade wasn't listening. His subconscious had registered something while Earley had been submitting her findings. It was so innocuous, so commonplace, that he'd almost missed it.

It didn't constitute proof of guilt. Yet, taken together with Earley's summary and his own suspicions, it pointed a finger in a direction that he'd never in his wildest nightmares considered until today. He looked again at the blackboard and scanned the words and phrases transcribed from the Angel tapes.

He saw now with clarity what he'd only half-seen before. Ironically, it was a snatch of the very first recording: the one made on Friday morning in Duffy's office. Earley had alluded to it that same day—yet had failed to quote the locution in full. She'd done so now, in writing.

It read: "Amn't I only just after telling you?"

Amn't I only just after telling you I do? Now come back to bed, will you?

Okay, Daddy.

Earley was right. To think that the bastard had been *here*, in Harcourt Square, right under their very noses; taking everything in, laughing his fucking head off at the lot of them the whole time. Jesus on a moped, it was unbelievable.

Blade checked himself; he bit his lip and allowed his professionalism to resume control. This was no time for private vendettas. Not when they were *this* close to baiting the monster in its lair.

The man was clever—too bloody clever. But Angel had slipped up, just as Blade had predicted, by providing him with a recording that none of the others—not even the omniscient bloody CIA—knew anything about.

And Macken wasn't telling them. He felt a rush of adrenalin, the surge of excitement of the soldier who is close, dangerously close, to the enemy's position. But Blade knew he'd have to have his wits about him, to keep a *very* cool head. For this was no ordinary enemy.

He'd to make a call first. As soon as Duffy was finished speaking, Blade excused himself.

"Peter?"

"Yeah."

"Where's the cockroach? Is he there with you?"

"Uh . . . no. He's working late at the office."

"At this hour? On a Friday? Are you sure?"

"That's what he said. Is there something the matter?"

"Never mind for now. You're sure now he's at the office?"

"Yeah."

"Thanks, Peter. I'll be in touch."

Twenty

Centurion Security was located on Crow Street, one of a number of narrow, cobblestoned byways that ring the area known as Temple Bar. The Irish equivalent of the Latin Quarter of Paris, it's the place where Dublin's young and beautiful come to shop, to eat, to drink, and to play. Two decades ago the street was a dismal, dilapidated part of the city; now it's prime real estate.

Blade walked quietly onto Crow Street a few minutes after ten in the evening. True nightfall was still some time distant, yet the mean street's dark buildings shut out most of the twilight, turning even the richest hues of the store signs and graffiti to indifferent shades of gray.

Jim Roche's premises were halfway down the street and Blade was pleased to see lights burning on the two floors above the store. He was also grateful for the fact that there was almost no traffic, and few pedestrians.

He stood for several minutes in front of the twin-windowed storefront. The steel shutters were down and he noted the array of security devices that kept a nocturnal watch on Roche's business assets. You name it, and it was there; the place was like a fortress.

Another door, however—to the right of the premises—was temporarily unguarded. It led to the apartment that extended to both the second and third floors. To be sure, it was watched over by a surveillance camera—but this was activated only when somebody rang the doorbell. The twin alarms were dormant, too; they would come into operation when the building had been vacated, or when Roche had settled in for the night, when he stayed late at the office and didn't return to Joan.

Blade waited for a break in the traffic on nearby Dame

Street, which would afford him a brief period of relative quiet. It came sooner than he'd expected. Taking advantage of the lull, he quickly picked the lock on the door and slipped inside.

He was wearing black Reeboks, a black canvas hunting jacket, and black pants. His cellular phone—in mute mode—was in a breast pocket.

The stairs were lighted but that didn't deter him. Blade had come for a confrontation and, if his quarry were to surprise him now, then that would do no more than hasten the confrontation.

Music was playing two floors up. It was muffled by intervening doors and the rich carpeting on the stairs. Jazz: slow and easy. Sensual. It was not the sort of background music Blade would have chosen when working late—but each to his own, he thought.

The neat office on the second floor was deserted and there was no sign that anybody had been using it that evening. A screensaver pattern of multicolored supernovae burst slowly and soundlessly across a computer monitor; a low hum came from fluorescent lamps in the ceiling. Blade glanced around, satisfied himself there was nobody in that section of the apartment, then padded slowly up the stairs to the next floor.

The hall of the topmost story belonged in a brothel.

Its walls were hung with red satin, illuminated by lamps held by naked, golden, *Jugendstil* nymphs. Macken's Reeboks sank into a coal-black carpet. Aspidistras and potted palms sprouted from a series of enormous gilded urns decorated with Grecian bas-relief, matching the frieze below the ceiling.

Blade stood before a door behind which the music was playing, now more distinct. He heard a male voice groan with either pain or pleasure. He turned the door handle noiselessly and stepped inside.

A trail of discarded items of clothing wound zigzag up to the end of a canopied, four-poster bed. Two people were on the bed, both glistening with perspiration. One was a man in his forties with a prominent beer gut. The other was Blade Macken's eighteen-year-old daughter Sandra.

And sweet suffering lamb of Judas, she was giving the motherfucker a *blowjob.*

Blade went to the stereo and turned it up full. John Coltrane's saxophone thundered and reverberated around the four walls.

Sandra sat up, stark terror written on her face. Jim Roche turned his head at the same time—and almost had a heart attack.

Though not a religious man, he would have gotten down on his knees at that moment and prayed, pleaded, cried out to the god of the Christians, the god of the Jews, of the Muslims, anybody's god. He would have paid that deity whatever tribute or sacrifice it demanded, in return for deliverance. Roche prayed he could be elsewhere at that moment—anywhere, *anywhere*: in a war zone, in a gulag, on death row, in hell itself—anywhere else but in that room, in that bed, with that girl.

"Get the fuck out of here, Sandra!" Blade bellowed above the wailing saxophone, drums, and double bass. "Now!"

The girl saw murder in her father's eyes. She left the bed, her nudity forgotten, and ran to him.

"Don't do it, Blade. Please, oh, please, don't do it!"

He averted his eyes. Jesus, how could he even *look* at her in that state? What did she take him for?

"*Go*, Sandra! Get out of my sight. For God's sake, go!"

She needed no more urging. Such was the fury in her father's face that she feared he was capable of anything at that moment. Almost in hysterics and sobbing, she gathered up her clothing and fled through the half-open door.

Roche had taken a marble statuette, one of a pair, from a bedside table. Naked, trembling with fright, he brandished it like a club as Blade bore down on him. When Macken reached one side of the bed, Roche scurried across to the other. He flung the statuette with all his strength.

But Blade had anticipated the move and dodged easily. At least two thousand dollars' worth of Italian marble shattered against a far wall. Roche tried to run for safety. Macken brought him down with a flying tackle, then kicked the door shut.

"Jesus, Blade—don't!"

A Reebok-shod foot connected violently with Roche's groin. He shrieked and nearly passed out.

Aitken was the bastard's name. Major Donald fucking Aitken. He'd almost forgotten, until now.

Roche writhed on the carpet in agony, hands held between his thighs. Blade leaned down and chopped him hard in the left kidney with the side of his hand. Roche's body convulsed; John Coltrane hit a triumphant high C.

He'd never expected it, that Aitken could do a thing like that. But you never knew with people—soldiers particularly; they were trained in aggression, in violence. It was part of their conditioning.

Roche's scrotum presented itself once again and Blade dealt it another vicious kick.

But Aitken had always become aggressive when he'd had a few. It was mostly punch-ups: harmless, really—almost what you'd call "friendly" fights.

Blade delivered a hammer punch to Roche's other kidney. This time the naked man went limp.

She'd been so young, too: fifteen, though you'd have sworn she was twenty. Jesus, she'd been far too young to have known what she was letting herself in for. And Aitken, fuck him, he wasn't going to tell her, was he?

Roche came to, only to find his tormentor gripping his right ankle in one hand and the twin of the broken marble statuette in the other. He screamed for mercy just before it connected with great force and accuracy with the upturned sole of his foot. He screamed even more loudly as Macken held his left foot by the ankle and struck that one, too. Then Blade repeated the punishment: twice, three times more. Roche began to blubber like a baby.

She was Norwegian—he remembered that. Very pretty. It had been her first visit to Cyprus and her first vacation away from her parents. She'd felt elated, free.

"Please, Blade," Roche moaned.

Macken decided that Roche's testicles were ripe for another mule-like kick—and obliged. John Coltrane launched into his closing, soaring solo.

He'd come upon them in an alley behind the taverna. The sounds of revelry from within had drowned out her screams. Men had been dancing solo, arms wide; plates were being smashed with abandon on the floor—part of the ritual. Her eyes had been like those of a wounded hind when she sees the hounds closing in for the kill. There'd been blood trickling down her bare thighs as Aitken had continued to thrust into her like a berserk pile driver.

Blade dealt each of Roche's kidneys a savage blow.

He'd thought of his eldest niece Rose. She was about the same age as the Norwegian girl. He'd imagined some bastard like Aitken doing those despicable things to Rose. He'd lost it.

The CD player was silent. Jim Roche lay moaning on the carpet. He'd passed beyond his threshold of pain some minutes before. A stream of vomit oozed from his mouth.

Blade squatted down beside him and spoke into his ear.

"Doesn't it feel good to be alive, Cock? Eh? And look, I haven't left a mark on you. Oh, you'll be bloody sore for days to come, I guarantee you that. But the thing is: Nobody'll know unless you tell them; you get me?"

No reply. Blade grasped a handful of Roche's hair and twisted it brutally.

"You *get* me?"

"Yes!" the naked man gasped.

"That's good. Because when I send for the men with the handcuffs and the blue van, I want to hand you over to them unblemished, not a scratch on you—which is more than can be said for those poor unfortunates you blew to fucking bits. There was a three-year-old-girl who lost both her legs *and* is blind for life. Did you know that, you cunt? Three years of age! And I'm not even talking about the baby that *didn't* make it. Fuck *me*, Cock, I always knew you were a prize prick—but this! You're an insane, twisted bastard, do you know that?"

Roche had shut his eyes. Pain burned through every part of his body. He could barely speak.

"Wh-what are you talking about?"

"Ah, please, don't insult my intelligence now, Cock—or would you rather I called you *Angel?*"

"What are you *t-talking* about?"

"Jesus, Cock, do you want me to start all over again? Believe you me, I'd be only too fucking pleased to do it. Except this time, it'd probably be the death of you. You see, I don't know how much more punishment them balls of yours can stand."

"N-no, please. . . . "

"You sniveling cunt. Next you'll be telling me you're not Angel at all. That you're *not* the fucker responsible for last week's bombing? Is that it?"

Roche's eyes opened wide.

"B-Blade, Jesus! You're wrong, you're wrong! I swear to God, Blade! On my mother's grave. Christ, I didn't even know it *was* a bomb."

Macken's blood was up; he himself knew that. Yet at that moment he wondered if he hadn't exerted himself above the limit of a man who drank and smoked as much as he did, because he felt palpitations in his heart. They came again—but this time he realized that it was the pulsating, double ring of his cellular phone.

He pulled it out, keeping his eyes fixed firmly on his victim.

"Macken. . . . "

"HELLO, BLADE. I JUST THOUGHT I'D GIVE YOU A RING AND SEE HOW YOU WERE KEEPING."

He'd felt like this only once before in his life. Cyprus again. His unit sometimes found itself sleeping rough; they used to bivouac in any old place, as long as it was flat and not too stony. He'd enjoyed it; made him feel like a Boy Scout again. Blade had risen one morning at first light, and had reached for his boots, going through the motions like an automaton. But when your toes expect to find empty space inside a boot— and don't? When they find, instead, something cold and coiled up, something that *wriggles* upon being roused from sleep . . .

Macken experienced the same crawling sensation now. He was too stunned to reply to the taunting voice. He stared in disbelief at the unclothed man who lay groaning at his feet, and felt as Macbeth had on seeing Banquo's ghost. Blade gazed stupidly at the phone in his hand.

He couldn't talk now; not to Angel, not to anyone. He broke the connection.

Five minutes later he was still at the window of Roche's love nest, looking down onto the empty street.

All the clues had led here: to this room, to this man. Now all was as dust. He would have to start almost from scratch again. His head was throbbing; he badly needed a drink.

Roche was lying where he'd left him; he would not be going anywhere tonight. Macken walked slowly to the door and opened it. He turned.

"It's not over, Cock," he said. "There's something about you I've never trusted. It wasn't because of Joan, either, and it wasn't because of Sandra. No, it's something else, Roche—I *smell* it, I know I'm close to it—and I'm going to find it before long."

He'd almost shut the door behind him when he opened it wide again.

"And listen, Cock," he hissed. "You lay another hand on my daughter and your balls won't be sore anymore. Because you won't *have* any fucking balls. Do you follow me?"

Jim Roche could only nod his acquiescence.

Twenty-one

Charlie Nolan breezed through the incident room in Harcourt Square, clutching a sheaf of papers. None of the detectives hunched in front of their terminals paid him more interest than normal. It was close to midnight; the Angel investigation was ticking over with the minimum number of officers manning the nerve center.

Nolan found three vacant work stations side by side in a corner of the big room and sat down at the middle one. There was no sign of Paddy Flynn; he'd made a quick check on that. He was nervous, very. He disguised the trembling in his fingers by shuffling the papers on one side of the keyboard, pretending to rearrange them in a different order. A telephone rang and Nolan was startled. But he recovered quickly and applied himself to the work in hand.

The previous user of the terminal had left a window open that read ARCHIVE 1992. Nolan shut it. He saw a list of folders, each bearing a date from 1980 to the present. Nolan opened that for 1989. He chose a month at random and began to type nonsense at the place where the cursor blinked on the screen. Presently he looked up and called out to the detective sitting nearest him.

"How's this you spell 'sapphire,' John?"

"Ehh, with two pees and a haitch, I think. Is it the Delahunt business, sir? The jewels?"

"Yeah. Pain in the arse, so it is."

"Nothing compared to *this*," the detective sighed, and returned to his own work.

Charlie Nolan had always approached computers with a mistrust bordering on awe. He was a man used to the traditional methods of police investigation, and was still convinced that legwork and steady, honest-to-goodness procedure were, in his own words, "your only man" in the solving of a case. In his heart he knew that officers like himself were becoming dinosaurs in the face of the technology embraced with great enthusiasm by younger members of the force. And so he'd made more effort than most men of his generation to keep pace with each new technological development at Harcourt Square. He'd even bought a secondhand PC to practice on at home.

As a result of his keyboard skills, it didn't take him long to locate the files that Flynn had brought up for his attention.

But he didn't delete them—as a lesser man would have, he thought smugly. No, Charlie Nolan *overwrote* each file with a line that he was particularly proud of.

It read: ACCESS DENIED: PASSWORD PLEASE?

There was no password, of course, because there were no more incriminating files. Nolan's nightmare had been banished forever.

The morning of Saturday, July 11, saw a slight change in the Dublin weather. It remained hot, but the humidity was lessened by a mild northwesterly breeze that rustled the leaves of the limes outside the American embassy.

Inside, in Seaborg's office, change of another kind was the subject of a heated discussion. The ambassador was on his feet, as was Lawrence Redfern. Seaborg's driver, Thomas Jones, sat to one side, filing his immaculate fingernails. Assistant Commissioner Duffy occupied one of the chairs facing the mahogany desk. His, he felt, was the "hot" seat.

"I think Mr. Redfern's right," Seaborg said. "Macken will have to go. He's been on the case now for more than a week and he's come up with nothing. I wouldn't say this, Mr. Duffy, if circumstances were different. But there's too much riding on it. I hope you understand."

Duffy felt powerless. Redfern he could cope with; the man was just a minion, not very much different from one of his own subordinates. But Seaborg had closed ranks with Redfern, and the assistant commissioner knew he was no match for the combined pressure of two such strong-willed individuals. It was the little, almost invisible, signs that passed between them that told Duffy he was dealing with men who'd fought battles together, had acted as a single unit to crush all opposition.

But Duffy was a fighter, too.

"I've stood behind Blade before," he said, "and I'm standing behind him now. You may think what you like of him, but I can assure you there's no better man on the force."

"Then why are we still no further than we were a week ago?" Redfern asked.

"Because we're up against something we've never had to contend with before." Duffy swiveled round to face Redfern. "You know that as well as I do. How's your own investigation coming along, eh? You people have half the intelligence services in America working on those tapes. What have *ye* come up with?"

Redfern stuffed his hands in his pockets. "Nothing so far, I agree. Which is why I'm recommending that we drop that line of inquiry and concentrate our resources right here. But I want somebody else to head up the investigation from your side, Commissioner. Macken's out, as far as I'm concerned. He hasn't even reached first base."

"Whatever that's supposed to mean," Duffy said dryly.

Seaborg saw the tension rising again and came between them.

"What about Superintendent Nolan, Commissioner?" he said. "Perhaps he could do better. We've less than three days, for crying out loud."

"The ambassador has a point," Redfern said. "Seems to me that Nolan is handling this better than Macken—and he's not even on the case. At least he produced a suspect."

"Which led Macken on a wild-goose chase, thereby slowing up the investigation," Duffy countered.

Seaborg ran his fingers through his hair. He laid his palms on the desk, seeming to tower over Duffy.

"At least he's doing something," he said, "even if it failed to get results. From what I hear from Mr. Redfern, Macken has done little except come up with a harebrained plan involving sniffer dogs—"

"When he hasn't been painting the town red at night," Redfern sneered. "I say we go with Nolan."

"Or you assign them both to the case," said Seaborg.

Duffy sighed. "You don't know what you're asking, gentlemen. That's the one course that *isn't* open to me. You might as well string two tomcats across a clothesline by their tails and let them fight it out."

"I'm not saying you should give them equal authority," the ambassador said. "Not at all. Put Nolan in charge, but let's not forget that Macken has a direct line to the bomber. Break that now and we might lose contact for keeps. So what I'm suggesting is that Macken's involvement ought to be confined to receiving and passing on phone messages. No more."

"My God, he'll love *that*," Duffy said. He stood up wearily. "All right, Nolan it is—alone. Now I suppose I'll have to break the news to Blade."

Seaborg came from behind the desk and offered Duffy his hand.

"It's for the best, Commissioner. I like Macken; he's a good guy. But I have to agree with Mr. Redfern. It's proved too much for him. We need fresh blood now. We're running out of time."

Duffy wanted to say something. Couldn't. He nodded gravely to the ambassador and left the room.

"Well? Happy now?" Seaborg said.

"No, Colonel, I'm not happy. And I'm sure not gloating either, if that's what you think. If you want the truth, I'm worried as hell. Sir, you've got to use your influence; get the White House to call off the visit. This situation is out of control."

Seaborg sat down. He picked up the jeep-shaped paperweight and balanced it on his palm.

"And on what pretext ought we to call it off, Mr. Redfern? Because there's been a gas leak in the city of Dublin? The president would be laughed right out of office."

Redfern was silent—if not for long.

"But that's it, Colonel! You've hit the nail on the head. A leak."

"Beg your pardon?"

"Don't you see, sir? Duffy has done his damnedest to try to keep the lid on this. What if we were to leak the real story to the press? Tell them the truth: that there's been a bomb threat on the president's life."

Seaborg laughed bitterly. He shook his head.

"Spoken, Mr. Redfern, like a true field agent, if you don't mind my saying so."

Redfern looked hurt. Seaborg's tone grew milder.

"You don't know what it's like to sit at this desk, Larry. You must think that what goes on behind closed doors here is all about who does or who doesn't get invited to cocktail parties in the ambassador's residence."

"No, sir, I certainly don't. I— "

"Let me finish now. What you're suggesting is that we blow the cover on a story that a foreign administration has been desperately trying to maintain for more than a week. Now, aside from creating an international incident should the leak be traced to this office, you'd most likely be exposing the president to even *more* danger than he's in right now."

Seaborg replaced the paperweight on his desk and began to roll the miniature vehicle back and forth.

"You're right," he went on; "there's still time for the White House to change its mind. The president can contract a bug, visit with his dying aunt, anything. He won't lose any credibility if he cancels now. Because there's no clear and present danger. And I wish to God he *could* cancel."

"Amen to that."

"But Larry, you know as well as I do that Duffy's story won't hold forever. Too many people know about the bomb— here and back home. It's only a matter of time before the press gets its hands on it. The White House knows this. More important, the president's political advisers know it. Everything is politics, Larry. You, me, Mr. Jones there: we're all part of the great political game. It's the World Series—except this one never stops. Did you catch the news Monday?"

He didn't wait for a reply but went to a cabinet and opened a pair of doors to reveal a television set. He took a videocassette from a rack and inserted it in the player.

CNN had the best coverage. The hollering match that was characteristic of the British House of Commons in session had gone on for more than three hours, as the prime minister tried to appeal to both benches for reason and restraint. He'd been shouted down. The most vociferous voices had belonged to his own party. Everything from the War of Independence to the Normandy Landings had been cited as evidence of a deeply rooted mistrust that lay beneath the veneer of friendly Anglo-American relations. The resident of the Oval Office had been branded a traitor, a coward—even a warmonger. The prime minister had been urged to seek an apology.

"Piss and wind, Larry," Seaborg said. "That's politics. Put one of those red-faced gentlemen in a combat zone and he'd soil his underpants."

He switched off the set. "But that's not the issue here. These people control the president as much as the voters in Libby, Montana, control him; make no mistake about it."

"Is he going to apologize?" Redfern asked softly.

"Probably. But not today, and certainly not according to Noah Webster's definition of the word 'apologize.' Diplomacy doesn't run off half-cocked; it takes its blessed time."

Seaborg sat down.

"You understand now?" he said. "The president's shot himself in the foot. He's damned if he does and damned if he doesn't. If he cancels the visit now and the truth comes out later, he's damned. If he doesn't cancel and the truth leaks out before Tuesday next—or, God forbid, if there's another bomb—then he's damned again. And he knows it."

"So he has to come, either way."

"That's right. Only an act of God can stop him now."

Twenty-two

When it appears that the whole world is against you; when everything you set your hand to works out wrong; when your best-laid plans go awry; when life seems bleak and indifferent, then there's always one person you can still turn to.

Mother.

Blade Macken was on the Wexford road, heading for County Wicklow on Saturday, the ninth day of Angel. The hum of the car engine soothed him; his CD player tinkled softly with the piano music of Phil Coulter and the cooling drafts of the air-conditioning on his face were in sharp contrast to the sweltering heat outside.

The bare, rugged limestone cone of the Great Sugar Loaf reared up ahead when he'd passed the southern boundary of County Dublin and entered the locality known affectionately as the Garden of Ireland.

He drove through places whose names matched their loveliness: Kilmacanogue, Glen of the Downs, Ashford. But the beauty of the countryside was lost on him; his thoughts were elsewhere. On dark angels of death, murdered children, child molesters, impending assassination. Only when he bore left at the village of Rathnew did Blade think long and hard on Katharine Macken.

He'd returned her calls at last. To his surprise, his mother had sounded bright and coherent, in contrast to the messages she'd left on his answering machine. What was she now? Seventy-three. But she'd sounded like a girl of twelve. That had cheered Blade considerably, even though an inner voice had reminded him that a regression to childhood speech and mannerism was a symptom of the dementia that was ravaging his mother's mind.

He stopped at Madden's newsdealer's shop in Wicklow

town and bought a pack of Hamlets and a box of Katharine's favorite chocolates.

She *lived* on the damn things: "What d'you mean, they'll 'rot your teeth'? I haven't *got* any teeth of my own left to rot." He always laughed to himself when he thought of her saying that.

Soon Blade was ascending a steep road south of the town. He looked in his rearview mirror and was gladdened by the sight of the harbor and the sea beyond, a panorama that presented almost the entire eastern coast as far as the peninsula of Howth. He never tired of the beauty of this vista.

On the CD player Phil Coulter began the intro to his masterpiece: "The Town I Loved So Well." When the chords of the first verse came, Blade loudly sang the lyrics in his bad baritone, confident that the closed windows of the car would spare the ears and sensibilities of anybody within earshot. But there was no one; as he negotiated the winding, hedgerow-lined road that led to Katharine's home, he passed only a solitary sheepdog.

The house was big: a three-story Victorian building with stables adjacent, set back from the road and approached by a climbing driveway. There was only one car out front: the small, battered Fiat belonging to Katharine's nurse. She had the hall door opened before Blade had cut his engine. He'd an enormous amount of respect for the woman; looking after his mother was a heavy task.

"How's she been keeping?"

"Ah, you know yourself, Blade, without me telling you. She has her good days and her bad days. But she was thrilled to bits when she heard you were coming down. Sure she's little else in her life these days, the creature." The nurse frowned a bit. "You really ought to try to drop by more often. You know how she dotes on you."

"I know," he said, as he looked about the hall that was filled with memories of the best of times and the worst of times. It was also filled with the smell of mustiness and decay and he wondered when the decorators had been in last. But who, Blade asked himself, was going to pay them? Louise and Barbara? You must be joking. Blade's older sisters hadn't seen their mother in years. The ferry from Wales took only ninety minutes now, but neither of the bitches ever bothered her arse to make the trip; Katharine was Blade's responsibility as far as they were concerned. He could never figure families.

"I know," he said again. "But I've been up to my eyes the past few weeks. Has she been eating at all?"

The nurse eyed the box of candy.

"Sure you're worse to keep bringing her those things," she admonished. "Ah, she's the same as always, I suppose. I can get her to eat the odd bit of meat for me, but she wouldn't touch a vegetable if you paid her." She paused at the double doors leading to the living room. "Maybe you can talk some sense into her, Blade. I'm sick trying."

He nodded, and went in.

Katharine Macken had made herself up for his coming. A mistake. She probably thought that the blue eye shadow, thick mascara, and bright pink lipstick made her look like a movie star. They didn't; Blade saw an old, painted crone, a travesty of the beautiful woman his mother had once been. But he pressed her hand and kissed her warmly on both cheeks as though she were his queen.

They drove to the lighthouse.

She enjoyed it so much when Blade brought her here. There are actually three lights: the oldest is a tall, massive, eight-sided structure, built toward the end of the eighteenth century. It fell into disuse when a newer tower was erected a hundred years later. That, too, is shut. Now Wicklow Head is guarded by an automatic light set halfway down the cliff face. Katharine linked Blade's arm as they descended the gently winding path.

They stood together at the low wall overlooking the old keeper's house and gazed out across the Irish Sea. A little distance out in the blue water, a small brown head appeared. A seal. Katharine grew excited.

"How adorable! One doesn't see quite so many of them as one used to." She turned to him. "Remember that time we saw a pair of them just off Killiney strand?" She sighed. "A long time ago now. You wanted to take a photograph, Blade, but they vanished before you could go and fetch the Brownie."

"Er, that was Dad, Katharine. Blade *senior.*"

"Of course it wasn't, silly! I recall the incident as though it were yesterday. We'd gone down for the day with that dreadful American and his girlfriend. What was his name? Slater, that was it. P. J. Slater. Whatever became of him?"

"It wasn't me, Katharine."

She shook her head in irritation.

"I do wish you'd stop contradicting me. Next you'll be telling me I'm *senile.*"

He'd persuaded her before they left the house that the garish makeup had been "too common" so she'd cleaned most of it off. She looked quite pretty now with a silk scarf tied around her head. He squeezed her hand.

"And that frightful Catacombs crowd!" she said after a time. "I was *ever* so glad when you stopped going to that place, Blade. It was nothing but a common drinking den; the constables ought to have shut it down. I simply can't imagine what you saw in those people. Boozers and ne'er-do-wells, every last one of 'em."

Blade said nothing. His father's ghost continued to haunt him. But he was relishing the afternoon, happy to be at his mother's side in this lovely, secluded place, where no dark angels ventured. He tried to put the investigation from his mind. To hell with Duffy, to hell with Nolan.

"And as for that Brendan Behan! How the young Salkeld girl could have thrown herself at a *person* such as he, I shall never understand."

"He was a bit of a character right enough."

"That's putting it mildly. When I *think* of what he got up to! I couldn't believe my ears that time when you told me that he'd had people eating human flesh for a bet." She shuddered. "You didn't make it up, did you? It really happened?"

"So Dad said, yes."

Some seconds went by. He heard her sniffling and when he looked, there were tears in her eyes. He put an arm around her shoulders.

"Oh I'm *hopeless*, Blade," she sobbed. "I don't know what's happening to me. The doctor keeps reassuring me that it's not so, but I think my mind is going. Is it, Blade? Tell me truthfully. Is it?"

Blade pressed her against him. There was a lump in his throat.

He drove her back to the house, along the little private road, past the green pastureland dotted whitely with sheep.

The nurse's car was gone when he pulled up. He helped her inside, the old house echoing to their footsteps and her walking stick. There was a fire burning in the living-room hearth.

"*Would* you straighten that picture, Blade?" his mother said, undoing her headscarf. "That woman has absolutely no eye to speak of. Hopeless."

He went to the fireplace and lifted the heavy frame that housed the oil painting. The artist had clearly been much influenced by Rosetti: the winged being, dressed in a flowing, white garment, had features and hair that glowed with an impossible beauty, and an almost pornographic sensuality. Its flat chest seemed at odds with the exaggerated femininity of the eyes and lips.

Something tugged at a corner of Blade's mind—something too intangible to be pinned down.

He straightened the picture and returned to help his mother to her favorite chair by the window.

His cellular phone rang the moment Katharine was seated. She looked around in confusion and showed surprise when her son drew the instrument from his pocket and put it to his ear.

"Macken. . . ."

"BLADE, THE VERY MAN! WARM FOR THE TIME OF YEAR, ISN'T IT? WE COULD DO WITH A DROP OF RAIN. WOULD YOU AGREE?"

Saint Christopher on a bike! Blade pressed the RECORD button on the back of the handset.

"I suppose so," he said softly.

"YOU CAN'T TALK, BLADE, IS THAT IT?"

"Yes, that's right."

Blade indicated to Katharine in sign language that he was going to take the call elsewhere. She frowned, yet still knew enough to appreciate that police business sometimes took priority over aged mothers. Blade went into the kitchen.

"All right," he said, "what can I do for you?"

"AH FOR FUCK'S SAKE, BLADE, SURE YOU KNOW WHAT YOU CAN DO FOR ME. WHAT'S THE STORY ON MY TWENTY-FIVE MILLION DOLLARS?"

"It's coming."

"YOU'RE SURE NOW?"

"Yeah, I think the Yanks have it sorted out. They've offered to pay the full whack themselves."

"YOU 'THINK' THEY HAVE IT SORTED OUT? WELL, THAT ISN'T GOOD ENOUGH, BLADE; IT REALLY ISN'T. IT'S—"

"Look . . . no. I didn't mean it like that. They're doing it. Believe me. You'll have your money on time."

"I FUCKING WELL BETTER. YOU KNOW WHAT TODAY'S DATE IS, BLADE, DON'T YOU?"

"The eleventh."

"THAT'S RIGHT. SO YOU JUST MAKE SURE THAT SEABORG AND THE OTHERS KNOW IT AS WELL. I HATE TO BE KEPT WAITING. DON'T YOU HATE THAT, TOO, BLADE, SOMEBODY KEEPING YOU WAITING? IT DRIVES ME SPARE."

"Yes. I do. The money'll be there, Angel. I guarantee it."

Blade heard the grandfather clock in the hall strike five times and glanced automatically at his watch. The clock was keeping perfect time. He guessed who it was who kept the mechanism oiled and in working order. It was not an easy job—by no means. Katharine's nurse rose a notch higher in his estimation.

Then, some forty-five seconds later, as Angel was still engaging in his dangerous small talk, Blade heard a whirring sound coming from directly behind him, and turned.

He was a child again: six years old. Or had it been his seventh birthday? He couldn't recall now. But he could remember the wall clock, and was surprised not only to find it here in the kitchen, instead of in his old bedroom, but still operating perfectly after all these years.

The timepiece was a beautiful piece of workmanship. It wasn't a toy; it was an exquisite example of the clockmaker's art. He remembered his joy when Katharine's parents had presented it to him, how his grandfather had taken Blade on his knee and given him a brief lesson on how to tell the time. Granddad had waited until a half hour before the hour before taking it out of its box, and thirty minutes later Blade had discovered why.

There was a semicircular path at the base, which ran from one little closed door to another, and a miniature grass border complete with a white milestone that read "London 10 Miles," the whole carved in wood and tastefully painted.

And at five o'clock exactly, the magic had happened. The little door on the left had opened and two diminutive figures had emerged and moved slowly in a semicircle, past the milestone, to vanish through the other door. Dick Whittington and his cat. Blade had known the story almost by heart; Katharine had read it to him more often than she would have wished. The young pauper who'd become Lord Mayor of the English capital. And his new clock had *played* the very song that Katharine had sung to the young Blade:

Turn again, Whittington, Lord Mayor of London!

Blade had carried that tune in his head for thirty-seven years. It haunted him. He sometimes woke with it in the morning; it disturbed his concentration when he was doing paperwork; it came—unwanted—when he was walking, driving, drinking. It was almost his personal anthem.

Now he heard it again. And the little painted figure of Dick Whittington, with its black tricorn hat and carrying a bundle on a stick over one shoulder, moved past the milestone and out of sight by way of the right-hand door in the base of the wall clock.

"ARE YOU DEAF OR WHAT?"

"Sorry?"

"IT'S LIKE I'M BLEEDING WELL TALKING TO MYSELF. LISTEN, I'LL RING AGAIN—WHEN IT'S MORE CONVENIENT FOR YOUR LORDSHIP. ANGEL OUT."

The line went dead and Blade cursed himself. So distracted had he become by the unexpected visitation from his childhood days that he'd barely listened to Angel's words.

But he had them on tape.

"Who was that, Blade?" Katharine asked.

"Ah, just business. The usual. They never leave me in peace."

"You work too hard. You don't get *that* from your father."

"No."

"What happened to the chocolates? Did that dreadful woman scoff them, as always?"

"Er, you ate them, Katharine."

"Don't be absurd! I'm hardly likely to have devoured an entire box."

He arranged the cushions behind her back. She patted his hand.

"You're a good boy, Blade."

"I know. I have you spoiled rotten. Listen, is there anything I can get you from town?"

Her look held contempt.

"I *scarcely* think so. One can't imagine what those clodhoppers could possibly purvey that should be of any interest whatsoever."

Blade grinned. He knew very well that his mother had fallen in love with Wicklow and its people from the moment his parents had moved here with him and his sisters. Katharine steadfastly refused to live anywhere else.

"I could get you a paper. . . . "

"Really, which one? The *Irish Farmers' Journal*? No thank you. I expect you'll be haring off again now? Done your duty."

"Er, actually I'll be here for another hour or so, Katharine. There's something I have to do."

Blade's voice had betrayed none of the elation he was feeling at that moment. He'd been turning the idea over in his mind, questioning whether he was heading down yet another blind alley. But the thing was so simple, so logical, that he couldn't bring himself to believe that it could fail.

By Jesus, he *had* the bastard! Angel had slipped up, and was about to give himself away. The hermit crab had ventured a tad too far out of its shell.

Blade waited until one minute before six. Then he excused himself and went back into the kitchen. There was one particular number he could call, he reasoned, that would ensure for him the silence he required for the experiment he was about to conduct. His own home number.

The grandfather clock struck the hour. Blade took his cellular phone in his hand and punched in the digits.

"This is Blade Macken. I'm not in at the moment. If you'd like to leave a message, please do so after the signal."

There was an electronic blip, then silence.

He hit the RECORD button.

149

Twenty-three

"I don't know, Blade," Dr. Barry Keogh said with a worried look. "I think we should have the Americans in on this." He gestured toward the battery of recording apparatus, speakers, and computer terminals. "They can handle this better. We can only go to eight-bit sound here. I've been pestering the commissioner for months for new stuff, but he says we're way over our budget as it is."

"To hell with the Americans. I'm not having Redfern take all the credit for this."

"What about Jim Roche?" Sweetman asked.

Blade glanced at her sourly.

"What about him?"

"Well, we might be able to borrow some of his gear. I hear it's the business."

He turned his back to her and studied the computer screens.

"Yeah, well we won't bother him just now. Somebody told me he was laid up for a couple of days. A severe chill, I think it was. We'll make do with what we have, Barry."

"You're the boss."

They watched in fascination—Macken, Sweetman, Duffy, and Earley—as Keogh pressed the PLAY button of the tape deck. Angel's voice issued from the stereo speakers.

"Right here," Blade said after a few seconds.

Keogh clicked on the RECORD "button" in the top left-hand corner of the screen. At once, a thin black line that had hitherto remained unchanged began to execute a succession of sharp spikes and troughs, following the modulations of the words. Then they heard the merry little tune, played over and over, as Dick Whittington and his cat trod their never-ending path to London. The notes were in stark contrast to the bomber's distorted words. When the tune had ended, Keogh stopped the recording and saved it.

No one spoke, but the air crackled with suspense. Out of the corner of his eye, Blade saw Sweetman look his way.

Keogh started the second tape and began the recording at once. This time, the notes played by the wall clock were crystal clear.

"What happens now?" Duffy said.

Keogh pushed his glasses higher up the bridge of his nose. "We isolate the tune from the first recording."

"Can you do that?" the assistant commissioner asked, eyeing the meaningless pattern that the computer program had generated.

The head of forensics chuckled. "*I* can't, but this baby can."

Almost more quickly than their eyes could follow, Keogh pulled down menus on the screen, clicking on submenus and paths whose designations Blade associated with the algebra he'd learned at school. But whatever it was Keogh had done, it achieved results. The waveform section of the screen went blank. A second later, more sharp spikes and troughs filled the window.

"Gotcha!" Keogh exclaimed with the delight of a boy.

He brought down another menu and split the screen in two. Side by side were two waveforms, identical in length, yet as dissimilar in character as chalk and cheesecake. The tension in the laboratory mounted; the soldier in Blade sensed the proximity of the kill.

Keogh changed the color of "Dick Whittington" to red. With another series of mouse clicks and dragging maneuvers, he superimposed the red image on the black one. Then he clicked on the word MERGE. The red waveform expanded and contracted with a blur of motion, until at last its jagged lines settled precisely over their dark counterparts like an inverted total eclipse of the sun.

"By Jesus," Blade breathed. "So it *is* possible."

"My congratulations," Dr. Keogh said. "It was a stroke of genius to think of it. How on earth did it ever occur to you?"

Blade reached into his pocket for his pack of Hamlets but, on seeing Keogh's horrified expression, thought better of it.

"Just luck, I suppose," he said modestly. "Remember last week outside the embassy, Sweetman, when the bastard was playing his bloody game of hide-and-go-seek?"

She nodded.

"Well, do you remember some silly twat in a red Mazda, who'd one of these horns that plays 'The Bridge on the River Kwai'? They ought to be illegal."

"They are," Duffy said quietly.

"That's what put the idea into my head. See, I'd heard the horn over the telephone, and then the real thing when the car was nearer to us. I didn't think any more about it at the time, not even when we listened to the tapes."

"Lateral thinking, Blade," Dr. Earley said. "It's what I teach them in college. There's no substitute for it."

Macken punched his palm.

"All right, people," he said, "let's cut the chat. Let's *get* the swine!"

Keogh grinned and fed the computer another sequence of arcane commands. He turned presently.

"We have the algorithm."

"If you say so, Barry," Blade said. "For all I know, you could be talking about African drum music."

"Now we apply the converse of the algorithm to the first recording. That way, we can remove all the distortion. We're nearly there."

He did as promised. And they listened. Keogh had turned up the volume, so that none of them would miss a single syllable of Angel's unscrambled words.

Blade heard those words that he'd recorded in his mother's kitchen as if he was hearing them for the first time. In the background, a little music-making mechanism tinkled prettily. The extraordinary thing was that voice and music blended so well. The real voice of Angel was sweet and melodious, belying the menace of the spoken words.

It was the voice of a young woman.

Twenty-four

Later they all sat in Keogh's office. Blade was allowed a cigar, though to be smoked with *both* windows open.

"I'll be damned," Duffy muttered. "I'll be damned." He'd said little else since leaving the laboratory. "A girl!"

Sweetman threw him a disapproving look. The man would never learn.

"It was Angel's trump card," Blade said. "She went out of her way to convince us she was male. The voice sounded so bloody masculine you'd never have dreamed it was a woman. Nolan wondered that first time whether we were playing it at the right speed. And how many electronics experts are women? How many *bombers* are women, if it comes to that. God, she must have been laughing up her sleeve at us!"

He ran his fingers through his hair.

"Angel. Over and over I wondered about that name. Why she'd picked it, of all names. I thought about 'avenging angels' or 'angels of death' and things like that. In the end I had to agree with you, Dr. Earley, that she'd simply chosen a name at random, that it hadn't any significance at all. But we were wrong. It had. It was her subtle way of saying: 'Guess my gender if you can.' "

He suddenly thought back to a living room in County Wicklow. Katharine's skewed picture had *spoken* to him, and he hadn't understood the words.

"It's what you said at the beginning, Blade," Dr. Earley told him. "People like our bomber invariably betray themselves. They think they're so incredibly clever, but that's exactly their undoing."

"So what happens now, sir?" Sweetman asked Duffy.

The assistant commissioner flicked a speck from the cuff of his dark uniform.

"We nail her. It's as simple as that. I want the two of ye to work intensively with Dr. Earley again, starting—"

"The two of us?" Macken said. "What about Nolan?"

"Don't mind about him, Blade. He's back on the Delahunt business as of now, plus a missing-person investigation that's just come in. You're in charge again." He looked a bit sheepish. "I shouldn't have taken you off it anyway. But we'll discuss that another time."

"Fair enough, sir. You were saying . . . ?"

"Yes, I want ye to work with Dr. Earley again, starting first thing tomorrow. I don't care if it takes all day and all night, we've got to find out who this woman is, or at least pin her down to some location by the day after tomorrow. We've only three days to go now—not even that. We *must* be able to identify the owner of that voice."

"I think we're halfway there," Earley said, removing her glasses and polishing them. "All right, I know I was mistaken about the age—and we won't even *talk* about the gender, thank you very much. Yet I stand firm on the district with which one associates her vocabulary. It's definitely Phibsborough." She squinted through one of the lenses and breathed on it. "With what we have now, we can probably narrow it down to a handful of streets."

"I'm impressed," Keogh said.

"I'm not a scientist, Barry," Earley said. "What you do and what I do are poles apart. I'm the first to admit that I make as many wrong guesses as right ones. But we are dealing with human beings, about as fickle an animal as you're likely to find."

"She could very well be older than she sounds," Blade suggested, remembering Katharine Macken's childlike voice on his answering machine. "I don't think we should rule that out."

Earley shook her head.

"No, the voice is young, take it from me. Someone in her twenties." She put on her glasses again. "At a guess—and it really is only a guess at this stage—I should say that we are dealing with a young woman who was an only child. She'd be more likely to adopt the speech patterns of her parents than the language of people her own age."

"Mmm," Blade murmured, "so we're dealing with a loner. A bit like the character they caught in the States a few years back. What's this they called him?"

"The Unabomber," Sweetman said. "Another fecking egotripper who tripped himself up with his own conceitedness."

Duffy had been doing more thinking than talking—an unusual departure from his regular pattern. He stood up and folded his arms.

"I'm still trying to puzzle this out," he said. "How could a girl learn so much about explosives? Could she have been involved with the IRA? Perhaps we should extend the investigation to cover that eventuality."

"Or she could have learned it from someone in the nick," Sweetman said. "Didn't we agree that she might have done time?"

"It was a possibility," Dr. Earley said. "And it's a line of inquiry that we could continue to pursue. But don't forget, Detective Sergeant, that anyone can find out how to build a bomb these days, simply by reading a book."

"She's right there," Blade said. "Wasn't it Ken Follett or one of the others who showed you how to make your own atomic bomb?"

"Fiction or nonfiction," Dr. Keogh said, getting up and going to a bookshelf, "you can get your information from all sorts of places."

He reached for a book and showed them the title: *Weapons and Defence Systems of the Royal Navy*. He flipped though its pages.

"A couple of nights tucked up in bed with this," he said, "together with a few service manuals, and you can build your own rocket launcher, grenade, antiaircraft gun. They have this at the National Library and the universities."

"Don't tell me about it, Barry," Duffy groaned. "I'd prefer not to know. There's too much of this stuff knocking around."

"So she's done her research," Sweetman said. "And maybe been in prison as well."

"*And* don't forget what I said about the possibility of her being on the force," Earley reminded them.

Dr. Barry Keogh shook his head in commiseration. "You people have your work cut out for you, so."

He ticked off his fingers one by one. "She's a garda; she's been to prison; she's an explosives expert; she's an electronics wizard; her taste in reading goes beyond Jackie Collins. Anything else I've missed?"

Duffy looked at his watch.

"It's nearly nine," he said. "We'll call it a day. You must be tired, Blade. Get yourself an early night—you, too, Sweetman. We'll call a conference with your team for half past nine tomorrow morning. Oh, and Blade, I'll be dropping in now to have a word with the commissioner. Stick around for fifteen minutes, will you? He'll most likely want to congratulate you in person for today's breakthrough."

There was a knock on the door and a uniformed garda put his head in.

"Excuse me, but there's a Mr. Redfern to see Superintendent Macken."

"He'll have to be told as well, Blade," Duffy said. "Don't forget the Yanks are coming up with the money, so we owe them something. And I'd rather he heard it from you."

"Well, I'll be damned." Lawrence Redfern echoed the assistant commissioner's words, almost causing Macken to wonder whether Duffy and he had been in secret communication. "A woman. I'll be damned."

Blade could afford to be generous. He wasn't gloating; his bonhomie had increased in the past few minutes.

"Your lads in the States would probably have cracked it sooner or later, Redfern," he said. "It was just a piece of luck really. A question of being in the right place at the right time."

As they strolled across the broad, tarmacked parking lot of

the Garda Depot, they watched the sun setting redly over the trees of Phoenix Park.

Redfern was silent for a minute, then stopped walking.

"Look, I don't know how to put this but . . . Well, I guess I misjudged you, Macken." He squinted into the sun. "Could be I'm a poor judge of people. I don't know. But you sure as hell surprised me." He turned to Blade. "Look, what I want to say is . . . is . . . "

"What you want to say, Redfern, is you're sorry."

The American nodded slowly at the asphalt.

"Well, there you are," Blade told him. "I've said it for you and saved you the embarrassment. All right? And apology accepted. You're not such a bad skin after all, apart from a few *minor* character defects."

"Thanks . . . I think."

He stuck out his hand. Blade shook it; then he clapped Redfern on the back and they strolled on.

"Now that we've got that sorted out," Blade said presently, "would you mind telling me what you're doing about the money? She's pest—God, I can't get used to thinking of her as a woman!"

"I know what you mean . . . Blade."

"Anyway. She's pestering me the whole time about it. I can't stall her forever."

"It's in Washington."

"Really? All of it?"

"Every last dime. They'll be flying it in tomorrow. In two planes. Safer."

Blade kicked a pebble with the toe of his shoe.

"Twenty-five million dollars! Someone's going to be out of pocket in a big way if she pulls it off."

Redfern shook his head and smiled.

"She'll never spend it. She can't. We can trace it."

"Used notes?" Macken stopped walking. "Jesus, Redfern! You're not thinking of marking them with invisible ink? She'd spot that immediately. She'd know about these things. She *must*."

Redfern smiled again. "Not this, she wouldn't. This is one scam she wouldn't know about. *I* didn't know about it until yesterday. We've got the best lab boys in the whole damn world at Langley."

"Tell all." Blade stuck a Hamlet between his lips.

But Redfern had no opportunity of disclosing the CIA secret that night and Blade was forced to return the cigar to the pack unlit. Because at that moment they heard a shout, and turned to see Sweetman running across the parking lot. She was out of breath when she reached them, and in high excitement.

"Blade," she gasped, "the bitch is after letting off another bomb!"

Twenty-five

She'd seemed omnipotent a week before. She'd had the Special Branch—the cream of Ireland's police force—groping in the dark. She'd thumbed her nose at the Central Intelligence Agency of the mighty United States of America.

Now she was making mistakes.

"It didn't go off, Blade," Captain Tom Fitzpatrick told him. "The detonators did, but the device itself didn't. It must have been the dampness down there, or maybe the explosives were contaminated; we won't know until we dig it up and run tests."

This time, a cluster of utility vans painted in the livery of Telecom Éireann surrounded an area of roadway that was cordoned off with yellow-and-black plastic tape. The "hard hats" were at work again, dressed now in an overall of a different color. They'd set up arc lights that bathed the site in a brilliance to rival a midday sun. Blade had to admire the speed with which Fitzpatrick had responded.

There was no uniformed garda presence—the commissioner had insisted on that—and now Duffy walked next to Macken, Sweetman, and Redfern, wearing his off-duty clothing. The assistant commissioner looked strangely vulnerable without the trappings of his rank.

Traffic moved slowly in a single line past the sealed-off section of Drumcondra Road, the road that led to the airport. The arc lights showed faces staring out of cars; but it was an incurious staring, without suspicion.

"Who reported it?" Blade asked, going over to inspect the damage. It was slight: hardly more than a crack in the asphalt—nothing unusual for a Dublin street.

"One of the local guards," Sweetman said. "It was a stroke of luck really. He just happened to be passing when he heard what sounded like a gunshot or a backfire. But it was still bright, and he saw smoke coming out of the road. That's what alerted him. It didn't smell like gas, he said; more like explosives."

"I shouldn't, by rights," Fitzpatrick said, "have you people within a mile of the thing." He looked grimly at the slow-moving traffic. "If we were going by the book, we'd have sealed off and evacuated most of the road. There could be any amount of explosive down there."

"What's the next step?"

"The next step, Blade, is that we *very* carefully tear up that piece of road. We could be at it till morning. After that, we'll freeze what we find, split it up, and have every expert in the country go over it with a fine-tooth comb."

"We'll get a sample, too, I hope?" Redfern said.

"CIA," Macken told Fitzpatrick in a half-whisper. "Major Lawrence Redfern."

Fitzpatrick almost saluted, but checked himself in time.

"Of course you will, Major. I'll see that the Guards get enough to split with you. Jesus, your president must be a brave man . . . I mean: not calling off the tour, when he knows what's going on." A pause. "He does, doesn't he?"

"We keep the White House well-informed, Captain. He knows. But he's the best."

Blade wondered if Redfern had served during the Nixon administration. No, he'd have been just a kid then—yet Blade was convinced that Redfern's blind loyalty would have elicited a similar accolade if Tricky Dicky were still in office.

Americans.

Macken's cellular phone rang. A shiver crossed his face; some sixth sense told him who the caller might be. He was not mistaken.

"BLADE, ME OLD FLOWER. HOW GOES THE BATTLE?"

Sweetman guessed, from her superior's expression, the identity of the caller and motioned to the others to remain silent. Blade pressed the RECORD button.

"Angel."

"THE SAME. I MADE A HAIMES OF THAT ONE, DIDN'T I? AH,
WELL, IT WAS ONLY MEANT AS A WARNING, ANYWAY. NO HARM
DONE. YOU CAN'T TRUST THESE ARMY SURPLUS STORES, CAN
YOU?" The jackhammer laugh. "BUT, BLADE, IT WAS TO TELL
YOU I MEAN BUSINESS. I DON'T WANT YOU FUCKERS GETTING COM-
PLACENT. D'YOU FOLLOW ME?"
"I follow you."
Redfern was whispering something to Fitzpatrick.
"THAT'S GOOD. I WOULDN'T WANT YIZ TO THINK I'M PICKING
ME NOSE. I'M WATCHING YIZ."
"For fuck's sake, Angel—we *got* the message the first time.
There's no need for this."
"AH, BUT THERE IS." Another grossly distorted laugh. "I HAVE
TO KEEP YOOZE ON YOUR TOES. THERE'S PLENTY MORE BOMBS
DOWN THERE, BLADE: JUST WAITING FOR A TEENY-WEENY TWIST
OF MY FINGER."
"I get you. But there's no call for this at all. You've made
your point, Angel. You'll have your money. It's all been taken
care of; I can tell you that for a fact."
"AH NOW, I'M GLAD TO HEAR IT. YOU DIDN'T SOUND TOO SURE
EARLIER. HAVE THE YANKS COUGHED UP? ABOUT FUCKING TIME!"
"They have it. All of it. They're flying it in tomorrow."
"AND IT'S THE WAY I WANT IT? USED NOTES?"
"Yes. Unmarked, untraceable. You have my word. It's the
goods."
"YOU'RE SURE NOW, BLADE? YOU WOULDN'T BE HAVING ME ON
NOW? IF YOU ARE, I SWEAR TO GOD I'LL—"
"It'll be there. Don't worry about it. Don't get your knick-
ers in a twist."
There was a long silence.
Oh, fuck. Blade could have bitten his tongue.
It had been an innocuous remark. It was an expression he
was accustomed to using in the course of a working day—
with both male and female colleagues. Now he realized that
the woman at the other end of the line might have construed
it as an indication that Blade was aware of her gender. Jesus.
He sought for words that might repair the damage.

"Are you still there?"

"I'M HERE."

"You'll have your money, Angel. God almighty, a man could live in the lap of luxury with that kind of bread. What are you planning on doing with it anyway? Buying yourself a harem?"

"AH, NOW, THAT WOULD BE TELLING YOU, WOULDN'T IT, BLADE?"

The line went dead. Blade walked slowly back to Sweetman and the others. He was just about to say something to Duffy when a flashgun flared.

Linda Doyle was waiting at the back entrance to Garda HQ in Phoenix Park when the army vehicle drew up and Fitzpatrick alighted. The night was not cold but she shivered. The spinning blue light on the roof of the truck cast her features by turns into shadow and glare.

The soldier threw open the rear door and ducked inside the vehicle. He reemerged carrying a large, metal box. A man wearing corporal's stripes followed him. Fitzpatrick moved slowly, stepping out of the van like a skater testing the ice after the first freeze of winter.

"Can I give you a hand?" Doyle asked.

"No, just point me in the right direction."

She led the way through a maze of corridors, all illuminated by fluorescent lamps. Uniformed police officers stood aside and allowed Doyle and her strange retinue to pass.

The Forensics Lab is actually a number of laboratories. There was no personnel at this hour, apart from a young man with a white coat and a bad case of acne. He pushed open a door that led to a room dominated by a metal table above which blazed an operating-room lamp unit. Fitzpatrick laid the metal box on the table, relieved to be rid of the burden.

"Can we stay and watch?" he asked.

"Sure. You'll be taking some of it with you anyway, won't you?"

Linda Doyle undid the clasps on the box and tilted back the

lid. Carefully, very carefully, she removed the top layer of Styrofoam chips. She looked at Fitzpatrick in amusement.

"What's this? A piece of your front garden?"

The object that lay exposed was a shapeless lump of dirt about a foot long. Part of it was blackened and glazed like anthracite. There was a burned-off wire visible.

"Clever, isn't it?" Fitzpatrick remarked. "She must have mixed soil together with some sort of glue and then wrapped it around the jelly. Once it hardened, you'd never know what it was. A workman could step over it and not be any the wiser—not when it looks just the same as any dirt you'd find under the street. Fair dues to her."

Doyle touched the crystallized area, ran a finger over the exposed wire.

"And this is where the detonator was attached?"

"Yeah. That's all that's left of it. That must have been a big enough bang in itself."

Doyle said no more but very slowly removed more of the polystyrene chips until the base of the clay lump was visible. Then she slid her hands under it, lifted it out, and laid it on the table. She angled the operating lamp for a better view.

"Are you going to freeze it?" the corporal asked.

"What do *you* think? I'm just wondering if we should try to remove some of the dirt first. Might be just as well."

Fitzpatrick shook his head.

"It's very securely bonded, whatever it was she used. I'd freeze the whole shebang if I were you. There's a good chance the glue will go brittle and fall off of its own accord."

"You're right," Doyle said.

She gave a sign to her assistant. The young man donned a pair of enormous gloves, went to a container, and lifted the lid with both hands. A cloud of vapor rose.

"Liquid oxygen?" Fitzpatrick asked.

"Yes. Nitrogen would shatter it into a million pieces in seconds. We want it cold, but not *that* cold."

Doyle motioned again to her assistant. He placed a circular, meshed-metal dish on the table. It bore an uncanny resemblance to a deep-fry basket. Doyle donned gloves, lifted the the camouflaged explosive, and set it gingerly in the dish. Her assistant carried it to the smoking container and lowered it gently in. A sizzle rose before he replaced the lid.

"Jayziz, just like in the chipper," said the corporal. "Only you won't find *me* eating anything out of that pan."

Doyle was looking at her wristwatch. "We'll give it twenty seconds, I think. That ought to do it."

She went to a rack on the wall and returned with a hacksaw.

"High tech," said Fitzpatrick with a smile. "That's what I like to see."

"Speed is the very last thing we want, Captain. A powersaw would generate a critical amount of heat. Ready when you are, Michael."

Her assistant retrieved the now-smoking lump and laid it on the table. Doyle brushed it lightly with a gloved hand. As Fitzpatrick had predicted, a coating of crystallized earth fell away. The two soldiers watched with great interest.

"Four pieces, Captain? One for us, one for the army, one for the Americans and one for the science lab at Trinity."

He nodded.

The operation was completed in less than thirty minutes. Four thick slices of a yellow substance resembling rock candy lay side by side on the table.

Jelly.

Some minutes later, Fitzpatrick and his subordinate left the way they'd come, the army captain carrying a less heavy, but no less lethal, burden.

Twenty-six

Another Sunday morning, another missed weekend for Blade's team. Yet not one of the assembled men and women was complaining. They scented the kill.

Redfern had summoned his full complement; more than twenty of his dark-suited colleagues had joined him; he himself was now seated close to Macken. There was an air of expectation in the incident room. Blade hadn't seen Duffy looking so good-humored in days. It was true: The assistant commissioner's moods made a tangible difference to the atmosphere of the bureau.

"Pluto," Blade began, "has showed her hand at last."

There were loud murmurs from some of the detectives on hearing this, the first reference to the bomber as a woman.

"Up until this morning," he went on, "we'd been unable to locate a murder weapon—at least enough of a weapon for us to follow up on. Now we have it."

He picked up two sheets of fax paper.

"We now have confirmation from two independent bodies that the gelignite found in Drumcondra is definitely industrial grade. Both reports match almost exactly. Both place the date of manufacture at a little over nine years ago; both indicate that the source of the gelignite is Irish Industrial Explosives in Enfield, County Meath."

The rear door opened and a middle-aged, uniformed garda came in. She excused herself and handed Blade another fax. He read it quickly.

"There's timing for you!" he told the room. "Confirmation from a third laboratory that IIE is the place of manufacture. Detective Sergeant Sweetman and myself will be making inquiries there later on today. In the meantime, I want every other member of the team working on the suspect."

"What have we got to go on now, sir?" somebody asked. "Apart from the fact we know it's a woman."

"I think Dr. Earley can answer that better than I can. Doctor?"

None knew better than Macken that Early's confidence in her abilities had been shattered by his revelations of the day before. Yet he knew, too, that the psychologist was made of stern stuff. She herself had always been the first to admit that hers was not an exact science. But, Blade argued to himself, what do we mean by "exact"? Is scientific advancement not a process of trial and error? How many patients had died of toxic transfusions before medical science became aware of the existence of different blood types? How many thousands of laboratory animals are sacrificed each day on the altar of faulty science? Nonetheless, Blade missed some of Earley's self-assurance as she addressed the gathering.

"Despite my obvious mistake with regard to the suspect's gender, certain key elements of my profile still stand. One: She is beyond doubt familiar with these headquarters, how a police investigation is conducted, and with certain members of the force, Superintendent Macken in particular."

She paused to consult her papers.

"Two: She remains an expert in explosives, as well as in sophisticated electronic apparatus. Three: She is a native of Phibsborough and may still be living there. I believe we should narrow that part of the investigation down to a radius of, say, half a mile from Dalymount Park."

Notes were made by Blade's team and Redfern's men.

"Four: She may have served time in prison, and consequently bears a deep resentment toward the authorities. Five: She is a young woman. My present estimation places her age between twenty-five and thirty."

"We're sure of that, are we, Doctor?" Duffy said.

"Quite sure, Commissioner."

But Blade detected a slight waver in Earley's voice. Sometimes Duffy could be a right pain in the arse.

"And last," she said, "the suspect is quite clearly a highly disturbed individual. Although at this time my hypothesis is open to dispute, I am nonetheless convinced that the suspect is suffering from schizophrenia, a mental disorder that makes her highly dangerous, given the present circumstances. I have already warned Superintendent Macken about this aspect of her personality and he will support me when I say that the suspect, if sighted, must be approached with extreme caution."

A hand went up.

"Do we do a house-to-house in Phibsborough or what?"

"Don't be ridiculous, O'Connor," Duffy said. "You know better than that."

"We have all the information right here in the Square," Blade said. "If you've been through it before, then go over it again. I've arranged with Mr. Redfern that you'll be receiving every assistance from him and his colleagues. Commissioner Duffy has also arranged for a direct link with Lyons. Anything we haven't got here, they'll have over there. But you're looking for a *woman* this time, probably with a home address in Phibsborough—though we don't know if she's still living there. She more than likely has a record, has done time. Start again in 1989—no, make that '86."

"But sir, if she's as young as twenty-five, like Dr. Earley says, then she was only a kid in '86."

"So bloody what? Are you trying to tell me that kids can't commit crime? Check the records of the juvenile courts, the magistrates' courts, the reformatories." He looked at his watch. "Off you go now."

Detective Sergeant Paddy Flynn stuck up a hand.

"Before we get going, sir . . . "

"Yes, Paddy?"

"You're asking us to go over the files again. I was wondering if it was you who gave the authorization to lock the files on the Chief Superintendent Merrigan murder."

"What!"

"They're locked. You need a password to get in, so you do."

Blade looked blankly at Duffy. The assistant commissioner shook his head.

"I know nothing about it," Macken told Flynn. He addressed the room. "Who's authorized to lock files?"

No one it seemed.

Blade pointed at a junior detective. "Get someone from the Park over here right away—whoever's in charge of the IBM mainframe."

"Right away, sir."

The Merrigan murder. The ghost that haunted Blade Macken. He stared absently at the faxes on the table. It made no sense. Why now? Why nine years on? Why *exactly* nine years on? No, it was impossible: What was then and what was now could in no way be related.

Yet an inner voice was telling him that it *was* possible, that there was indeed a tide in the affairs of men, that the flood was rising again. He'd been asked if Angel could have an accomplice in Harcourt Square. He'd dismissed the idea.

Now Blade wasn't so certain.

Twenty-seven

Sweetman drove. They followed the Grand Canal past Old Kilmainham Jail and merged presently with the traffic flowing westward on the dual carriageway. Lucan was a blur as Sweetman hit the gas pedal. But Blade didn't comment; they were running out of time. Some minutes later they raced past the village of Leixlip; then Kilcock—and Macken thought suddenly of Jim Roche. He doubted if the fucker would dare show his face again at the Square. Good riddance.

The speedometer was at ninety miles per hour and climbing. Grazing black-and-white Frisian cows turned to dirty gray streaks.

The freeway ended and the road narrowed. They were passing through rolling, green countryside, tree-rich and pleasant. The road grew winding but that didn't deter Sweetman; Macken gritted his teeth as she overtook two cars on a particularly dangerous bend.

Enfield, like most midland Irish villages, consists mainly of a single street lined with stores and bars. They had to stop and ask directions to the explosives plant. It was in the township of Clonagh, some six miles to the south. Sweetman found the turning and slowed to thirty in deference to the sharp corner. Blade smelled burning rubber.

As the terrain grew progressively more rustic, Blade mused on the facility and its isolated location. It made sense, of course: it wouldn't be smart to build an explosives plant close to civilization. Somebody at the Square had told him that, at any given time, there was enough gelignite, dynamite, and TNT stored at Irish Industrial Explosives to blow a sizeable hole in County Meath.

No wonder Angel had been drawn there.

* * *

The facility was enclosed by an eight-foot-high chain-link steel fence. A gate, topped with razor wire, opened onto a long inspection bay and a second tall gate. There was no one manning the blue, prefab security hut to one side. There didn't need to be: They suddenly heard the barking of many dogs. Lithe, black shapes bounded along a footpath toward the outer gate.

"Jesus, Dobermans," Blade breathed. "I knew we should've brought along a sack of dog biscuits."

He instinctively wound up his window as ten slavering beasts pummeled the steel of the fence. Their bared fangs looked as though they could gnaw through the thick metal, given time. Blade liked dogs, but there were limits.

Then, as if by some magic, the animals fell silent and, as one, dropped to a crouch. Their brown eyes grew soft and gentle. Blade found himself almost wanting to pet them.

A man approached from the direction of the main building. He wore a dark blue uniform with a cap perched jauntily on a head of snow-white hair. He took his time, stretching in the heat of the afternoon, as if just roused from sleep. A half-smoked cigarette dangled from one corner of his mouth, a dog whistle from the other. Blade heard nothing, but the cigarette flared at regular intervals as the man expelled air between his lips.

"Dr. Doolittle, I presume," Macken murmured half to himself. Sweetman grinned.

The gates opened and Sweetman drove on through. Blade kept his window tightly shut.

"Mr. McCarthy's in his office," said the old man, pointing to a neat, one-story building surrounded by lawns, trees, and flowering shrubs. "Round the side, first door on the left. You can't miss it." He leaned down and patted a panting head. "Good girl, Queenie." To Macken and Sweetman he said: "Did they give yiz a fright? Ah, sure they're only playing, so they are. They're bored stiff, God help them, with shag all to do all day."

Blade rolled his eyes heavenward.

170

McCarthy met them at the entrance. He was unshaven and dressed in a jogging suit.

"Sorry to get you out on a Sunday," Blade said.

"No problem at all. I had to do some paperwork anyway. Come on in."

"Should the old guy be smoking?" Blade asked.

McCarthy laughed. "What did you expect, Superintendent? Kegs of gunpowder lying all over the shop? No, we're a bit more advanced than that here. Besides, old Tom never comes near the works; he has his own little place beside the kennels."

He showed them into an office that was immaculately tidy and modern. One wall was hung with a large map of Ireland, speckled with brightly colored pins. There was a quarrymen's calendar; July's pin-up was a gigantic primary crusher, located in Colorado.

"I can't offer you anything, I'm afraid," McCarthy said. "My secretary has the key to the tea cupboard."

"That's all right," Blade said.

He took a sheet of fax paper from his pocket, laid it on the desk, and smoothed it flat. "This'll probably mean more to you than it does to me."

McCarthy produced a pair of reading glasses and studied the document. He frowned.

"This is from the dark ages," he said. "We haven't manufactured anything like this since . . . since . . . "

"Nineteen ninety?" Sweetman said.

He threw her a sidelong look. "Since thereabouts, yes."

"Could you trace it?" Blade asked.

McCarthy turned in his seat and activated a PC.

"Our records are perfect," he said. "My secretary keeps track of every paper clip—in a manner of speaking." He called up a file and scrolled down it.

"Oh, dear."

Blade's heart sank. He glanced at Sweetman. "Something wrong?"

"No, no. Not really. It's just that . . . " McCarthy went to another list. "We had that spot of bother with Slattery then.

Had to let him go. He'd made a right pig's mickey of things. Sorry, miss."

"That's okay," Sweetman assured him. She had notebook and pencil in hand. "What do you mean by a 'spot of bother,' sir?"

McCarthy turned to face them. He removed his glasses.

"He was incompetent. Cost us a lot of money, as well as good will with a big client of ours. Ballsed up five different orders, if I remember rightly. One customer got too much, another got too little; that kind of thing."

Blade was thoughtful. "Did anything go missing?"

"If it did, we'd have reported it, Superintendent. At least we would have, if we'd known for certain. But that's just it: We didn't. Slattery had jiggled things around so much that we had to go over everything by hand. It's a big warehouse out there, y'know. But we got it sorted out in the end." He looked sharply at Macken. "Or so we thought. Are you saying that something did go missing after all?"

"This Slattery," Blade said. "Where can we find him?"

"He lives with his mother in Johnstown Bridge. Or he used to anyway, when he was working for us. I'm sure I have the address somewhere." He returned to the terminal. "Yes, here it is."

Sweetman made a note.

"Colm Slattery?"

"Yes. . . . "

"Special Branch," Macken said. "We'd like a word."

The man, who looked to be a few years Blade's senior, held the door half-open.

"Uh, me mother's sick upstairs."

Blade commiserated, then pushed the door fully open, practically knocking Slattery off his feet.

"You can't do this!"

"I've just fucking done it, head. File a complaint later."

The cottage was tiny. The first floor consisted of a single room with a small kitchen beyond; a staircase ascended at an angle of forty-five degrees. Although the sun shone brightly, the little room, crowded with worn furniture, was gloomy and cold.

"Sit down, Mr. Slattery," Blade ordered.

Slattery sat.

"What do you want? I haven't done anything."

Blade said nothing. Silence was best when dealing with a nervous suspect. Maintain silence long enough and he'll be the first to break it. Birdcalls from the backyard and the ticking of a clock on the mantelpiece were the only sounds for almost a minute.

Slattery broke the silence.

"I'd nothing to do with it. Honest to God."

Sweetman had her notebook out. "To do with what, Mr. Slattery?"

His eyes were wild. "Nothing!"

"Fair enough," Blade said. "We'll talk about this 'nothing' later on. What we want at the moment is information on the gelignite that disappeared in 1989."

Slattery went white. "I know nothing about that."

"Right. That's why McCarthy fucked you out, is it? For knowing nothing?"

Blade stood up and walked slowly behind Slattery's chair. Before the man knew what was happening, Blade had grasped him by the left wrist and wrenched Slattery's arm viciously up behind his back. He screamed.

"Sir!"

"Don't worry, Sweetman. I'll leave it in its socket like God intended it."

"Is that you, Colm?" came a faint voice from upstairs. "Is everything all right?"

"Answer your mammy now, Colm," Blade said. "Tell her you're fine." Another wrench.

"I'm fine, Ma!" Slattery gasped. "Everything's okay."

"I thought I heard voices."

"Tell her it's the telly."

"It's only the telly, Ma."

173

"Sir, this is *wrong,*" Sweetman said, as Blade forced the unfortunate man down on his knees, left arm still firmly pinioned at his back. Slattery moaned.

"So is mass murder, Sweetman. And we haven't time for niceties."

He forced Slattery farther down until the man's nose was touching the pile of the thick, sheepskin rug on the floor. Then he placed a foot on his head.

"I want answers, Slattery. I want them quick and I want them now. Who took the gelignite?"

No answer.

Blade rammed his foot down hard on Slattery's head. There was a muffled shriek as his nose burst asunder on the rug.

"Sir, for God's sake!"

He ignored Sweetman and wrenched Slattery's wrist higher until his thumb touched his neck.

"*Who,* Slattery? Who took the fucking gelignite?"

"I don't know!"

Blade kicked Slattery's face down again, harder. Blood spattered the white sheepskin. Macken stomped down on the back of his head; once, twice. The man went into convulsions.

"One more time," Blade said coldly. "Who took the gelignite?"

Slattery said something. His voice was barely audible.

"What? Speak up."

Blade removed his foot from the man's head and pulled him up by the left arm. Slattery cried out and Sweetman turned away in horror when she saw the gory ruin that was Slattery's face. Blood flowed freely down his shirt front, staining the white rug. Some of his teeth were missing.

"Carol," he moaned. "Carol."

Sweetman saw something bestial cross Blade's face; it was the feral look of a carnivore. It would haunt her dreams for weeks to come. She knew at that moment why Macken never talked about his time as a soldier. Oh yes, he would mention the places he'd visited during his tours of duty: exotic places that she'd probably never see. The bars, the clubs, the beaches. But never the combat. And now Sweetman knew why.

"Carol," Blade said in a half-whisper. "Carol who?"

"I d-don't know. I don't know. She never told me her second name."

"Okay," Macken said, and allowed Slattery to fall to the rug amid his own blood.

So Angel had a name: Carol. Blade relaxed, went to the little window, and stared out past the flowerbox on the outside windowsill. Carol, Carol.

When he turned at last, Sweetman was wiping the man's face with a tea towel. Already Slattery's right eye had swelled and purpled. He was whimpering softly like a puppy.

"Colm Slattery," Blade announced, "I'm arresting you on suspicion of being an accessory to murder."

Twenty-eight

"Came as soon as I could," Humphrey Bell told the assistant commissioner in an accent that never failed to set Duffy thinking of boating on the river Cam, girls in white hats and frocks, and champagne picnics on green lawns. "Traffic accident at Loughlinstown. Cars backed up for miles."

"Sunday drivers," Duffy said equally laconically. "But we shouldn't complain; they're our bread and butter. And thanks for coming at such short notice, Humphrey. Cup of tea?"

Bell waved a hand impatiently. "Let's get it over with, Mr. Duffy. We've some friends coming by later this afternoon."

Paddy Flynn and four other officers were clustered around a computer terminal in the incident room. They stood aside to make space for the IBM programmer from the Park. He sat down to the left of the keyboard.

"Right," he said. "Show me these 'locked' files of yours."

Flynn showed him. One by one, he brought up the offending files contained in the folders of 1989 and 1990.

ACCESS DENIED: PASSWORD PLEASE?

"I see what you mean," Bell said. "Except that these files aren't locked, Sergeant. We're actually *in* the file you have up at the moment. What you see is what you get, as they say. That's all there is; no more, no less."

"I don't follow you, Mr. Bell."

"Don't you? What I'm saying is that the file as it once was is no more. Somebody has written over it."

Flynn scratched his chin. "Deleted it?"

"I'm afraid not. Whoever did this knew exactly what he was about. Had he simply deleted it, then we'd have stood a reasonable chance of retrieving most—if not all—of it. You see, a deleted file remains on the hard disk for a limited time, even though you'll not find it listed in the directory. Overwrite a file, however, and the original is gone forever."

"Jesus."

Humphrey Bell smiled. "But all is not lost, Sergeant. Would somebody get me the Park on the telephone?"

Bell was shortly put through to the IBM room.

"Declan? Humphrey here. No, no, I'm at the Square. Would you mind terribly if I asked you to fish out last week's backup tapes for me? No, not all of them; '89 and '90—serious crimes. Good man."

He turned to Flynn.

"Our friend was clever. But not clever enough. What he didn't know is that we back up the IBM once a day. It's a precaution that has paid dividends from time to time. You see, all the contents are saved on tape. So, should anything go awry, then it's simply a matter of working from the copy. Our friend may have wiped the files from the network, but their replacements should be on line in a minute or two."

Flynn shook his head in admiration. Then he said: "Those weren't the only files, Mr. Bell. I was cross-referencing some data from other sources."

"We'll get to them presently. First let's retrieve your own."

The files came on line as Bell had promised. Another phone call led to the retrieval of the information that pointed a finger at Jim Roche. Bell stood up.

"Time I was getting along, gentlemen. I've some guests whom I can't keep waiting. Any idea who the culprit might be?"

"No, sir," Flynn answered, "I haven't the foggiest."

But when Bell had shut the door behind him, the detective sergeant turned to the others and told them of his suspicions.

"Christ! Do you know what you're saying, Paddy?"

"I know, I know. But who else could it have been? He was sitting right there when I was going through them files. He even asked for a printout."

"Fuck *me*. Duffy'll have to be told; you know that, don't you?"

"Jayziz, what happened to *him?*" the desk sergeant asked as Blade escorted a battered and handcuffed Slattery into Harcourt Square. There were wisps of white wool sticking to the matted blood on his nose and cheeks.

"Walked into the back of a bus. It'll probably need a respray. Is there an interview room free?"

"It's a busy day, sir. We've that shooting in Tallaght and two rape cases." He consulted his book. "Number two is free. He ought to get that face seen to, sir."

"I'll take care of it. Listen, can you ask someone to get hold of last Saturday's paper and have it sent down there?"

"Which one, sir?"

"It doesn't matter. The *Times,* the *Herald,* anything."

Sweetman opened the door of the interrogation room, admitted Macken and his captive and locked it from the inside. Blade unwrapped a Hamlet and lit it. Sweetman started the recorder.

"Sunday, the twelfth of July, 1998, approximately 4 P.M. Detective Sergeant Orla Sweetman here. With me is Detective Superintendent Blade Macken and the suspect Colm Slattery—"

"—and the forecast for today," said Blade, "is for right thundery showers of hail, followed by blustery gales, and belts of depression."

"Sir, *please.*"

"Sorry, Sweetman."

He frogmarched the suspect to the two-way mirror that extended the length of a wall and held Slattery's face in front of it. His unswollen left eye opened wide with horror.

"Look at the state of you, Slattery! Go on, have a good look at yourself. Believe me, you'll look a hundred times worse if you fuck with me now. I'm telling you, your poor sick mammy'll be a lot sicker when she sees you after I'm through with you. Do you follow me?"

He unlocked the handcuffs and propped Slattery in a chair. "Right. This Carol woman, how did you meet her?"

"In the pub."

"Which pub?" Blade asked.

A pause. "The Hamlet."

"It's in Johnstown Bridge," Sweetman assisted. "We turned off there for the factory."

"Oh . . . right. I remember now."

"We all used to drink there after work," Slattery said.

"We?"

"The lads from IIE. Every Friday mostly."

"Did she approach you, or did you approach her?"

"I . . . I don't remember. I—aagh!"

"Suspect has just fallen from his chair," Blade said, "and Superintendent Macken is helping him to his feet. Are you okay, Colm?"

Sweetman looked appalled.

"Who made the first move?" Blade asked.

"Ehh, I did. But she was kind of leading me on, y'know."

"I know. Did you go to bed with her?"

"Yeah."

"Often?"

"Yeah."

"How often?"

"Uh, I don't know. A lot."

There was a tap on the door. Sweetman opened it and accepted a folded newspaper from a young officer.

"Was she good?"

"Jayziz, yeah."

"Fucked like a baboon in heat, did she?"

"I . . . I don't—"

"The best fuck you ever had, eh Colm?"

"Hmm, yeah."

Blade paused then; something about Slattery had struck a chord. How old was he? Older than Blade, that was for sure. Forty-eight, forty-nine? Yet, despite his earlier show of bravado, there was something innocent about Colm Slattery. Nine years ago, a forty-year-old bachelor is living with his mother in the one-horse town of Johnstown Bridge, where the world revolves around a job at the explosives facility, the football club, and a pub called The Hamlet. *Nothing ever happens in Johnstown Bridge*. It could have been a book title. Blade saw it all in his mind's eye: a young woman, a stranger, cunning as a vixen, walks into a country bar on a Friday evening, sits down in a corner with a glass of beer, and observes.

The men from the plant cluster at tables and line the counter, released for two days and three nights from the tedium of their jobs. They drink, make merry, and engage in the mating ritual with the local women.

The predator scans the faces of the drinking, laughing men; sees through the cigarette smoke a man who drinks faster and laughs more shrilly than the rest; catches his eye, and holds it. It's the first time Colm Slattery has ever been so blatantly propositioned with a look. He's hooked.

"Would I be right in saying that Carol was the *only* fuck you ever had?" Blade said. "You were a virgin, weren't you, Colm, before you met Carol?"

"Ehh . . ."

"It's all right, Colm. Nothing wrong with being a virgin. I used to be one myself, you know."

Slattery bowed his head.

"What did she want the gelignite for? Did she say?"

"Yeah. She said it was for East Timor."

"What!"

Slattery was scared that Macken would hit him again. His words tumbled out in a torrent.

"That's what she said—East Timor—she was helping the rebels there, her and some friends of hers—they were fighting for their freedom against the Indonesians."

"I see. And you believed her, did you, Colm? You thought she and her friends were going to use the jelly to waste a few nasty little slant-eyed soldiers? No skin off *your* nose—if you'll pardon my indelicacy."

"Uh, yeah, I did."

"Do you know what she really wanted it for, Colm? Have a look. Have a *good* look."

"Superintendent Macken," Sweetman said, "shows suspect the front page of the *Evening Herald,* dated Saturday, the fourth of July."

"You see these pictures, Slattery? Take a good fucking look at them. You see that little kid? He was two years of age, Slattery. Blown to fucking bits with the gelignite that *you* stole, that *you* gave to Carol."

"Jesus, I didn't know. Honest to God, I didn't know. It was nine years ago."

"So you'll help us find her then, will you, Colm? Because she's going to blow up more people if you don't."

"Suspect nods his head in agreement," Sweetman said.

"Now," said Blade, "we'll have a doctor look at those little scratches of yours, before they turn septic."

"Charlie, a word."

"Right away, sir?"

"Yes, Charlie. Right away."

Nolan found Duffy in his office, studying a length of perforated computer printout.

"Sit down, Charlie."

Nolan could not read his superior's expression. Something was up, that much he guessed. But what?

Duffy folded the printout back into place. He steepled his fingers and fixed Nolan with a basilisk-like stare.

"I'll come straight to the point, Charlie. Why did you tamper with the Merrigan files?"

Nolan blanched. He attempted to speak. Couldn't.

"That's enough for me," Duffy said. "You've just as good as admitted your guilt. And let's *please* not go through the rigmarole of you trying to convince me otherwise. I've been at this game as long as you have, Charlie. I know all the tricks." He leaned back in his ergonomically designed chair. "Now, take your time. But for fuck's sake Charlie, don't lie to me, all right?"

Charles Nolan had always considered himself a tough man. It was why he'd joined the force. He'd been through the mill, as they all had: Duffy, Merrigan, Macken. He'd played rough when circumstances demanded it, and had no regrets. Thus, when he broke down in the assistant commissioner's office, he himself was more surprised than Duffy.

He didn't protest when Duffy summoned an officer to bring him away. He'd no words to describe the sensation of having a cell door shut behind him, as it had shut behind so many of his own detainees.

Rob McGrath looked up in mild surprise when Macken and Sweetman led in the man with bandages covering half his face. The right eye was shut, lost beneath a terrible, purple swelling. "Car-wreck victim" were the words that came to McGrath's mind.

"Rob's an artist, Colm," Blade said. "He's never had a show at the Municipal—or anywhere else for that matter—but he's still one of the best in the business."

Slattery nodded glumly as he was given a chair to one side of McGrath's twenty-one-inch computer screen.

"Rob," Blade went on, "is an expert in portraits. He couldn't do much with *your* mug at the moment, but that's not what we're here for. I want you to tell Rob everything you can remember about Carol's appearance, do you get me? Every detail: the color of her hair, her eyes, the shape of her mouth, etcetera. Is that clear?"

"Uh, yeah."

"Good. Got your colored crayons and tracing paper ready, Rob?"

McGrath opened a new window on his big screen.

"Ready to go, Blade."

McGrath had written the program himself, and worldwide sales of the software had made him a relatively wealthy man. It went beyond Identikit insofar as the images generated were not two- but three-dimensional. McGrath knew that a witness could sometimes remember a profile far better than a frontal view.

Sweetman was in awe of McGrath's brainchild, could freely

pass an entire afternoon just watching a "virtual" human head taking shape and acquiring texture in the cyberspace behind the screen, as McGrath spun it slowly through 360 degrees. She considered it art.

"Age?" McGrath asked. He leaned back in his chair. "It doesn't have to be exact."

"Nineteen or twenty," Slattery said.

"Shape of face? Fat, thin, long?"

"Uh, medium. No, sort of uh . . ."

"Full?"

"Yeah, that's it. Full."

"Something like this?" A hairless white head revolved slowly from left to right and back again. There were no features. It was as lifeless as a marble bust in the sculptor's preliminary stage.

"No. Not as fat."

"This better?"

"Uh, yeah."

"I can't smoke in here, can I Rob?" Blade asked.

"No. Color of eyes?"

"Greenish blue."

"Hmm, that's unusual. Let's see what we can do about that."

McGrath reached into a menu, plucked out two eyes, and colored them from a palette at the base of the screen.

"That about right?"

"Yeah. Bang on." Slattery was beginning to enjoy it, his swollen and damaged face almost forgotten.

"Hair? Did she wear it long or short?"

Slattery had to think about this.

"Uh, long, I think. No, short." He paused. "Look, it was a long time ago, all right?"

"*Think*, Colm," Blade urged and Sweetman heard that the menace had returned to his voice. She was still very shaken by the brutality she'd witnessed back at the cottage.

"No, it was long. Sometimes she wore it in a ponytail. I remember now."

"Color?"

"Sort of mousy."

"*Sort* of mousy?"

"Uh, light brown. It's hard to describe. . . ."

McGrath dipped into his palette.

"Something like this?"

"No, browner than that."

And so it went for an hour or longer, as Sweetman watched in utter fascination. The sculptor's marble gradually assumed the skin texture and contours of a human head, until the eyes that looked out at her from the screen held *life:* a sentient being stared back at her in recognition. She almost swore she saw those eyes blink, those lips move.

"That's *her,*" Slattery said at last. "Jayziz, that's Carol."

"You're sure now?" McGrath asked.

"As sure as anything. I can practically hear her voice. It's unbelievable."

"Okay." He saved the simulacrum and turned to Macken. "D'you want me to age it now?"

"You mean," said Colm Slattery, "like they do with missing kids?"

"That's it. Blade?"

But Blade was entranced. He stared at the slowly revolving head and, each time the eyes met his, a thrill passed through him. He knew those eyes, remembered eyes like those looking into his. Another image tugged at a corner of his mind. He dug deep among the brachiate strands of his memory.

Nothing, nothing is ever lost. We are better than soulless computers.

"Blade?"

"Can you do the reverse, Rob? Can you go in the opposite direction?"

"Make her younger, you mean?"

"Yes."

"*Pas de problème.*"

McGrath pulled down a menu and clicked on a command labeled ENJUVENATE.

184

"Enjuvenate?" said Blade.

"Do you like it? Made it up myself. I'm rather proud of it, actually. How many years?"

"Try eight. And give me a full frontal."

Like melting wax the image dissolved slowly. The cheeks grew chubbier, the chin receded, the nose lost its sharp edges. Only the eyes remained the same. The face of a little girl took shape on the screen.

It was not exactly the face as Blade remembered it, yet was so uncannily similar that he caught his breath in astonishment.

The face was that of Carol, Chief Superintendent Gerry Merrigan's daughter. A young girl once so fond of Blade Macken that she used to call him "Uncle."

Twenty-nine

Her diary was her best—her only—friend. No one, no one in the whole world but she, had ever read the neat, handwritten lines contained in its pages. She seldom reread what she'd entered. She dared not. She swore that several of the diary's passages had been written by another person. They read so queerly. They frightened her.

Carol Merrigan stared at an entry, written in her own hand.

Saturday, 4 July

Dear Mammy and Daddy,

I hope your both keeping well and that God is good to you. I miss you Mammy and Daddy I dont know how much longer I can be without you.

I did a terrible thing yesterday. I think I am going to burn in hell for it but I dont care. It was for you and I am not a bit sorry I done it. But they said on the news that I killed little babies and I cannot believe that. they must be lying I wouldnt do a thing like that believe me.

Oh ask almighty God and the saints in heaven to forgive me will you Mammy.

I am leaving the house next week and going to the docks to live. Its a horrible place but they don't know me their and its the place where Im going to get revenge because of what they did to you. I know its wrong but I am going to do it.

Will you pray for me?

Your Angel

Carol Merrigan shut the front door gently and carefully behind her and walked the fifteen-feet distance to the gate. She paused on the sidewalk and gazed back over the overgrown yard of the little public-housing dwelling. She'd thought about this moment for longer than was healthy. It had sustained her through the black years following her parents' deaths; it was to have been, in another sense, the final closing of a door. Yet home, be it a fifty-room mansion or a shack in the boondocks, is always hard to say goodbye to. Carol looked up at the dirty glass panes of her bedroom window, then at the peaks of the Dublin Mountains, plainly visible to the south, and experienced a sadness she'd never expected.

A sudden thought struck her: She'd left the radio on in the kitchen. She always did; left one or two lights burning, too. She'd never had a break-in, unlike most of the residents of the area. Yet you couldn't be too cautious in this neighborhood. Carol wondered whether she should go back and turn off the radio. A waste of electricity now. She decided against it. What did it matter when you were never going home again?

"There's the witch!" a young voice called out, and Carol turned.

A group of boys were kicking a football around on a circular grassed area opposite the house. At seven in the morning—the boundless energy of the young!

"Hey, witch! Where's your fucking broomstick? You fucking freaker!"

Carol didn't mind the taunts. They reinforced her own opinion that her disguise was perfect. She swept her unwashed hair back from her forehead and tucked it under her plaid shawl, clutched her bundle more tightly to her chest, and walked slowly away. There was no hurry.

As she turned into Eamon Ceannt Park, Carol reflected on the events of the last ten days.

She caught herself smiling—as well she might smile. She'd fooled them all. All of them: the fuckers at Harcourt Square, the army of the Republic, the CI-fucking-A. It *was* the CIA;

she'd no doubt about that. And she'd beaten them, too. Daddy would have been proud of his angel. Yes, yes.

No. *Was* proud, *is* proud. Carol paused and looked up at the sky, blue and cloudless. Up there was where Daddy was. When you split the sky into four equal parts, and split it further and further until you had 360 degrees, then Daddy lived in the eastern quadrant—there—at thirty-three point six degrees. He watched her by day from behind the blue, and at night from behind the reddish black that was the night sky above Dublin.

Carol crossed over the bridge at Clanbrassil Street and turned onto the footpath that ran beside the Grand Canal. There were swans on the water, a family of them, and she regretted not having brought that stale bread in the kitchen. Maybe tomorrow? Oh God no; it was beginning to sink in now. She was never going back to Crumlin.

The shade under the trees was welcome. She passed a white-haired woman seated on a bench, rocking a baby carriage, making cooing noises. Carol had to laugh, remembering. The sound caused the woman to look up. She frowned on seeing Carol, and her face took on the blank expression that decent people reserve for beggars who shouldn't, by rights, be sharing a city with them.

Carol continued to chuckle to herself, on recalling Blade Macken's bewilderment that Friday afternoon outside the American embassy. It had been foolhardy what she'd done: call attention to herself like that. But Blade! Blade, the great detective, the Pride of the Square: he'd looked right at her, looked right through her, past her, as she'd spoken those words through Dolly's mouth. Dolly had enjoyed the joke as much as she. Dolly hadn't had so much fun in twenty years.

Today was a good day, she thought. No spillage, no leaking out.

Carol hesitated at the corner of Charlemont Mall and Charlemont Street. Would she or wouldn't she? Harcourt Square lay in that direction, just a few hundred yards away. It was tempting—one last time. But she decided against it; best not to tempt providence on this, the last day before payday. She'd had her fun at the Square, squatting on the sidewalk opposite the entrance, watching Duffy, Nolan, and Macken come and go, their ugly faces growing more ugly and worried with each passing day.

Dolly had enjoyed that, had called "Mommy!," "Daddy!" each time Blade Macken and his young, dark-haired whore emerged, speeding in pursuit of a new false lead. Once or twice Carol had hoped that the reckless hussy might crash the car and kill them both. Had hoped it only for an instant; Blade belonged to Carol, not to God or the Devil.

No leakage today. It was good.

The Voice was actually soothing. She is strolling, it said, along the path by the canal; she is leaving home; she is looking in wonder at the beauty of the city, its walks, its paths, its trees, its greenery, its buildings of centuries, its uninterrupted links with the past, its age, its agelessness; she is hearing the hum of traffic; it does not detract in any way from the sweet calls of the songbirds; it augments them; she is smelling the water, ripe and beautiful; she is tasting the carbide in the air, the metallic tang of glorious industry, the desiccating of steel in the drying sun; she is . . . she is . . .

And so Carol continued eastward along the canal path, under the weeping willows, past strolling mothers and unemployed young men, once spitting in the face of a leery-eyed wino who'd the effrontery to proposition her.

The Devil resided in every drunk, just as he resided in Blade Macken, the most murderous drunk of all. The Devil was all around you and had to be fought at every turn.

Carol was on the side of the angels.

Thirty

Blade had a full complement in the incident room that Monday morning. He'd stopped counting, on reaching one hundred twenty, and that didn't include Duffy and almost thirty members of the CIA. Pride of place had been given to the men of the Emergency Response Unit; Blade detected a restlessness among them, a restlessness he recognized from his soldier's tours of duty. Macken and some of the other detectives had already completed the paperwork required for the issuing of firearms. Gareth Smyth's team had no need to do the same; these were men who *slept* with their weapons.

One of Redfern's operatives shifted his position, causing a ray of sunlight to slant along the front of his double-breasted suit, betraying a slight bulge under the left shoulder. No forms-in-triplicate to fill out there, Blade thought. Did Duffy know? Blade was almost certain this constituted a grave breach of security at the Square.

But he dismissed it; it was none of his business. Blade had more pressing matters on his mind.

"What's the story from Clonmacnoise Road?" he asked an officer.

"We've had it under surveillance since eight this morning, sir. A squad car and two plainclothesmen."

"Any sign of the suspect?"

"No, sir. No visual show. But she's there all right. Our man round the back reported lights on and a radio playing."

"Fair enough," Blade said.

He turned to a large-scale map of Crumlin that showed an area of two square miles, stretching from the Grand Canal down to Terenure. Somebody had drawn two concentric red circles; they radiated from a point slightly north of the circular green enclosed by Clonmacnoise Road.

"Detective Inspector Smyth of the ERU recommends that we evacuate every house within this radius," Blade said, indicating the outer red circle. "I'm inclined to agree; we don't know how much explosive Pluto has stashed there. There may be none at all. Then again, there could be enough to wipe out the whole housing estate. We simply don't know."

"Do you realize what you're asking?" Duffy said. "You're talking about upwards of two hundred families. Are you proposing that we carry out the operation in broad daylight? It's madness. She'd be on to us like a flash."

"I've thought of that, sir, but I don't think we should postpone this till this evening. Pluto tends to move around, as we know. At the moment we have her where we want her, and if we don't move now we might lose her."

Duffy considered this. He went to the map.

"What about a partial evacuation?" he said. "Say, two or three houses on each side. Could we do that without attracting attention?"

"It's extremely risky, sir, in my opinion. I'd hate to take responsibility if anything were to go wrong."

"Leave the responsibility to me, Superintendent. We run a far greater risk of detection if we try to get everybody out at once. It can't be done without us calling attention to ourselves. Not in broad daylight."

"I agree," Blade said. "But I have to say that I don't like it one little bit."

"That's settled then."

"Fair enough. We're going to need covering fire from the ERU. Gareth . . . ?"

The chief of the armed unit joined them at the map.

"Right. We can mount sharpshooters on the other side of the square," he said, "*here, here* and *here,* and in the rear of the houses at the back. On Leighlin Road. It'll be easy enough to evacuate the occupants: They can slip out the front."

"Grand," said Blade. "It only remains to us to find a way of getting the people out of those adjoining houses without showing our hand. It'll have to be plainclothesmen of course."

Orla Sweetman held up a hand.

"What if we were to try the same thing as we did in O'Connell Street, sir? Let on we're the gas company."

"What, you mean go round checking the meters? No, we're going to need more than that, Sweetman."

"No, sir. I meant Mr. Duffy's idea." The assistant commissioner looked interested. "We can tell them we suspect there may be a minor gas leak somewhere in the street. That way, we can ask them to leave their houses without alarming them too much."

"Hmm. I wonder if—"

"Well now, *I* think it's a marvellous idea, Macken," Duffy said. "The detective sergeant's hit the nail on the head. Look at it this way: Half of Dublin's worried about gas leaks since the explosion. They know Bord Gáis are checking all the mains in the city, thanks to that, ahem, TV interview last Friday. If we were to send a van round there today it wouldn't look at all suspicious. We could get the people out in dribs and drabs—and quietly, too. All we need do is say it's a routine check."

"Fair enough," Blade said. "I'll go along with that." He pointed. "I want Detectives Dunphy and McArdle to handle it, okay?" The two men nodded. "Yes, Paddy?"

"What happens, sir," asked Sergeant Paddy Flynn, "when they knock on Pluto's door?"

"They won't. The local Guards say the place looks deserted. The front garden's overgrown with weeds. You'd never think anyone lived there, so our boys can skip the house without raising suspicion."

He turned to the map again. "Dunphy and McArdle'll cover the road, starting from *here*, opposite Pluto's house. They'll work their way round, just pretending to inspect the fittings, nothing more. But once they come to the six houses on either side of Pluto's, they explain about the suspected leak." He turned to Dunphy and McArdle. "On no account are you to alarm them—but you know that without me telling you."

The two men nodded as one.

"Ask the people to leave so you can get down to business. Oh, and tell them that they mustn't take anything with them, otherwise Pluto'll be on to us. Try to get them to leave their houses at separate times: say, at half-hour intervals, and in ones and twos—no more. Get the kids out first. We don't want it looking like an exodus." Blade pointed to the map. "And tell them to walk or drive in the direction of Bangor Road, north and south. That way, there's a chance they won't be spotted from Pluto's house." He looked at his watch. "With any luck we should be able to have everything in place by lunchtime."

Gareth Smyth called for Macken's attention.

"What do we do if we see her leaving, sir? If we have a clear sight on the target?"

"I wish you wouldn't put it that way. She's not a target yet. Nor will she be unless we've good reason to believe she's carrying a weapon or weapons, and is attempting to use them."

"But what if she's carrying a radio-transmitting device, sir? If we show our hand she might use it to detonate a bomb."

"I know, I know. But can you imagine the stink if we were to gun down an unarmed woman in cold blood? We're in enough trouble as it is. Remember what happened with the Brits in Gibraltar? No, leave her to me. I've a feeling she wants to talk—why else would she keep phoning me? If I can get her alone I might be able to talk her out of whatever it is she's planning next."

Smyth looked decidedly unconvinced.

The editor of the *Sunday Courier* held a tabloid newspaper between thumb and forefinger as though it was something offensive he'd found while cleaning the bathroom.

"And where were you, Elaine," he asked sourly, "while this was going on?"

Elaine de Rossa didn't have to look at the picture that took up a third of the front page, or read the huge headline that exposed what the paper called COVER-UP NUMBER TWO. She'd seen it. And it hurt.

"Duffy, Macken, a 'high-ranking army officer' and a member of the CIA," Brian Cusack said, "looking like they were caught coming out of a brothel."

Cusack turned the front page to him, still holding the paper as though it might bite at any moment.

"Listen to this: 'We believe that no police force has the right to withhold information if that means putting lives at risk.' 'We are determined to bring you the facts.' 'Come clean, Commish!' "

Cusack let the paper drop into his wastebasket in disgust.

"*We* should be running that story, Elaine. Why aren't we? What happened to your direct line to Blade Macken? Eh?"

Elaine looked sheepish. "It's still intact. But he can't be reached, Brian; I don't know how many messages I've left for him. He doesn't return my calls."

"Get him to, Elaine. You're a bright girl; use any means, fair or foul. We've missed this week's edition, fuck it, but if you can get Macken to come across with the full story, then we might still beat everyone else to it."

"Right. Can we offer him money for an exclusive?"

Cusack's look was withering. "Don't be stupid, Elaine. Do you want all of us—Blade, you, and myself—put behind bars? That's called police bribery, you know. No, Elaine, you can offer him anything you like—anything at all—as long as it's not money. As I said, you're a bright girl. You'll think of something."

Thirty-one

Carol reached Leeson Street Bridge in time to share the market in alms from the lunchtime suits and ties. On, on down to the corner of Baggot Street and Fitzwilliam Square: That was the spot she liked most. It wasn't taken either. Somebody was falling down on the job.

Carol found a convenient milkshake container in a garbage can, poured out the residue, and wiped the inside clean with the hem of her dress. Then she took up a station against the wall, beaker on the sidewalk beside her. Diagonally across, on the far side of the intersection, young business people sat sweating in the sun at tables in front of Larry Murphy's pub, convincing themselves that this was the chic thing to do. Carol pitied them, she genuinely did.

A twenty-pence coin dropped into her cup. She looked up to see the back of an elderly woman disappearing hurriedly. God is good. She laughed aloud; this was the best part of the masquerade.

"Spare a few pence for a bit o' food for the child?" she inquired of a fat suit. Blank face. Then another and another and yet another. Carol was enjoying herself; she was the Invisible Woman.

Two nuns in rimless spectacles passed by. One hesitated, said something to her companion, returned to where Carol squatted, and deposited a handful of change in the milkshake beaker.

"God bless ya, sisther."

The nun's eyes became opaque. Her holy duty to the poor was done. One didn't speak to invisible people.

It was a good lunch hour. By two o'clock the beaker rattled pleasantly with coins, both copper and nickel. It was time to go. Carol got up, paused to ease the cramp in her legs, and made her way to the far side of the street. A little boy in rags reigned there. Carol sidled up to him.

"Howya," she said.

His eyes were those of a middle-aged man. "Fuck off, y'oul' wagon!" he snarled.

"Had any luck today?"

"Would ya ever fuck off, y'oul' cunt, or I'll bleedin' burst ya!"

Carol smiled. Without another word she put her beaker on the ground next to the boy's own. He looked, looked again. Carol was already turning the corner into Lower Fitzwilliam Street.

"Hey! T'anks; t'anks very much! I'm sorry for callin' ya an oul' cunt."

An elderly gentleman looked startled. Carol grinned.

She passed the Archbishop Ryan Park and crossed the road, down past Holles Street maternity hospital. Another intersection later and she entered the darker side of Dublin's inner city.

The Voice . . .

She is in the place where nightmares begin; she is gazing at the frightful faces of the people in the street; she is close to where the fuckers in Harcourt Square wished her to go—her and her mammy and daddy; she is remembering places past; she is remembering opportunities lost forever, big chances dashed, education wasted, things that should have been and were not, brilliance sacrificed for the . . . She is . . .

The towers of tenements seemed to absorb the sunlight. In another climate the washing hanging from balconies might have lent life and color to this depressing place; here it had the opposite effect. Parked cars stood amid a frozen river of broken glass, the thousands of shards sparkling like crystal. Every night was *Kristalnacht* here for the car thieves and joyriders whose playground it was. Carol Merrigan saw some of them now: groups of youths in baggy jeans and expensive trainers, killing time until the sun went down and their victims ventured along these streets.

* * *

Carol reached the river a half-hour later. She sat down in the shadow of a warehouse, looked across at the Custom House and the green, glass towers of the Financial Services Centre. From farther down the docks came the deep note of a ship's horn. She allowed the cooling breeze from the northwest to blow for a time on her face, then stood up and crossed the cobbled street.

The door was unlocked, as always, but you had to know how to open it. Carol didn't mind the stench of urine on the stairs, or the presence of the heroin addict who lay fast asleep on the landing. This was her new home. Here she was more anonymous than in Crumlin. Here she would lure the great Blade Macken. Nine years of planning had led to this.

She hoped that her preparations would meet with Blade's satisfaction.

Thirty-two

"Where is he now?" Blade asked quietly.

"In cell four," Duffy said. "But I'd rather you didn't talk to him for the time being. Let him cool his heels for a day or two, until we've got this other thing out of the way. Will you do that for me?"

"No, sir, I can't. And if you were in my shoes, you couldn't either."

"Blade, I don't want you going in there. Please don't force me to order you to stay out."

"Five minutes."

"No, Blade."

"For fuck's sake, sir—sorry about the language—it may have a bearing on the investigation. In fact, I'm bloody sure it does. Don't you see, sir? It's Gerry's daughter we're dealing with."

"I know. And I still can't believe it."

"Just five minutes, sir; that's all I ask. There'll be no rough stuff, I promise you that. Word of honor."

Duffy laughed without humor.

"And the Slattery character? Come on, Blade; I know you too well. If he files a complaint, then don't expect my full and unbiased support. My God, what did you *do* to the man, reverse your car over his head?"

"I promise you, sir, I won't lay a hand on Charlie."

Duffy sighed and looked at his watch.

"Very well. Five minutes, and not a second more. I'll have two men posted outside the cell—and the door stays open. If you so much as lay a finger on—"

"I won't."

"You better not, Blade; I'm warning you."

He thanked Duffy and strode down the corridor while the assistant commissioner telephoned the front desk.

The cells were located one floor lower and Blade took the steps two at a time.

Duffy was mistaken: this couldn't wait. For Blade suspected that Charlie Nolan held the key to Carol Merrigan's capture. He wasn't sure why. And yet he felt certain there was more than just coincidence involved.

Nolan, Roche, Merrigan—and Merrigan's daughter: each knew—or, in Gerry Merrigan's case, had known—something that Blade did not. The pieces of the puzzle were rapidly clicking into place on this, the eleventh and penultimate day of Angel.

The cell door was opened.

He hadn't expected that Nolan would be so bloody *meek*. His demeanor took Macken aback. The detainee was seated on the narrow bed; he looked up blankly as Blade was let into the cell. His eyes were red and puffy, in contrast with his skin, which appeared to have already assumed a prison pallor. This, Blade thought, is what they called a "broken man." A cliché; but sometimes clichés spoke the truth better than anything he himself could dream up.

Blade had steeled himself for this encounter. You cannot banish ghosts easily; they have a habit of coming up behind you and tapping you on the shoulder when you least expect them. The murder of Gerry Merrigan haunted him as no other of "his" unsolved slayings.

Gerry had been, Blade always thought, the only genuine human being he'd ever had the privilege to share his life with. Gerry had been tough, had taught Blade about the fine line between compassion and understanding, and letting the bastards know that you weren't to be fucked with. He'd been gentle, too, a side of his personality he'd shown to few men other than Blade. Perhaps some part of Gerry Merrigan lived on in his protégé.

"Charlie."

"Blade."

"I don't like seeing you like this. Really I don't."

Nolan managed a weak smile. "Nor me, Blade. I've made a right fucking cock-up of things, eh?"

"Listen, Charlie: Duffy's only let me have five minutes. He thinks I'm going to beat the living crap out of you. But I'm not. I wouldn't."

"I know, Blade." He looked around him. "I'd offer you a chair but as you can see there aren't any. Makes you think, doesn't it?"

"I'll stand. Look Charlie, is there anything you want to tell me?"

"About Roche?"

"For instance."

"He's bad news, Blade. Bad fucking news."

"Ah, tell me something new. Did he screw you as well?"

Nolan inspected a thumbnail. It had been chewed.

"You may as well know—it'll all come out sooner or later anyway—you may as well know I've been putting business his way for years now."

"I hope you were charging the cunt plenty."

"I was. But Blade, it wasn't for me! If *you* don't believe that, no one will."

Nolan reached into his inside pocket and produced a wallet. He riffled through its contents.

"It's okay, Charlie."

"No, I want you to see this. Listen to me, Blade. Listen now. It's important."

Nolan found what he was looking for and passed it to Macken with a trembling hand. It was a color photograph, taken in a small room with floral-patterned wallpaper. The flash had cast a black shadow behind the subject and the wheelchair he sat in. It was difficult to guess the man's age: he could have been twenty, he could have been twice that. The hair was gray yet the face held a boyish look.

"That's Fintan. My youngest brother."

"Handsome devil."

"Ah, a real heartbreaker he was—until the illness got him. Muscular dystrophy."

Blade continued to gaze at the photograph.

"Is that something like MS?"

"It's similar. Except with MD it's only the muscles that're affected. They just waste away, slowly, until the patient is bedridden. It won't be long now until Fintan reaches that phase."

"I'm sorry," Blade said, returning the photograph.

"I'm all he has. There's no one else. And I did it for *him*, Blade. Jesus Christ, the kid's been in and out of hospitals half his bloody life, had every specialist in. They cost a *fortune*. The money had to come from somewhere, y'know."

"I understand, Charlie."

"No, Blade, you don't. Why do you think it was so important for me make promotion, to head the unit? It was the pension! They'll be retiring me in less than three years' time." He closed his eyes. "At least, they would have been, if I hadn't a been so fucking stupid. I needed every penny of that pension, Blade. For Fintan. God knows what'll happen to him now."

Macken was silent, uncomfortable. He noticed then that Nolan's shoelaces were missing.

"You have to understand me, Blade. I'd never anything against you. It was never anything personal. Christ, you helped me out of some scrapes in our time, you really did."

Nolan looked pensively at the armored glass of the cell window, remembering.

"But I *had* to get there first, and when Duffy put you in charge of the Angel investigation, I saw my whole world caving in. I was desperate."

Blade nodded. Then he said: "We'll work something out, Charlie. I'll speak to Duffy. I'll go to the commissioner himself if needs be. Christ, thirty-two years' service must count for something."

An officer poked his head in.

"Sir, I'll have to ask you to leave now. Mr. Duffy was very specific about that."

"Tell Duffy it's okay, Dan," Nolan said.

"Are you sure, sir?"

"Very sure. Give us five more minutes, will you?"

The cell door was left ajar again.

"Listen, Charlie," Blade said, "you know something that I don't. About Roche. About Gerry's murder. I can't guarantee it'll let you off the hook completely if you tell me, but I'll do my best on that score, I promise you."

Nolan nodded. "I believe you. You're a good sort, Blade. Get Roche for me, will you? That's all I ask."

"What was his part in the murder? Why didn't you want us to reopen the case?"

Macken unwrapped a Hamlet and lit it. Nolan the censorious nonsmoker hardly seemed to notice.

"He had me over a barrel, Blade," he said. "The fucker had tape-recorded every transaction we'd made—going back years. I was afraid . . . But that's all in the past now. I've nothing to lose by telling you. Would you mind blowing the smoke in the other direction?"

"Sorry. I'm listening."

"Roche has any amount of contacts in the underworld. It's natural in his line of work. If you're dealing with new alarm systems, new types of safes, then you get them tested by people who know what they're doing."

Blade nodded. Then Nolan gave him a brief account of the facts surrounding the BMM file.

"So Roche hired the heavies, did he?"

"There wasn't supposed to be any rough stuff, Blade. Roche was as shocked as I was. Those two fuckers were either new to the job or they were a pair of homicidal maniacs. Jesus, poor Gerry!"

"I'll find them, Charlie; don't you worry. I'll beat it out of Roche if I have to."

"You do that, Blade. And while you're at it, give him one for me."

*   *   *

One of Roche's salesmen was demonstrating to a customer a Truth Phone, a device that monitored stress in your caller's voice, when Macken pushed through the door of Centurion Security.

"Is Roche in?"

A mask of professional, icy detachment descended like a visor over the salesman's features. "*Mister* Roche is not available."

Blade pointed upward. "Is he in or isn't he?"

The man caught the menace behind Macken's words and gesture. It unnerved him.

"I-I'm sorry, but Mr. Roche left instructions that he's not to be disturbed."

Blade smiled. "Thanks for answering my question." He headed for a door marked PRIVATE to one side of the store.

"You can't go in there!"

"Watch me."

"I'll call the Guards!"

"I *am* the fucking Guards." The door swung shut behind him.

Weak daylight filtering through the landing window gave a feel of faded glory to the upper floor of Jim Roche's apartment. Specks of dust on the black carpet reinforced the impression of neglect. Macken made straight for the bedroom and flung open the door.

Roche had been reading, sitting up in his four-poster bed. His jaw fell.

"Hello, Cock," Blade said pleasantly. "How are the balls? Jockstrap not too tight, is it?"

"Keep away from me, Macken!"

Blade sat down on the bed. Through the comforter he grasped one of Roche's feet, but gently. Roche gasped.

"There there, Cock. Nothing to be afraid of. You know I wouldn't kick a man when he's down." His voice hardened. "That is, not unless you give me reason to. You follow me?"

"Wh-what do you want?"

203

"Names, Cock. Who killed Gerry Merrigan?"

Bombshell. Roche's jaw became slack again.

"I know you know, Cock. Nolan told me all about it."

"Nolan . . . ?"

"He's down in the cells. And he's willing to swear on his mother's walker that you were behind it."

Blade casually turned back the comforter, exposing the soles of Roche's feet, swollen and discolored. Roche flinched and tried to move farther up the bed. Blade caught him by an ankle.

"You think your feet are sore now, Cock," he hissed. "By Jesus, you don't know what *real* pain is. Ever heard the expression 'opening old wounds'? Believe me, you wouldn't want me to do that."

"Please, Blade . . . "

"The names."

"I can't. They'll *kill* me. They'll find me, no matter where I am, and they'll kill me. You don't know what you're asking."

"No they won't, Cock, I promise you that. You see, when I'm through with them they won't be in any state to kill anyone. Now: the names."

"The Price brothers. Paddy and Dominic Price."

"Where can I find them?"

"I don't know. They move around a lot."

"You're not being very cooperative, Cock. We could play a bit of footsie again, you and me. . . . "

"Christ, Blade, that's all I know. I swear it. All I had that time was a phone number. It was probably disconnected ages ago. They may not even be in the country."

"All right." He let go of Roche's ankle.

If there had been any fight left in Jim Roche, then not a trace remained now. He heaved a deep sigh and closed his eyes.

"You're going to arrest me now, aren't you? Well, fucking do it and get it over with."

Blade smiled. "No, Cock, I've no intention of arresting you. No, you're the man who likes to do deals. Ever since I've known you, you never stopped going on about the deal-to-end-all-deals. Well, Cock, I've got good news for you: You're finally going to do it. And when you've done it, I don't want to hear about any other rotten deals you make, 'cause if I do, I'll see that you're banged up in the Joy for the rest of your life. You follow me?"

"Yes."

Blade took a folded paper from his pocket and smoothed it on the comforter. It was police stationery, regular Harcourt Square issue. The typed text comprised a single, short paragraph. It began with the words: *I, James P. Roche.*

"You're going to sign this, Cock, and I'm going to witness it. Perfectly legal. In it you state that you're cohabiting with Joan—*and* supporting her financially."

Roche read the words, and Macken was intrigued to see that his lips moved at the same time.

"That's all?"

"That's all, Cock."

"And there won't be any comeback?"

"No. Not for me—and by Jesus not for you either."

Roche signed. It was not his best or most assured signature.

Thirty-three

Elaine de Rossa, on returning from a long lunch, found an unusual E-mail waiting for her. It was from a company in Buenos Aires.

She frowned. Only when she'd scrolled down to the sender's name did she see it had come from her father.

Dear Elaine,

Don't give anybody this address, right? I don't want people bothering me here. I've little enough time to myself as it is and Carlos is being a right pain with his bloody haggling about the stallion. I wouldn't bother you either love except that there's something I think may be of interest to you. Give me a ring will you?

Dad

Elaine looked at her watch. It was a little after two in the afternoon—early morning in Argentina.

She was answered by a woman who spoke almost flawless English, a servant. Presently her father came on the line. He sounded tired but in good humor.

"Elaine! You got my note, did you?"

"Yes, Daddy. How are you? What's the weather like in Buenos Aires?"

"I'm grand and it's raining, but never mind about that. Listen, I didn't want to say too much in the E-mail; I'd be afraid someone else might read it."

"All very mysterious. . . . "

"You could say that, Elaine. But I think I have a story here that you could use. Who knows, it might earn you a few more bob a week. Are you listening?"

"Fire away."

"The thing is, I thought about getting in touch with the gardaí about it, but then I decided I'd put it your way first."

"Hmm."

"You see, Carlos is a first cousin of the chief of police here and he told me that they'd picked up three Irishmen the other day. They have them down in the cells—God knows what they're doing to the poor bastards; I don't *want* to know. They're a rough lot; even Carlos will admit that. But do you know what the three lads were charged with, Elaine?"

"Umm, a robbery?"

"No, better still. They were trying to pass off fake jewelry. They tried to con a collector here with masses of the stuff. He was completely taken in, too—though you'd have thought that someone like him would have been able to spot the difference. Apparently not. It was very well done. Glass or paste, or whatever they make these things from. I saw it myself. Brilliant job."

"Excuse me, Daddy, but I don't see what all of this—"

"Will you wait now a second? God, you're as bad as your mother. What I'm saying is that Carlos took me to see the stuff, and I got the surprise of my life. You weren't there when your mother threw that big dinner party last year, so you wouldn't have seen Patsy Delahunt's emerald necklace. Your mother never stopped admiring it all evening, and she wasn't the only one. Well, it's here, Elaine—in Buenos Aires."

"What!"

"You heard me. Except it isn't the real one, just like the rest of the haul. All fake. So the question is: What happened to the real jewelry? Now get this: here's the good part. I overheard Don Delahunt a week or two ago telling his cronies in the Paddock Club that he'd had the wife's precious baubles insured to the tune of two-and-a-half million and he'd make damn sure the insurance company shelled out."

"Very interesting."

"Isn't it though? I never liked that man, Elaine. Too much unaccounted-for income. Not that I begrudge him that; I'm no saint myself. I just never liked his manner, that's all. He's an uncouth bastard."

Elaine sighed. "You don't have to tell me, Daddy. I know."

"I think it's worth looking into, don't you? But you better do it quick; they'll be getting in touch with Dublin soon, if they haven't done it already."

"I'll get onto it right away. Thanks for the tip, Daddy."

"Don't mensh."

"When will you be back?"

"Uh, next week, I think. It depends. Be sure to give Cusack a boot in the arse for me."

"I will. Bye, Daddy."

Thoughtful, Elaine went to the big table at the back of the office. She delved into the untidy, scissored pile of back numbers of the *Sunday Courier* and found a copy of the issue of two weeks before.

The story had merited a mention on the front page, together with a full account on page four. The home of Don Delahunt, former government minister and friend to the famous, had been burgled. The intruders had gotten past some of the most sophisticated antitheft devices in the country and made away with Mrs. Patsy Delahunt's collection of jewelry. Sure enough, the items—a badly registered color photograph showed the gems in their platinum and gold settings—had been insured for more than £2.5 million.

Elaine had wondered at the time why Delahunt had drawn so much attention to the robbery—and to the value of the stolen jewels. He was known as a man who was ever reluctant to disclose any details of his personal fortune. Yet Elaine's colleague, the reporter who'd filed the story, had told her that Delahunt had informed the radio and all the papers within an hour of discovering the break-in.

She believed Don Delahunt might not be so forthcoming with regard to the follow-up story she planned.

Elaine made two phone calls. One to the Delahunt mansion in County Kildare, the other to Blade Macken. As usual, he could not be reached at Harcourt Square. Elaine left a message for him to call her. Urgently.

She'd missed yesterday's paper. She was determined that the following Sunday's edition would carry the story that would be the watershed in her career. Blade Macken had, she was certain, the goods that she needed. And now Elaine had something worthwhile to trade.

Thanks, Daddy.

Thirty-four

Gareth Smyth and the others were good, Blade had to concede. He scanned the top stories of the houses opposite Angel's lair through a pair of high-powered binoculars but saw nothing out of the ordinary. Yet Blade knew that at least twenty telescopic sights were trained on that house and that the men whose fingers were on the triggers could light a match at two hundred yards.

Blade heard the sudden approach of a helicopter. He tensed.

"Fuck. Who ordered that? It wasn't us."

"Nor us," Redfern said.

But the chopper was headed in another direction and Blade saw it was a commercial aircraft. He relaxed. He returned the binoculars to the car and looked over the street.

There was a big, circular green in the middle, where a number of very young trees grew; two paths formed a cruciform shape on the green. The only sign of life was an old man walking a mongrel dog.

They were at the intersection of Bangor Road South and Clonmacnoise Road, and the unmarked cars they'd come in were backed up for a hundred yards, out of sight of Angel's home. The public-housing estate was like so many that ringed the center of Dublin: mean and primitive, not the kind of place you'd choose to raise your children in. Most of the cars in the tiny driveways looked barely roadworthy. Yet the houses were well-kept; many had little front gardens planted with flowerbeds, rosebushes, and shrubs.

Macken's radio squawked.

"We're in place round the back, sir. No sign of any movement in the house. The radio's still on though."

"Okay. Stay there. I'm going in now."

"I'm coming with you, sir," Sweetman said.

"No, you most certainly are not, Detective Sergeant. You wait here and maintain radio contact." He addressed the others. "The same applies to the rest of you. The last thing we want is to panic her into doing something rash."

"But sir, do you not think she might be more cooperative with a woman along?" Sweetman persisted.

Macken thought about this. He didn't wish to expose Sweetman to unnecessary danger, yet knew she was probably right. Her presence had helped before, in other confrontations. But with Carol Merrigan?

"All right," he said at last, grudgingly. "But let me do the talking. Don't open your mouth unless she speaks directly to you."

They set off down the curving street. Blade was acutely aware of the weapon he carried in the waistband of his pants: a .22 semiautomatic. He thought of the last time he'd been issued a gun, more than two months before. He hadn't used it then and had been glad of that fact. Blade didn't like guns, had seen more than most men what guns did to people—to their victims *and* to their bearers.

The Crumlin police were right: the house definitely looked abandoned. There was a graffito sprayed in white paint on the low wall out front. It read BURN WICH BURN!!! The weeds in the little garden reached waist high; dumped cola and cider cans sparkled metallically among the fronds. The path was strewn with dog shit and the trash of many years. There was even a discarded diaper. Was there, Blade wondered idly, something symbolic about that?

There were two windows at the front. The bigger downstairs window had cracked panes; the net curtains behind it were gray and filthy; they hadn't been washed in a long time. The upstairs window was pasted on the inside with newspaper.

Stepping around the dog turds, Blade went to the front door and carefully pushed back the flap on the mail slot. He saw little more than an empty hall, but heard the voice of a radio chat-show host ask a guest something about a new and revolutionary diet. Macken shut the flap and pressed the doorbell.

Nothing stirred. He looked at Sweetman, waited a full minute, then pressed the bell a second time.

"I don't think there's anybody home, Blade."

He waited another minute, then tried again. He heard only the echo of the ring and muffled voices from the radio. He activated his own.

"We're going in."

"Do you want backup, sir?"

"No, stay where you are. I'll call you if I need you."

Blade had the door open faster than it took to pick Jim Roche's lock on Crow Street. He held his breath as he drew the handgun from his waistband and took a step over the threshold. He didn't know what he was going to find. It came as a surprise therefore when a very, very commonplace little house confronted him. It had not been tidied in a long time and smelled stale and airless.

Blade saw nothing out of the ordinary. There were cheap prints on the walls of the hall, a mirror framed in fake gold leaf; a worn, floral-patterned carpet and a hat rack, empty. Sweetman followed him into the cramped front room.

Again, nothing unusual. The room, too, was in need of dusting. The chairs and couch were old but looked comfortable. There was a glass-fronted case with crockery, drinks glasses, and silver ornaments, the kind of stuff that elderly people are fond of accumulating. There was even an old-fashioned radiogram in a corner, together with a collection of Perry Como and Dean Martin record albums. A television set, small. The whole room was so damn ordinary that Blade felt a rising sense of disappointment. He moved to check the rest of the house.

It was then he saw the potted plant next to the door.

The following thoughts occurred to Blade Macken in less time than it takes for the heart to skip a beat and start pumping again. But his subconscious had given him a head start, had registered the anomalies almost as soon as he'd entered the room.

The thoughts were: The plant did not belong there, on a

small, low table: the carpet below the table was bright and clean, a sign that a bigger piece of furniture had stood there for many years: bits of earth speckled the table and the portion of clean carpet: the plant stood crookedly in fresh soil: sunlight filtering through the grayed net curtain reflected off an almost invisible strand of clear material: the strand led in the direction of the front door.

"Get out of here, Sweetman," Blade urged in a hoarse whisper. "Out of the house. Don't run, or you might panic one of Smyth's lads."

"What is it, Blade?"

"For fuck's sake, go, go! Don't argue with me now."

Sweetman left without another word.

He'd come across the trick in south Lebanon. The Hizbollah were experts at it. You worked with two timers, the first attached to the front door. It was triggered when the door was opened, snapping a semitransparent thread. The timer was designed to set off a *second* timer after the intruder had entered, when he was well within the house. This second timer activated a concealed detonator some minutes later.

Blade knew where that detonator was.

His mouth was dry as he grasped the stalk of the plant and pulled it slowly up out of the pot, bringing half the soil with it. The exposed timer made no sound but Blade knew that its mechanism was counting down the seconds.

He raised it. Two thin wires led to a small detonator embedded in a lump of smooth material resembling candle wax. Blade reached for his car keys and the miniature Swiss Army pocketknife attached to the ring. He extracted one of its four tools and carefully used it to slice through the wires. Then he gasped for air; without being conscious of it, he'd been holding his breath for more than forty-five seconds.

Forensic testing of the second timer might reveal how many minutes—seconds—Blade had had left, how close he'd been to annihilation. He didn't think he wanted to know.

"Sweetman?"

Her voice came over the walkie-talkie at once.

"You can come back in now. Tell the others it's all clear."
Blade sat down heavily on the couch and lit a Hamlet. He was still perspiring when Sweetman came back in the room with Redfern and two of his associates. She eyed the wrecked plant and the devices, went to the pot, and studied its contents; frowned.

"Nails," Blade confirmed. "Dirty great four-inch nails. If that gelignite had gone up, then the place would have been like a shooting gallery, nails flying everywhere. We'd have died instantly. Fucking hell, I don't know where she learned it but she's a dangerous bitch and no mistake."

"Booby trap," Redfern said superfluously, inspecting the flowerpot. "And enough gelignite to take out the entire house—maybe two, three of these houses. This lady plays rough."

The house was full of men now, in bulletproof vests, many armed with assault rifles and handguns. Walkie-talkies chattered; somebody had switched off the radio in the kitchen. Blade heard boots tramping up the stairs. Presently a voice called out.

"Sir, I think you'd better see this." It was Gareth Smyth.

Sweetman, Macken, and Redfern ascended to the second floor. It bore no resemblance to the first.

Angel's lair was a shrine to two people from Blade Macken's past. There they were, smiling down on him from pictures on the walls: Gerry and Breda Merrigan. Gerry and Breda on their wedding day, young and hopeful; on vacation in the west of Ireland; somewhere in Spain; on a Greek island. Gerry and Breda at a party, among friends; at some child's christening; posing for a formal photograph; in their twenties, thirties, in middle age.

The worst was yet to come. Blade joined Gareth Smyth in the main bedroom.

It had been converted into a work area. The walls were almost totally covered with press clippings, enlarged on a photocopier. They had three themes: a bank robbery in 1985, a woman's suicide in 1987, and a double murder in 1989. What all three had in common was the name Merrigan. Blade was familiar with the contents of the news stories. Just as well, because most of them were now illegible. An angry hand had partially obliterated them with graffiti; executed in spraypaint, marker, and crayon. The least offensive of them read: MACKEN THE DEVIL MUST DIE!!!

"Why do I get the impression," Redfern said softly, "that she doesn't much like you, Blade?"

Macken had enemies—what police officer hasn't? Most were serving sentences in Mountjoy and Portlaoise, some were still at large. Yet few of those enemies, he knew, bore such a degree of animosity toward him. Such blind, uncompromising hatred. He let his eye wander over the messages on the walls, and felt his skin crawl.

Redfern was examining Angel's workbench. There were two computers, models that Blade didn't recognize; half-assembled pieces of electronics lay on the table; there were hundreds of loose components. Yet all had been sorted with painstaking attention and color coded. Assembly tools were arranged in neat rows according to size. Everything was laid out with meticulous care, fanatically.

"Most of this stuff isn't store-bought," Redfern said. "She put it together from pieces you pick up in a Radio Shack. Take these terminals, for instance. I haven't seen this kind of hardware in ten years or more."

He pointed to a primitive-looking device. "And I guess this is a modem of some kind. It's a goddamn dinosaur." He shook his head. "You know what she's done here, Blade? She's created a Frankenstein's monster, all made up of junk."

"A very effective monster, though," Blade muttered.

"I'll give you that. That's the reason your Dr. Earley was fooled right from the beginning. She'd profiled some rich guy who could afford the very best in hardware—and the whole goddamn time we were dealing with a college kid who knew exactly what she wanted and how to assemble it. It didn't cost her a thing. Well, not much anyhow."

Redfern powered up one of the computers, the one linked to the modem. He grunted when the desktop filled the screen. "That's what I figured: She'd access to the Net. Any weapons information she couldn't find locally, she could obtain from all kinds of sources—anarchists, militias, left-wing revolutionary groups." He turned to Macken. "The Pentagon and the Fibbies have been trying to shut these people down for years. What do they call the monster with a hundred heads?"

"The Hydra."

"Right. Shut down one website and two more grow in its place. You can't stop these guys."

Blade went to a small bookcase. It contained a mixture of hardbacks and paperbacks, photocopied books, college texts. Almost all dealt with two subjects: electronics and explosive devices. He pulled out a ring binder. Redfern looked over Macken's shoulder.

"Those are printouts of stuff she downloaded from the Net," the American said. "She did it all from this crummy little room. Roamed the world and found what she was looking for. Jeez, it gives me the creeps."

There was more. There were copies of the *Garda Review*, stretching back decades. Blade thumbed through them. Carol Merrigan had highlighted stories—stories dealing with promotions, with the comings and goings of members of the force. There they were, highlighted with yellow, fluorescent marker: Duffy's promotion; Macken's and Nolan's rise in the echelons of the Special Branch.

More stories, and all of them highlighted.

Gareth Smyth and his men had been making a preliminary search of the rest of the house and the backyard. He returned to the bedroom.

"There's no trace so far of any more explosives, sir."

"How much did the guy in Meath say was gone missing?" Redfern asked Macken.

"He doesn't know; they never found out. Slattery had messed with the records in some way. Fucked everything up."

"That's too bad. No, it's worse than too bad, Blade. We're

dealing with an unknown quantity here. Maybe she used up everything she had—here, in Drumcondra and on O'Connell Street. And maybe she didn't. Could be there's twice that amount still out there. Hell and damnation."

"I'll question Slattery again. Maybe I can jar his memory a bit."

Blade's cellular phone throbbed just then.

"Macken."

"BLADE! DID I CATCH YOU AT A BAD TIME AGAIN? YOU WEREN'T HAVING A SHIT OR ANYTHING, I HOPE? I WOULDN'T WANT TO IN-TERFERE WITH YOUR MOVEMENTS IN ANY WAY, HEH HEH HEH."

Blade shut the door, put a finger to his lips, and thumbed the RECORD button.

"Not at all, Angel," he said. "I was just going through some paperwork." He saw Sweetman frown. "You know how it is."

"INDEED I DO, BLADE. DUFFY WAS ALWAYS A WHORE FOR THE PA-PERWORK, WASN'T HE? A RIGHT BOLLIX. BUT BLADE, I'M GLAD YOU MENTIONED PAPER BECAUSE THAT'S JUST WHAT I'M RINGING YOU ABOUT."

"The money."

"YES. ARE YOU LOOKING FORWARD TO TOMORROW, BLADE? IT SHOULD BE GREAT GAS ALTOGETHER. I CAN'T WAIT TO SEE YOU AGAIN, SO I CAN'T. I'M SURE YOU FEEL THE SAME WAY."

"I might if I knew who you were, Angel." He winked at Sweetman; she relaxed. "But do I understand you want *me* to deliver the money?"

"YES, BLADE. NO BETTER MAN. NOW THEN, LISTEN CAREFULLY, BECAUSE I'M GOING TO GIVE YOU HALF OF YOUR INSTRUCTIONS, AND I WON'T REPEAT THEM. DO YOU HAVE A PEN HANDY?"

Blade paused. "Right here. I'm ready."

"GOOD. THE FIRST THING IS: YOU'RE TO COME ALONE. BY THE WAY, BLADE, DID YOU HEAR THE ONE ABOUT THE BOY WHO'S BEING HELD TO RANSOM? THE KIDNAPPER PHONES THE FATHER AND SAYS: 'YOU'RE TO COME ALONE. LEAVE THE MONEY IN A HOL-LOW TREE AT THE PAPAL CROSS IN THE PHOENIX PARK.' WELL, THE KID'S FATHER BRINGS THE MONEY ALL RIGHT BUT HE GETS HIMSELF A HERNIA CARRYING THE HOLLOW TREE!"

217

"That's a good one, Angel. Ha ha."

Insane cow.

"ISN'T IT? BUT LET'S BE SERIOUS, BLADE. FIRST, I WANT YOU TO ARRANGE FOR THE MONEY TO BE DELIVERED TO THE VAULTS OF THE BANK OF IRELAND IN COLLEGE GREEN."

"All right."

"LEAVE IT THERE OVERNIGHT. IT SHOULD BE SAFE ENOUGH. NOW: TOMORROW MORNING AT EXACTLY HALF PAST SEVEN I WANT YOU TO PICK UP THE MONEY AT THE BANK. YOU'RE TO USE YOUR OWN CAR. HAVE YOU GOT THAT?"

"I've got it. My own car."

"BUT FIRST, BLADE, I WANT YOU TO MAKE SURE THE RADIO'S TAKEN OUT OF IT. IN OTHER WORDS, THERE'S TO BE NO RADIO CONTACT BETWEEN YOU AND THE SQUARE. YOU'RE TO GO TO THE BANK ALONE, AS I SAID—NOBODY ELSE, BLADE. IF I SO MUCH AS SMELL ANYBODY FOLLOWING YOU, OR IF I THINK YOU'VE GIVEN AWAY YOUR POSITION IN ANY WAY, THEN THE CONSEQUENCES ARE YOUR RESPONSIBILITY. AND BLADE . . . ?"

"Yes, Angel?"

"I'LL MAKE BLOODY SURE THAT THE PAPERS AND EVERYBODY ELSE KNOW YOU WERE THE CAUSE OF IT. DO I MAKE MYSELF CLEAR?"

"Crystal."

"GOOD. NOW, WHEN YOU'VE PICKED UP THE MONEY, YOU'RE TO PUT IT IN THE BOOT OF YOUR CAR AND DRIVE TO THE CUSTOM HOUSE. PARK YOUR CAR EXACTLY OUTSIDE THE MAIN ENTRANCE ON THE QUAYS, AND WAIT UNTIL YOU HEAR FROM ME. IS THAT CLEAR? DO YOU WANT TO READ IT BACK TO ME?"

Oh fuck. Think, think. "Ehh, what if I'm held up in traffic? Have you thought about that?"

"MAKE SURE YOU AREN'T, BLADE! USE A FUCKING SIREN. JESUS, DO I HAVE TO BE YOUR MAMMY, TOO? HONEST TO GOD!"

Bad slipup, Angel: your mammy. But it didn't matter now.

"I'll take care of everything. Is there anything else?"

"NOT AT THE MOMENT. I'LL BE IN TOUCH."

Blade rewound the tape and played it. There was silence when it ended. Redfern was the first to speak.

"Seven-thirty. That's cutting it fine. The president is scheduled to arrive at the city center at nine o'clock. Where's the Custom House?"

Blade told him.

"So she wants you to meet her on the O'Connell Street side of town?"

"D'you think that has any significance?"

"Hard to say. Could be that's where she's holed up, on that side of the river." He rubbed his chin. "I can stake out the area, have a—"

"No you bloody well won't, Redfern! That's the very last thing we want. The front of the Custom House is about the most exposed place in the city. Any movement there that's the least bit out of the ordinary and she'll be on to us. Come to think of it, that's probably the reason she chose the spot."

Redfern looked at the murderous slogans written on the walls.

"You don't know what it is you're letting yourself in for, Blade. She'll have you right where she wants you."

"I know. But she wants me all to herself. And that's just what she's going to get."

Thirty-five

Most of the lunch-hour patrons had left by the time Macken and Sweetman got to the bar on Purcell Street. Joe's assistants were removing plates, glasses, and dirty ashtrays from the tables, and wiping the surfaces with damp cloths. The interior was muggy, hung with stale cigarette smoke and no-nonsense perfumes. He left Sweetman seated and went to the counter.

"Blade!" Joe called in greeting. "Bit on the early side for you. The usual?"

"Nothing thanks, Joe." He leaned across the counter. "You told me last Sunday you'd keep your ears open, right?"

"I did. Only I haven't heard a thing." He gestured toward a tabloid newspaper on the counter. ANOTHER GARDA COVER-UP? read the headline. "Did you see the *Mirror* today? I wonder what *that* was all about now."

"I wonder, too. Listen, Joe, you know everybody. What can you tell 's about the Price brothers?"

The bartender's eyes narrowed. "Paddy and Dominic Price? They're bad news, Blade. Sell their own grandmother for the price of a pint and twenty Marlboros. What is it the fuckers have done now?"

"I can't say. Do you know where I can find them?"

"Let me make a phone call, Blade."

Joe returned two minutes later and passed a slip of paper across. It was an address on Sheriff Street.

"Sound, Joe," Blade said. "And give 's five Hamlet while you're at it."

Sweetman asked no questions when they set out to walk the short distance to his car, parked nearby, opposite the grand façade of the Shelbourne Hotel. She knew that this inquiry was one that Macken wished to keep to himself for the time being. All the same, she asked herself how her superior could afford to take time off from the investigation in hand. Four American flags fluttering slightly in the light breeze that blew past the hotel reminded her how close they were to the visit of the U.S. president.

"Spare a few pence for the child?" a beggar-woman, squatting against the wall near the hotel entrance, pleaded. Sweetman barely saw her.

But Blade had taken note. He stopped walking.

"Who are the most invisible people in Dublin?" he asked. "I'll tell you who: the beggars, the tinkers, the travelers, call them what you want. Nobody looks at them; we're *ashamed* to look at them. We think: There but for the grace of God go I. They're dirty and ragged and smelly and when they say, 'Misther, can you spare some change for a bit o' food?', we turn our heads the other way and walk on. When there's a little girl sitting on the pavement in the rain, we don't even want to look, because it might upset us."

"I know what you mean, Blade."

"And even if we do look, we don't see a *person*. Listen, you've been trained to remember faces, Sweetman. Would you recognize that beggar-woman if you saw her again? Just a couple of yards back—No no, don't look round."

"You mean the one with the baby?"

"Yes. You noticed she'd a baby—what woman wouldn't? But if someone tidied her up and gave her some clean clothes, would you be able to pick her out in a lineup?"

"Uh . . . I don't know, Blade."

"You probably couldn't. I know *I* couldn't."

And Blade knew with near-certainty that he'd passed Carol Merrigan many times on the street. He'd been so close to Angel that he could have touched her. He turned to Sweetman.

"Look, can you give me a few minutes alone?" He handed her his keys. "Take the car. I want to have a stroll in the park; clear my head."

"Sure, Blade."

He watched her go, dark hair bouncing on her collar, then turned into the gate of St. Stephen's Green. Time to think.

He found Sweetman in the office in the company of Lawrence Redfern when he got back to Harcourt Square a little after three-thirty.

"Somebody's been trying to get in touch with you for ages," his assistant said. "She rang again an hour ago. Says it's urgent." She passed the message to Macken. He read it. The number told him it belonged to a cellular phone.

"Would you excuse me a minute?"

Blade went out into the corridor and made the call.

"It's Blade."

"Gosh, at last. You do like to keep a girl waiting, don't you?"

"Busy times. Sorry. I got a message saying that you need to speak to me urgently."

"I do, darling," she replied in a voice that caused a slight distention at the front of Macken's trousers. "And it can't wait. Are you free this evening?"

"Ehh, no. Sorry, Elaine; it's really out of the question. It'll have to be some other time."

"Criminals to catch again?"

"Yes."

"Then what I have to tell you ought to interest you, Blade darling."

"I don't get you."

"Criminals, Blade. If I say the name Don Delahunt, does that get your attention?"

And she told him some of what she knew. About her meeting an hour earlier with the mistress of a country mansion in County Kildare; about her growing suspicions. Elaine had Blade's attention.

"Look," he said, "I really want to see you."

"Then why don't you?"

The manufacturers of French cigarettes had a lot to answer for, Macken decided. But: "It's not the best time, Elaine. It really isn't. Look, can I call you on—"

"I have the goods, Blade. On Delahunt, and more. It won't wait. Nor will I."

"Elaine, please try to understand. I'm trying to do a job here."

"So am I, darling."

At last Blade understood. He should have cottoned on sooner—he knew that. In other circumstances he might have done so, but . . .

"You're a journalist, aren't you? Why didn't you tell me that before?" He was peeved, very.

"Let's not talk about it over the phone, yeah? Why don't you come to my place this evening? Forty-six Upper Mount Street. Say about nine?"

Blade's relative privacy was abruptly disturbed by the appearance of the assistant commissioner. He was accompanied by Gareth Smyth of the Emergency Response Unit.

"In my office, Macken," Duffy said. "Two minutes."

Blade nodded, flustered. Then he told Elaine: "I'll come. But only for half an hour."

"That's sounds good enough for me, darling," she said, and hung up.

Sweetman and Redfern were also present. The bulletin board in Duffy's room had a new addition: a large photograph of a woman in her late twenties. Macken was drawn to it.

Angel.

"The lads in Crumlin talked to as many of the neighbors as they could," Duffy said. "They called her 'the witch,' did you know that? Rob McGrath used the descriptions to put that together. It's probably the nearest we'll get to the real thing."

The head was shown three-quarters on, yet McGrath had contrived to have the eyes staring straight into the "camera." It was eerie; they followed you about the room. Tangled, unbrushed hair framed the face, a face lined like that of an old woman. Blade didn't know that face any longer.

"Every station in Dublin should have a copy of that picture by now," Duffy said. "If Pluto is on the move, then we might just spot her. But I've given strict orders that she's on no account to be approached."

"Very wise," Blade said.

"There's one other thing." Duffy consulted a typed report on the desk. "It's puzzling. Some of the neighbors insisted there were *two* people living in that house."

Macken had a sense of dread. "Two?"

"Maybe we shouldn't attach too much significance to it, Blade. You know yourself how unreliable witnesses can be. But the fact remains that at least four people claim they saw somebody else come and go. On more than one occasion. They described her as being an elderly woman. White hair. With a pram."

"May I see that, sir?"

Duffy handed him the report. Blade read it quickly.

"I think it was her, sir. Pluto. It must have been. I think she was using more than one disguise." He turned back to the picture on the bulletin board. "This is what she normally looks like. A knacker. It's good; it had me fooled. But we've no guarantee that this is the disguise she's wearing at the moment."

"Are you trying to tell me that half McGrath's work was for nothing? Are we going to have to put out a picture of her looking like an old granny as well?"

"No," Blade said resignedly. "No, don't bother, sir. I don't think we're going to find her, one way or the other. I think she has us beaten on that score. She holds all the cards. When she wants to speak to us, she phones. When she wants to see us, we do it on her terms. Our hands are tied."

"My God," Duffy said quietly, "I never thought I'd hear defeatist talk like that from you, Blade."

Blade want to the "photograph" again. The eyes seemed to mock him.

"No, not defeatist, sir. No way. She's won a couple of rounds, but the real fight is still to come."

Thirty-six

The residents of the neighboring apartment blocks called it "Beirut." Aptly, because the place looked as though it had taken heavy and prolonged shelling. Few of the building's windows were intact. Fires, whether accidentally or deliberately started, had gutted several of the apartments. The open space in front, at ground level, was every mother's nightmare: the garbage was a hell of broken glass, discarded car batteries, putrid waste, and hypodermic needles.

There was no sign that anybody was living there, yet Blade knew that the apartment block housed at least one crack house. If you wished to disappear from sight for a while then that address on Sheriff Street was where to do it.

Blade had wanted four men, including himself, for the operation. It had to be fast; he needed men who knew the place, could get in and out in double-quick time. He'd approached the drug unit at Store Street police station, the obvious choice, but they could put only two officers at his disposal.

Lawrence Redfern had volunteered his services.

"Let me come with you, Blade," he'd said. "I've been twiddling my goddamn thumbs for days here. I could use some action. Besides, I like to see how you guys work."

Blade had agreed. On one condition.

"No guns, Redfern. That's not the way we do things here. You'll have to check in your piece, like it or lump it. This isn't—"

"Grenada. I know."

Blade had smiled at that. "Actually what I was going to say is: This might not be the best time to mention it, but are you people authorized to carry weapons here?"

It had been Redfern's turn to smile. He hadn't replied to Blade's question. But at least he'd left his hardware behind.

So here they were, Macken at the wheel of a "company car"—a battered old Ford, used in a robbery and impounded at the Square. The two Drug Squad men sat in back; young detectives whose appearance allowed them to pass unremarked on in these surroundings—shaved heads, earrings, the clothing of the street. John and Joe.

Redfern had swapped his double-breasted suit for a soiled anorak and jeans; a mariner's cap was perched on his head. Blade was in his Reeboks again.

He parked the car between two similar wrecks at one side of the apartment block and turned to the men in the backseat.

"You have the mug shots. Dominic is the one to look out for—the one with the beard. He's a dangerous fucker, mad as a March hairball. But don't underestimate the brother either."

"Right, sir. Do we all go in together?"

"No, we'll do it two floors at a time. You lads take the ground floor and Redfern and I'll take the first, then you the second, and so on."

"Can you run that past me again, Blade?" Redfern said with a puzzled look. "I thought you wanted to cover two floors at the same time?"

"I do."

Understanding dawned.

"Damn, I forgot you Americans had it arseways, as usual. Oscar Wilde was right: We're separated by a common language. Let's try it again. The lads search the ground floor—that's the *first* floor in the States—while you and me search the one above it—*second* floor to you—at the same time. Then they search the . . . Jesus, this is giving me a headache!"

One of the men in the backseat patted Macken's shoulder. "It's all right, chief," he said. "We've got it. Just for convenience' sake, we'll do it the American way. So we'll take the first floor—the ground floor—and yooze'll take the second, okay?"

Redfern was sizing up the building. "Is there a back way? If that's so, then maybe we ought to split up further."

Joe shook his head.

"You can only come and go from the two sides. There's stairs up to each floor and balconies along the whole length of the building."

"No elevators—lifts?"

Joe laughed. "They were out of action a week after the very first tenants moved in and they haven't worked since."

"Okay," Blade said. "You and John take this entrance; we'll take the one at the far end. And be careful. We'll maintain radio contact at all times."

He watched the two move through the debris, past a group of ragged, ill-fed children who were burning something on a small bonfire. Blade was almost sure it was the corpse of a dog.

Redfern and Macken waited until the narcotics men were inside. Then they left the car and crossed to the other entrance, taking their time. The children ignored them.

The doorway was almost blocked by a stinking mattress whose cheap stuffing lay partly exposed. They stepped over it and entered a stairwell. Heaps of flyblown excrement littered the steps. The stench was horrific. Redfern, though, seemed to take it all in his stride.

Macken wondered where the American had been, what he'd experienced in the service of the CIA. Then he remembered reports of the agency's clandestine work in a number of Latin American countries. The worst of their inner-city slums were probably not very much different from "Beirut," Sheriff Street. Human degradation looks and smells the same the world over.

They came upon the first of the crack houses about halfway along the second floor. It had no door; that had most likely been used for firewood a winter or two before. The apartment was gutted of furniture and hangings; all that remained were two more evil-smelling mattresses and a packing case, its top scorched in many places. The concrete floor was littered with shards of glass: the remnants of capsules that had carried the deadly crack cocaine.

Blade found a wallet, mildewed. It contained no cash or credit cards; nothing except a passport photograph of a well-dressed man, and a medical prescription. He tossed it back among the junk and thumbed his walkie-talkie.

"Anything, lads? Over."

"Not a thing, sir. We're nearly through down here. Over."

"Right. Watch your arses now. Over and out."

Redfern was trying to decipher something scrawled on a wall. He gave it up. "We could be wasting our time, Blade."

"We could. But my sources are reliable. If the Prices haven't popped out for a quick pint, they'll be here right enough. It's just a matter of finding their rathole."

"Wait." Blade stood rock-still and put a finger to his lips. He'd heard something moving on the floor above. Then the radio squawked, as his young colleagues called in, and he learned that the footsteps had been theirs.

The fourth floor was somewhat more habitable than the second, with no sign of a crack house or other indications of recent activity on that level. Nevertheless, Redfern and he made sure to tread as silently as they could, skirting carefully each broken bottle and crushed beer can.

A radio was playing.

In the corner apartment, the last one on the block. It commanded a clear view of the area, right up to Connolly train station. The song was "Every Breath You Take," an old '70s number by The Police. Blade heard part of the lyrics—"Every move you make, every step you take, I'll be watching you"—and thought the words strangely appropriate, given the circumstances.

The apartment still had a door but there was no glass in the windows. Blade ducked low and crept to the nearer one. He raised his head and looked in.

The place was a pigpen. It showed signs of having been used by a succession of vagrants, each of whom had left something behind to add to the filthy accumulation of old clothing, bedding, broken utensils, bottles, food containers, and beer cans. Somebody had taped a poster of Pamela Anderson to the wall years before; others had daubed the image with obscene graffiti and impossible additions to an already impossible bustline.

A man was seated with his back to the window. He was dressed in a dirty, white singlet and brown cords. His hair was red, and when he moved his head slightly to one side, Blade caught a glimpse of a full beard. Dominic Price.

The ghetto blaster announced the range of bargains to be had at Power City: a portable television set for less than one hundred pounds, a washing machine for a similar sum. Macken motioned to Redfern to join him.

"They're inside," he whispered. "One of them at least."

"What's the procedure here? Do we bust the door down?"

Blade smiled. "It'd probably fall in of its own accord if we leaned too heavily on it. No, we'll be polite and knock."

Redfern seemed not too happy with this.

"Umm, it's your show, Blade, but I hope you know what you're doing, is all."

"Trust me."

"Okay, but shouldn't we call the boys?"

"I'm way ahead of you," Blade said. His walkie-talkie was in his hand. He was about to give the word when a shadow came between him and the early evening sun.

"Well, well," a voice said, as Blade squinted, "what have we got here? On your fucking feet, gentlemen!"

A shotgun is an unsettling weapon. Never, ever argue with a shotgun when it's pointed at close range. The user doesn't even need to aim a shotgun properly; it will punch a gaping hole right through you, especially when its barrel has been sawed off. And, at close quarters, it'll take out anybody crouching behind you as well.

It had been several years since Blade had looked down the barrel of a weapon raised in anger. He appreciated now that it was an experience you had to relive from time to time in order to keep your nerve. He rose slowly to his feet, hands above his head, and was conscious of Redfern's heavy breathing at his back.

They should have checked round the side of the building. Sloppy, very sloppy.

"In the house," Paddy Price ordered.

The door was open now and his brother made way for the unexpected guests.

"Drop the radio," he said to Blade.

It bounced and came to rest next to an old pizza box. Dominic picked it up and studied it.

"Well, well. I believe we've been honored by a visit from the Guards, Paddy. Isn't that nice?" To Macken and Redfern he said: "Down on yer knees, boys, and hands behind the heads."

Paddy passed the gun to his brother. Dominic pulled a rickety chair nearer and sat down facing the captives, the weapon resting in his lap. His pale blue eyes were inscrutable.

"What were yiz looking for?"

"Drugs," Blade said. "We heard there's a crack house here."

"Is that a fact? A shame now—we smoked the last of the crack for breakfast. The most we can offer yiz is a nice cuppa tea."

"I'll go and stick the kettle on," Paddy said. He grinned, and Blade noticed that the teeth on one side of his jaw were missing.

"How many of yiz are there?" Dominic asked.

"A dozen. We're combing the building."

"I on'y saw one car, Dommo. I think there's on'y four of the cunts."

"We've more men round in back," Redfern said. "The place is surrounded. Best put the gun down; it'll make things easier."

Merciful hour, Blade thought, why couldn't the Yank just keep his bloody trap shut? But the damage had been done. Dominic Price's eyes narrowed.

"Ah now, what have we here?" He moved the shotgun into an upright position, holding a finger curled around its twin triggers. "Who's your furry friend? Dick fucking Tracy?"

"Sergeant Larry Redfern of the DEA," the American said. "That's the Drug Enforcement Administration to you."

"I know what it is," Dominic Price said. "But what the fuck are you doing here?"

"Special assignment," Redfern answered evenly. "Now put the gun down and there won't be any trouble."

Price cackled. "Jayziz, for a guy who's on his fucking knees you've got some fucking neck. Now tell me why I shouldn't just waste the pair of yiz and have done with it."

Redfern had no time to reply because Macken's radio crackled at that moment.

"Sir, we're done on this floor. No sign of the Prices. Over."

Shite.

Dominic was on his feet, eyes wild, gun pointed now at Macken. His brother stared at the instrument in his hand.

"What'll we do, Dommo? It's *us* the fuckers are after."

Dominic's eyes were flickering from side to side. He placed the gun under Blade's chin.

"Talk," he said. "Tell your mates you're still looking. No codes, just plain English, or your brains'll be decorating that wall behind you."

Paddy Price held the radio to Blade's ear. Both men were sweating.

"Nothing here, either," Blade said into the mouthpiece. "Try the fourth floor. Over."

"The *fourth*, sir? Are you sure? Over."

"Yeah, you heard me: the fourth. We're just about done on the third. Over and out."

Paddy Price moved the radio away from Blade and nodded, satisfied. Blade's mouth was dry and his limbs were beginning to ache. He started to alternately tense and relax the muscles of his arms and thighs, keeping the circulation going. Numbness was the last thing he needed. He became aware of Redfern's breathing; it was slow, deep, and measured. Out of the corner of his eye he saw that the American was now squatting on his heels.

Dominic Price had returned to his chair. "Right. You did grand, copper. Just as well, too. Now, let's have some real answers. So it's us, is it? Why?"

"Murder."

"Oh. Really?"

"Really, Dommo."

"And who are we supposed to have murdered?"

"Gerry Merrigan and Michael Byrne. On the first of July, 1989."

Dominic, without taking his eyes off Macken, addressed his brother. "You hear that, Paddy? I take everything back I ever said about the Guards being a slow bunch of fucks. On'y nine years and they've already cracked the case. Fucking marvelous. Do we have an alibi for that day, Paddy? I'm sure we do."

"Ah yes," said his brother with a smile, "I remember distinctly. Weren't you and me making our Confirmation that very day? Or was it our Holy Communion? I do get confused between the two sometimes. Mind you, I still have the tenner Aunt Cora gave me."

Play for time, Blade; keep the shaggers talking.

"You probably got the dates mixed up," he said, "so I'll jog your memory. It was the little job you did for Jim Roche. In Kildare House."

Dominic Price had stiffened. "Roche?"

"Certainly," Blade said with a confidence he was far from possessing. "Roche was only too happy to talk about it. I suppose it's been on his conscience this past while. Maybe you can look him up when the pair of you are out of the Joy. That's if he hasn't died of old age by then."

"Jayziz, copper," Dominic Price said, "you've the brass balls of the fucking Devil. If you think—"

He stopped. All four men had heard a sound from outside—the unmistakable, metallic clatter of an empty beer can kicked by a careless foot. John and Joe.

The brothers' attention directed itself at the window, an action of a split second's duration. It was enough for Lawrence Redfern. Macken saw only a blur of limbs; the Americans' body uncoiled like that of a cobra, as he launched himself from the floor.

The shotgun roared deafeningly and blew a ragged hole in

the ceiling, both barrels spent. It spiraled out of Dominic's grasp as Redfern took him full in the chest and the chair toppled backward. Blade was on his feet and throwing himself at Paddy Price's legs.

But Price's brother had delivered a blow to Redfern's chin, sending him reeling. Dominic was on his feet again, lashing out with his foot at Redfern's ribs. The American rolled away. Blade, meanwhile, had forced a knee into the small of Paddy's back and had twisted the man's arms behind him. He was powerless. Macken could observe Redfern in full battle frenzy.

He saw two shaved heads appear outside the window.

Redfern had regained his footing. His hands dropped loosely to his sides. He emitted a cry, leaped in the air, feet level with Dominic's belly, and kicked the man full in his beard. Dominic staggered. But he was a fighter and dodged Redfern's next attack, sidestepping as the American's kick scythed the air harmlessly in the place where Dominic's head had been.

The door opened and the two narcotics men came in. They saw the flailing arms and legs of Redfern and his antagonist. They stepped aside, out of the way.

Redfern screeched again, pivoted on one foot, sending the other in a lethal arc that glanced off Dominic's head.

Dominic slipped on some food remains and lost his balance. He pitched sideways—and blundered into Blade. Blade's grip on Paddy Price's arm loosened. Paddy took full advantage. He rolled out from under Blade. A knife appeared in his hand.

The brothers became a deadly fighting duo. Paddy Price skipped nimbly to one side and struck out at Joe while Dominic lunged at John. The knife missed its target. John was less fortunate: Blade heard bone snap as John went down, taken by Dominic's brutal kick to the side of his knee. John screamed in agony.

Blade picked up the rickety chair by the backrest and stalked Paddy Price. The knife was ineffective now. Blade used the chair legs to keep Paddy at bay, forcing him back against the wall and farther from the door. Joe prepared a flank attack.

"Come and get it, cunts!" Paddy roared. "Come on. I'll gut the pair of yiz like fucking mackerels." But his eyes betrayed his desperation. He was cornered. Knew it.

Blade lunged with the chair. Paddy dodged and slashed out at Joe.

The knife sliced his jacket sleeve but failed to connect with flesh. Blade lunged again. This time one of the chair legs slammed into Paddy's ribs. He cursed.

Dominic Price emitted a blood-curdling yell and launched himself at Redfern again in a classic karate assault, both feet aiming for the stomach. Redfern rolled with the kick.

Blade and Joe were working as a unit. Blade thrust the chair under Paddy Price's swinging knife hand and caught him in the ribs again. Joe kicked him in the shin. Paddy faltered. Blade swung the chair like an ax. The knife flew from Paddy's hand. Joe punched him in the stomach—at the same moment Blade brought the chair down on his head. It splintered. Paddy dropped to the floor like a poleaxed steer.

His brother made for the door.

Redfern had anticipated the move. Macken saw the CIA operative turn his back. Then Redfern was a tumbling acrobat, turning once, twice, three times in a flurry of motion.

Dominic Price was over the threshold when the soles of Redfern's shoes caught him square in the back. The force of contact lifted him off his feet and sent him hurtling toward the balcony. He cried out—and disappeared with a scream over the edge.

"Christ on a trampoline," Blade heard Joe say; "Bruce fucking Lee isn't in it!"

Redfern was looking down to where the bearded man had fallen. He shook his head slowly, then returned to the apartment.

John was on his feet again, pale and limping. "I hope the

fucker isn't dead, is he?" he asked. "I was hoping to be around when they put him away for good."

"No sign of movement down there," Redfern told him. "I guess his neck broke his fall. Poor bastard."

But when Blade escorted the handcuffed Paddy Price out of the building, he saw a group of children clustered around a battered, bloodied, but very much alive Dominic. The bearded one was trying to get up off the filthy mattress that had saved his life.

"We really need someone from the press office," Blade said. "There's no point now passing this on to the evening papers but we can make tomorrow's dailies. We might even get it on the front page."

"I can do better than that, Blade," Duffy said. "I'll have the crime correspondent from the *Independent* over here right away. Get your report typed up and I'll brief him myself. I owe it to Gerry."

Blade went to the "photograph" on the bulletin board and looked into the eyes of Carol Merrigan.

"What's she up to? Why doesn't she ring—just when I want her to ring! She's rung me at least twice a day for the past week. Fuck it. I don't know if she'll buy it, sir, I really don't. It's all so neat. She waits nine years to take revenge for her father's death, and we get the men responsible, the day before the payoff. It's all too bloody neat. I don't think she'll buy it."

Duffy had come behind him. "Go home, Blade. Get some rest. Your nerves must be in shreds. It's half-eight now and you've an early start tomorrow. Get some rest."

So Blade took Duffy's advice, mumbled his goodnights to the others and headed for home. When he'd reached the top of Harcourt Street, however, he suddenly remembered an appointment he'd made earlier that day.

Upper Mount Street was only minutes away, and rest was the last thing on his mind.

Thirty-seven

He'd never seen her in trousers before. But this was more than trousers: Elaine was dressed in an exquisitely tailored pantsuit, dark blue with a broad chalk stripe. She wore a white shirt and a red necktie; her hair was gathered back severely and tied high. When she opened the front door, Blade felt as though he was stepping into a Greta Garbo movie.

She kissed him on both cheeks. At least the perfume was the same. As always, it did things indefinable to him. But the circumstances were different now, he reminded himself. This was business.

"Gosh, you look as if you could use a drink."

"I could but I don't want one, thanks. Just coffee, if it's not too much bother."

"No bother at all. Come in."

She appeared to own or rent the entire ground floor of the Georgian building; through an open door Blade saw a big sitting room before she ushered him into another room on the other side of the hallway.

Its bareness surprised Macken. He'd been expecting a room whose furnishings would be in keeping with the house's age; instead he found himself in something resembling an art gallery. The walls were white and hung with three gigantic canvases done in primary colors: geometric shapes that were by no means restful on the eyes. Yet you found yourself drawn to them again and again. There was no carpet on the floor, just very light, bleached and gleaming pine boards. There were three chairs—at least Blade assumed they were chairs. They were narrow and tall and black, austere in the extreme, not the sort of chair to lounge in with a six-pack and a bag of potato chips. Designer stuff; probably cost a fortune.

Minimalist music (what else, Blade mused, would it be?)

seemed to fill the room. He'd trouble tracking down its source. Then he saw the buttonless Bang & Olufsen tower near the glass drinks cabinet and the almost invisible, sandwich-thin speaker boxes.

"Take a seat," Elaine said, disappearing through a far door. "I've fresh coffee, just brewed. Turkish."

The black chairs were actually very comfortable. They forced you to sit upright and your spine seemed to relax more the straighter you sat. The arm supports were at precisely the right height and angle. A sudden vision of an ancient Egyptian pharaoh flashed through Blade's head.

The blinds were drawn and the room's illumination came from a massive, semiglobular lamp hung above a low, black table and from a triad of concealed spots in the ceiling.

Elaine de Rossa returned with a small, steaming cup of black coffee. She was having nothing herself.

"So you're a journalist," Blade said bluntly. "What paper?" She told him.

"At least it's not the *News of the World*."

Elaine made a face. "Look, I feel pretty shitty about deceiving you, Blade darling."

"Please don't call me that."

"I thought you liked it."

"I did before. Not now. I don't like people having me on. It rubs me up the wrong way."

"And I suppose," Elaine said carefully, sitting down opposite him, "you've never deceived anybody in the line of duty?"

"That's different. That's work."

"So's mine."

"Maybe. And you're right: It was pretty shitty." He sipped some coffee; it was like molasses, but good. "So let's keep things strictly on a professional footing from now on, okay? Tell me about Delahunt."

He'd hurt her feelings, that was obvious. But she'd done the same to him; far worse. Macken hadn't come here to score points. He was glad when she cut the charm and grew serious, businesslike.

"I spoke to his wife today," she said. "All sweetness and shite. Until, that is, I mentioned Buenos Aires." She told him of her father's unexpected discovery.

Blade sipped more coffee, then put the cup and saucer aside. "There's no mistake, is there? They were fake?"

"So the experts there say. It certainly put the wind up Mrs. Delahunt. More so when I asked her the name of the firm that had insured the jewels. That's when she showed me the door. But it shouldn't be hard to find that out."

"Hmm. Delahunt is going to love you."

And so, Blade thought, is Charlie Nolan. He was already figuring out how the loose ends were about to be tied up. There was something poetic about the whole thing: first Roche, then the Price brothers, now Delahunt and Nolan. The game that had been set in motion nine years before was in its final stage of play.

"Look, Elaine, would you do me a favor? It's in your own interest as well."

"Sure."

He took his notebook from his pocket and began to write, talking as he scribbled the words. "This is a note for Detective Superintendent Charles Nolan. You probably won't know him but he's conducting the Delahunt investigation."

"Nolan? Yeah, I think his name's been mentioned a few times in the office."

"Well, you're to take this note to him. He can open doors for you. And *you* can open a door for him, too." Blade signed the note, tore out the sheets, and passed them to her.

"What do you mean, I can open a door for him?"

"It's complicated. You'll find out when you get to Harcourt Square." He hesitated. "Leave it till tomorrow afternoon though, will you? The morning isn't a good time."

Elaine put the note in her purse without reading it.

"You're sure you wouldn't like a drink?"

No! No alcohol. Not now. He couldn't risk it. Not now.

"Well, maybe just a drop of whiskey in the bottom of a glass."

She'd already risen when the telephone rang in the adjoining room. She shut the door behind her. Blade heard her voice, muffled.

The minutes ticked by. Blade grew restless. He no longer heard Elaine's voice on the phone. The music had ended some time before.

"Blade!!"

Her scream jolted him. He leaped from the chair and made for the door to the adjoining room. The scream came again, the scream of a woman in mortal danger. He flung the door open.

The room was a bedroom, vast. The bed itself seemed to hover above the floor, an illusion created by the indirect light beneath it. Other light bathed the room in a deep pink that changed the white carpet to the color of cotton candy. There were animals ranged around the room's sides; soft toys; pandas and koala bears; cats and dogs and monkeys as big as sumo wrestlers; squirrels and rabbits; a life-size, white plush pony; plush cranes and pink flamingos with outstretched wings were suspended from the ceiling.

So, too, was Elaine de Rossa.

A pair of gymnast's stationary rings had been secured by metal bolts in the middle of the high ceiling. The rings were adjustable and hung now at the level of Blade's chest. Elaine de Rossa had set them in motion by the momentum of her body and they swung slowly back and forth. Participants in this branch of gymnastics will tell you that there are various positions you can assume, making use of the rings. The forward and backward start are popular and require only a little practice. The backward uprise, cross, and cross hang are exercises that shouldn't be attempted by beginners. The inverted hang, however, is one of the most difficult feats of all. You slip your knees through the rings and suspend yourself solely by entwining your legs in the ropes—and all this must be accomplished without spinning or jerking horizontally. Done well, it's spectacular.

Done nude, it's breathtaking.

Elaine de Rossa swung slowly upside down in the soft, pink light, eyes closed and mouth open, perfect teeth bared. She was singing to herself: "Swing low, sweet chariot, coming for to carry me home. . . . "

Blade approached her slowly, like a man in a trance. He'd never seen anything so beautiful. In the pink light her body glowed with a sensuality that awakened in him emotions that had lain dormant for over forty years. Pink, the color of babyhood, of warmth, of mothering, of innocence.

He'd never seen anything so beautiful—or so vulnerable and challenging all at once. Her blonde hair, loosened, swept the white-pink carpet as she swung. Her round breasts and hips were the same hue as the rest of her torso, tanned evenly. Her nipples were taut and their shadows lengthened and contracted as her body swung from the rings. Her navel was a vertical line.

At the bifurcation of the long thighs that rippled in the light, Blade saw a smooth mound. Liquid trickled from the parted lips; they were almost purple in the light.

"Kiss me," Elaine said. "Kiss my fanny. Kiss my lips."

They were on a level with Blade's own. He caught her hips as they swung toward him, held them, heard Elaine moan, and pressed his tongue deep into that moist recess.

"Oh God!" she cried and he felt her hands grip his shins.

Then he was thrusting down deep, exploring her warm, secret places with circular movements of his tongue. She hadn't allowed any soap or other foreign substance to penetrate those depths and he tasted only the magnificence of Elaine de Rossa. He felt her hands clamber up his thighs, unbuckle his pants, slide them down his legs, work his underpants out over his erection. Then her mouth was slowly, slowly engulfing his cock; her chin brushed against his soft hairs. He shuddered. The shuddering caused Elaine to climax and warm liquid flowed down Blade's chin.

She was humming the chariot song now, and Blade felt the vibration in her larynx transfer itself to his penis. He swelled

240

so much that he thought her jaw might burst. He came up for air.

"Jesus," he gasped. "Enough. Bed. Now."

But suddenly there was the sound of a phone ringing. It was not Elaine's house phone; the ringing came from close by, from Blade's jacket pocket.

Angel.

The long-awaited call. But God almighty, why *now?* He felt his erection wither in Elaine's mouth. She released him and looked up at him questioningly.

"Golly, Blade, you're not going to take that?"

He had the phone in his hand already. "I have to, I have to. It's business."

"Blade!"

"I'm sorry, Elaine. I'm going to the other room."

Blade left her hanging in the rings and shuffled to the door, trousers held up with one hand, phone in the other.

Don't stop, he urged the phone; don't hang up now. He shut the door and leaned against it, panting. He took a deep breath.

"Macken. . . . "

"Blade, it's Peter."

He blew his top. The little gobshite. He said things to his son that he'd never said before, things that no father has a right to say. When Blade had finished, Peter's voice was small and nervous.

"You weren't at home. I tried you dozens of times. I know I promised I'd never ring you on your mobile again—but I had to."

There was no sense being angry now. The damage was done. He sighed heavily.

"All right, Peter—spit it out."

"Er, the cockroach is gone, Blade."

"Gone?"

"Lock, stock and barrel. He came around in a taxi today and moved a load of his stuff out. Joan was in bits."

"Did he say where he was going?"

"No. And he didn't say when he'd be back either. I heard them arguing in the kitchen. He was on crutches, too, Blade. He looked as white as a sheet. I think he must have been in an accident."

"Poor chap. How's your mother now? Is she all right?"

"She's gone to a friend's house. You know what I think, Blade? I think Roche is gone for good. That's why I had to ring you."

Macken relaxed. Through the timber of the door he heard music. Not minimalist this time but something that took him back to his Arabian days and nights. The impossible bending of high notes, the throb of goatskin drums, soothing and enervating at the same time.

Of all the people who should call him now, it had to be his son. Blade felt love.

"Take care of your mother. Will you do that, Peter?"

"You sound funny, Dad."

"I'm grand, Peter. Believe me, I'm grand. Good night, son."

Thirty-eight

Elaine de Rossa was lying on the bed when he returned. The rings still swung slightly. Her eyes were glassy. Blade smelled something pungent in the room. Hashish, very strong, very African. From hidden speakers came a song in Arabic, North African, a mesmerizing chant sung by boy sopranos, with violins and pounding drums rising in volume, then receding. Blade was back in the desert, under a black sky filled with painfully beautiful stars. This was where lust began.

"Get your kit off," she murmured huskily. "And no more police business tonight."

He struggled out of his clothes, felt passion return. Elaine thumbed a switch behind her head and the music increased in volume. He joined her.

"Fuck me, Blade," she said. "Fuck me now."

Blade's thrusting began slowly. His hands alternately squeezed and relaxed on Elaine's buttocks, her vagina kneading his erection. She called his name and the name of God. The voices of the boy sopranos entwined round an inconceivable note as the African drums beat more loudly and insistently. He thrust faster and deeper, felt his first juices emerging. Time to think about the Girls from Brazil.

The Girls from Brazil. There'd been three of them. And what they'd taught him in 1980 beat the hell out of thinking of ice and vinegar.

The African drums pounded wildly, their rhythms seeming to resonate in an echo chamber; now came the violins, bowed upright, Maghreb style, like an old-fashioned viol. Elaine was thrusting her pelvis up to meet his every stroke. Their bodies were soaked.

He'd replied to an advertisement in a German newspaper during an especially idle and boring weekend. The three

243

women had been purveying tantric yoga. Blade had known nothing about it, but they'd sold it well. The lessons, they'd said, would be costly, but he'd emerge from them a new man. What had clinched it for Blade was that the lessons were practical ones: seldom had the term "hands-on" been more appropriate.

They'd given him his own mantra, one easily memorized. You chanted it first, over and over, until it spun in your head, looping like the outgoing tape of an answering machine. Then it really *was* in your head; you didn't need to chant it aloud. It released the power of Shiva and Shakti, the male and female opposites, what the Buddhists call samsara and nirvana.

The mantra was only a preliminary. The yoga itself did things to Blade Macken's libido that a live, personal group session with every *Playboy* centerfold girl couldn't hope to rival.

The hours passed.

"Gosh, Blade," Elaine gasped at last, "where did you learn this stuff?"

He didn't think it was prudent to tell her. Instead, he turned Elaine over on her belly and began to massage her buttocks. She trembled at his every touch, kicked her feet in ecstasy. Blade's hands went to the lips of her vagina and he parted them tenderly. Holding her open as wide as possible, he slid his cock between his fingers and entered Elaine. He was deeper than he'd ever been. She moaned loudly. There were more drumbeats and African violins playing; they merged with the mantra that revolved in Blade's head. Time lost its meaning for him. He felt that only seconds had gone by, but knew from experience that his perceptions had altered.

Now his cock was slowly massaging Elaine's parted labia. Blade no longer knew where he ended and she began.

"My God, Blade," she whispered, "it's like you're fucking me and licking me at the same time. This is unreal."

No, he thought, this is real. Unreality was the domain of the woman who called herself Angel.

Another unreal thing was: he felt her presence close at hand, almost in this very room.

*   *   *

The nights were the worst.

When the traffic passing along the wharf had trickled to a few stray passing cars, when the voices in the adjoining building and below her were silent, when only ghosts were there to keep her company, that was the worst time of all.

Carol couldn't sleep at a time like this, when the sins of the world came to call on her. She knew she was responsible; her diary had told her so. But *she* had written that diary, if only to remember herself as she'd once been, to chart her day-to-day sinking, to her becoming this other person. It was her and it wasn't her; that was the most puzzling part of all.

When her daddy's voice spoke to her during the hours of darkness, telling her things, Carol heard his voice sometimes from outside her, sometimes from within. His voice told her things she knew and many things she couldn't have known. She was damned; she knew that. Each day brought fresh horrors, as she descended lower and lower, felt herself being pulled apart, felt the contagion in her head sallying out into the world.

Her daddy knew about the wickedness, had tried to help her stop it. But even from where he sat behind the sky, watching over her, he was powerless. Her thoughts were escaping. She couldn't keep them inside. Out, out they poured, the flow growing daily. She'd looked on—helpless—when the wicked thoughts had gone out and entered her mammy. Carol had watched her mammy trying to fight the evil that seeped out of her daughter's mind.

The children on the street were right: She was a witch. The Devil had taken control of her and was using her for his evil ends.

He'd made her murder her mammy.

Oh, God! Carol had seen the horror in her mammy's eyes when realization had finally dawned. But she hadn't been able to do a thing to stop it; neither of them could have stopped it.

The whiskey helped sometimes. It kept the wicked thoughts from leaking out. How much of it had she drunk now? Half

245

a bottle? It helped. When she'd drunk this much, Carol was aware of how the thoughts ran around inside her head, searching for some means of exit. But Carol knew they couldn't escape so easily then—because they kept returning; that was the proof. They couldn't harm anybody but Carol.

A foghorn sounded low and menacing in the distance. It shocked Carol; shocked her because she imagined that she'd dropped her guard, allowed the wickedness to fly out of her and take the souls at sea. Blade Macken, the Devil, had been right about the souls on O'Connell Street: It was Carol who'd taken them. More evidence of her power. She'd made the men who'd made the gelignite that made the bombs. She couldn't stop it. She couldn't stop it. She couldn't stop it. Those men had picked up her evil thoughts. She was responsible.

She was the Angel of Death.

Carol went to the canvas bag, unzipped it, and took out the funeral shroud. She stripped off all her clothes, threw them in a corner, and slipped the gown over her head.

She was Mammy now. In the dim light of the candles and the forty-watt bulb—forty jewels per second!—she studied the front of the white garment. It was gone, the blood was all gone; no trace remained.

She remembered the voice inside her head, on that other night. It had been her father's voice, guiding her steps.

She is going upstairs, Daddy's voice had said; she is turning the handle; she is opening the door; she is screaming silently, looking at the dead woman on the bed; she is seeing the empty sleeping-pill bottle on the nightstand; she is seeing the kitchen knife on the floor; she is seeing the red ruin of the woman's wrists; she is touching the still-warm blood on the front of the nightgown, bathing her hands in it; she is reaching down and pulling up the gown, up over the woman's head; she is going to the bathroom and throwing the death shroud in the tub; she is scrubbing and scrubbing and scrubbing and not feeling the scalding water blistering her hands; she is scrubbing until the water turns pink and the gown becomes white again. . . .

Carol took her hairbrush and went to the cracked mirror on

the wall. She began to brush slowly. Only lightly, just enough to take her hair away from her mammy's face. It was tangled and dirty, but so was she. So was her mind.

The gown was practically sheer at the front, where the blood had been; the material had been worn to a thread by the scrubbing, the bleaching. Carol laid the hairbrush aside and cupped her breasts in her hands. She squeezed and felt beautiful.

She is squeezing her exquisite breasts, her mammy's voice inside her head said; she is closing her eyes and moaning; she is growing wet in her private place; she is trembling all over her wonderful body, Mammy said. She is coming, Mammy said.

Carol wiped herself carefully with the last of the tissues. She felt cleansed, purified. This was one power that couldn't leave her. When she'd welcomed men in her private place it was *their* power she'd taken; she'd given nothing of herself away—just as it should be.

She stripped off the nightgown, rolled it up carefully, and stowed it in the canvas bag. Would she dress again? There seemed little point now; it had grown hot in the room; she'd just crawl between the thin blankets. She was tired, thought she could sleep now.

Dolly wants to speak to Blade.

It was not her mammy's voice; it was Dolly's.

Dolly wants to speak to Blade, wants to speak to Blade.

Carol went to Dolly's bed and looked fondly at the closed eyes. She couldn't understand why Dolly wished to talk to Blade just then. There would be plenty of opportunity in the morning. No, Dolly should sleep now; it was better.

Carol went to the window and drew back the boards. A rush of air entered the room, cool and refreshing: the wind from the northwest. She craned out and delighted in the feel of it on her bare skin, breasts. The lights on the far quay danced in the black water. The Custom House, white in the floodlights, looked like a sculpture of sugar icing. Its beauty saddened her for reasons she couldn't articulate.

Carol began to weep uncontrollably. Dolly simply could not talk to Blade now. He'd misunderstand.

Elaine was weeping. She lay on her belly and Blade saw her shoulders jerk with every sob. He stroked her back tenderly.

"What's the matter?"

"Nothing. Nothing's the matter. I'm crying because I'm happy. I've always done that. It's silly."

"No, it's not, Elaine. Cry all you want."

"What happened to me, Blade? I seemed to be in a place I'd never been before. It was weird. No one's ever made me feel things like that before."

Blade said nothing, just ran a hand up under Elaine's long hair, now heavy with perspiration.

Angel hadn't called. He couldn't understand why. This should have been her big night, her last chance to twist the knife before the rendezvous, before the kill.

He thought of sex and death—how close they were. The freaks sometimes hanged themselves in order to experience the ultimate hard-on: the one you were supposed to get on the gallows. Blade had investigated one such incident less than a year ago; they'd thought at first it was murder.

"Mind if I smoke?" he asked suddenly. Elaine murmured.

Blade got up and went to where his jacket lay, found his Hamlets and lit one.

He went naked to the window, raised a slat on Elaine's venetian blind and looked out on the lamplighted street, at the Georgian houses on the other side.

The little death is a preliminary to the big one. It sharpens the senses, forces you to evaluate what you are: a journeyer, nothing more.

Macken was prepared for his journey. As he looked out Elaine's window, he thought back on his life. Katharine, Joan, Anne, Peter, Sandra: all way stations on the journey into night.

"Blade . . . " Elaine's voice was drowsy.

He went to her. She lay on her side, eyes shut.

"What is it, Elaine?"

248

"I wasn't deceiving you."

"It's all right."

"When we met . . . when I saw you first, I didn't know you were a guard. Business came later."

"Don't talk about it. Go to sleep."

"Hmm. Will I see you again? Ever?"

Elaine de Rossa. Beautiful Elaine de Rossa. The final way station before night.

"Yes," he said.

He returned to the window. Carol hadn't called him because she'd wanted him to savor the little death, to wrest all he could from life while he was still vital. They were joined together by place and circumstance. And by death. Death to Blade meant utter annihilation, the snuffing out of *all of this*. When he went, the world would disappear with him.

Vanity? Perhaps. But these were the thoughts of the condemned man. Blade looked out on what he sensed was his last night. The day had been his swan song, the tying together of the loose ends. He didn't think he'd see night again. Nor did he care all that much.

Elaine de Rossa's breathing had deepened. She was asleep. Blade finished his cigar and dressed leisurely. He went to the bed and planted a soft kiss between Elaine's shoulder blades. She sighed in her sleep. Blade covered her with the comforter. From the sides of the room the plush animals stared at him, eyes of glass, dumb.

There was a lightening of the night sky when he stepped out onto the street. A delivery truck passed by. The last night of Angel was over.

Thirty-nine

They didn't offer the condemned man a last meal, Blade reflected. What would he have ordered? Something he'd never tried before in his life, that was it. Roast swan stuffed with truffles; a terrine of Seychelles swordfish; pâté of polar bear liver and red wine; elephant's balls, lightly grilled. . . .

What they offered him instead was a Kevlar vest. It was so light that Blade had doubts that it would stop a BB shot from an air rifle, never mind a real bullet fired at close range. But Gareth Smyth assured him that it would do exactly that, and was backed up by Redfern.

"The worst injury you can sustain is a bruise," the American said. "We use these all the time in the field. Incidentally, that's the same model the president will be wearing," he added with a touch of pride in his voice.

"Pity they can't," Blade said, buttoning his shirt over the bulletproof garment, "make a face mask out of this stuff. *Then* I'd really feel safe."

"They're working on that, but so far they can't get the porosity right," Redfern said, and Macken decided it was yet another example of the CIA man's morbid humor. "What are you carrying, by the way?"

Blade showed him the .22-caliber police issue. Redfern looked unimpressed.

"At least you can stash it away where it won't be seen," he said with disdain.

The vest was warmer than Blade had anticipated; that was its main drawback. Hardly had he put on his jacket when he felt a glow on his chest that quickly turned to a sticky, uncomfortable feeling; it was like wearing a nylon shirt in a heat wave.

He caught Sweetman looking at him. Her expression was

one that he couldn't immediately identify. He read concern there, yes, but there was something else as well.

Was this how the condemned man felt? Did he suddenly, in the last hours—minutes—of life, discover that people he'd taken for granted had harbored strong, emotional feelings toward him? At six-thirty on the final day of Angel, Blade Macken saw Orla Sweetman as she really was: a warm, loving person whose loyalty to him had always, perhaps, concealed a more powerful sentiment.

"I have a bad feeling about this," Smyth said, derailing Blade's train of thought. "There's still time to deploy my boys. We could have the—"

"No, Gareth," Blade said. "We can't risk it. Look, we know who she is, we know what she's done. But what we still don't know is what she's capable of. To be honest about it, nothing she could do would surprise me anymore. She chose the Custom House for a reason and I think it's because she can keep an eye on it, wherever she may be. She'll be watching my every move. No, let me do this her way."

"Do you still think you can talk sense into her, Blade?" Duffy asked.

"I doubt it."

He picked up his copy of the morning newspaper, read again the item on the front page. He found himself wishing they'd made more of the story: it occupied too little space. More information might have helped win Carol's trust. Yet all the names were there: of the victims, the killers—and the arresting officers. Gerry Merrigan had received due prominence. Blade folded the paper and stuck it under his arm.

"It may work. If not, I'll think of something."

They watched presently as Blade started up his car, moved slowly to the checkpoint and passed the raised barrier. The garda on duty saluted. In his rearview mirror Blade saw Sweetman wave a farewell, concern now more clearly written on her face. He turned out onto Harcourt Street.

He was on his own now. Twenty-eight CIA operatives and

more than one hundred garda detectives could do nothing to aid him.

As Blade sped down Camden Street, he reflected on the quarry who called herself Angel. Carol Merrigan had never been other than a very normal little girl. Brighter, perhaps, than most of her schoolfriends, but nobody special. She'd never given Blade reason to believe that one day her mind would become so twisted that, for her, mass murder would be nothing more than a means to an end. Frightening. How easily we can be tripped over the edge of the abyss into insanity.

Yet Blade thought that he might still be able to reach her, to extend a hand across the abyss.

The weather was changing. The breeze from the northwest had grown during the past three days; now it whipped up the garbage that littered Aungier Street and sent cooling drafts of air through Blade's car window. It was two hours before most of the stores would open; a number of delivery trucks with flashing hazard lights stood at the curb; the traffic was light.

There was also a considerable garda presence. As Blade swung right onto Dame Street, he saw the steel barriers at College Green. In less than three hours, flag-waving Dubliners would be massed behind those barriers as the motorcade of the president of the United States wound past.

He took the side entrance to the Bank of Ireland. It is one of the city's most imposing structures. Built early in the eighteenth century, it had once housed the Irish Parliament, before that body voted itself out of existence and was absorbed by Westminster in 1801. The giant pillars that circle the building flung the cobbled laneway into gloom. It was cold there and Blade saw a waiting cabdriver rub his hands together. He drove on past and stopped at the arched gateway. The door was open. Blade left the car unlocked and entered the courtyard on foot.

His arrival had been announced; a sharply dressed young man came out to meet him.

"You're early, Detective Superintendent. We hadn't expected you for another half hour."

"I didn't want to get caught in the rush-hour traffic," Blade said. "Little did I know there wouldn't be any."

The man smiled. "Give them time. You won't know the place in ten minutes. It's always the same. Would you follow me, please?"

He led the way past a guard and down a corridor to a locked door. It opened when he keyed in a code and they entered an elevator. It was the heavy-duty kind, designed to take many tons of weight. Blade thought of gold bullion. They descended into the bowels of the bank. It was difficult to know just how far down they went, so slowly did the elevator seem to travel. Then the door slid back with a siss of hydraulics and Blade looked out into a corridor, brightly lit and vigilant with surveillance cameras.

The bank official made no attempt to conceal from Blade the code he punched into the second numeric pad, located on a steel door a little way down the corridor. That door opened onto yet another—steel, with a third security pad. Finally they entered the vault proper.

It was flanked by the sort of safety deposit boxes you see at post offices, airports, and train stations; rows of them, reaching to the ceiling, in ascending order of diminishing size. The bank official went to a big one at floor level. He unlocked it with a key chained to his wrist, reached in, and lugged out two large suitcases. Their locks had been sealed and imprinted with a date and the circular seal of the Central Intelligence Agency.

"Are they heavy?" Blade asked.

"Not as heavy as you'd expect. Banknotes don't weigh all that much."

Blade tested this. It sent a thrill through him, lifting a suitcase that contained—what? twelve-and-a-half million dollars? The lottery. A childish part of him saw himself heading straight for the airport with a one-way ticket to Rio. "What is in ze suitcases, senhor?" "Oh, just money." "*Assim!* Welcome to Brazil, senhor." All his worries over.

Dead easy.

253

But the bank official was calling up reinforcements on his cellular phone, and when Blade and he reemerged on ground level with the two cases, there were three security guards to escort them to the car.

"Sign, please?" the bank official said, and Macken put his signature to a piece of paper that bore more zeros than were decent. Helped by one of the guards, he stowed the cases in the trunk of his car. There were no more waiting cabs at the curb.

The garda presence in College Green had increased in the interim, as had the number of sightseers behind the barriers. People had come with their families; already small children were perched on fathers' shoulders, although there was nothing to see except their counterparts behind the barriers outside Trinity College.

Dame Street was cordoned off at this point. Blade showed his ID to a uniformed police officer and was escorted by a squad car up the wrong side of the street. Some time later, he turned into Eustace Street, headed down to the Liffey, and turned left. He glanced at the clock on the dash. Not yet seven-thirty.

O'Connell Street was cordoned off as well, and alive with milling crowds, the early birds come to secure the best places before the show began. Excited children waved little American flags; adults waved camcorders. Blade heard a pipe band rehearse an ancient Irish marching song.

On learning Macken's identity, an officer pulled back a barrier and allowed the car through. Blade couldn't resist a quick look to his left as he crossed the wide street, passing the O'Connell Monument. The scene bore an eerie resemblance to that of a morning eleven days before: the crowds of people, the police cars, even the helicopter overhead. Only the mood had changed and the roadway was bare and gray.

Up Eden Quay now, past Beresford Place, and under the massive railroad viaduct that overshadowed Butt Bridge. The bright stone of the Custom House reflected the morning sunlight.

Blade stopped at the appointed place, on the white tiles in front of the building, and cut the engine. He wound down the window and received a putrid smell from the murky river, invisible under the quay wall. Gulls screamed and dived in the sun. There was a faint hum of traffic from the opposite side.

Blade waited.

"Bravo-niner-two-eight sealed and secure, sir," the American barked into his walkie-talkie. "Over."

"Did you double-check? Over."

"Affirmative, sir. Six to go. Over."

They'd been busy since first light: two score of CIA men, assisted by some of Redfern's team and Dublin police officers. Every manhole that Macken's dogs had entered had been reentered by humans and its culvert searched thoroughly. Following inspection, each manhole was sealed, and patrolled at regular intervals. The inspection team was now halfway through Nassau Street, a stone's throw from the Irish houses of parliament.

A helicopter pilot flying above the city would have noted the presence, too, of armed men standing on the rooftops at places where streets turned corners or intersected, places where the presidential motorcade would be forced to slow.

All this was standard procedure. Angel ruined the neat equation.

The call came at eight o'clock precisely.

"BLADE! TOP O' THE MORNIN' TO YOU. I SEE YOU GOT THE CAR WASHED, TOO. WAS THAT IN MY HONOR? I'M FLATTERED."

As was the case that Friday afternoon eleven days ago outside the American embassy, Blade found himself looking every which way in an effort to spot the enemy. But there was no one on foot in the vicinity and his was the only parked car.

"Let's just get this over with, Angel," he said curtly. "I'm not in the mood for small talk." There was no more need to tread carefully; Carol was in the home stretch now and wouldn't jeopardize her own plan at this stage. The Kevlar vest was beginning to torment Blade with its clinging stickiness.

"AH NOW, BLADE, SURE I'M ONLY TRYING TO BE NICE. NO NEED TO GET ON YOUR HIGH HORSE. A SHAME TO SPOIL THE LOVELY MORNING THAT'S IN IT. WELL, HOW DOES IT FEEL TO HAVE ALL THAT CASH WITH YOU? I BET YOU THOUGHT OF DOING A BUNK. A ONE-WAY TRIP TO RIO, EH? WOULDN'T THAT BE GRAND?"

Jesus, Mary, and Joseph, was she psychic as well as crazy?

"Let's just get on with it, Angel. Where do you want me to go?"

There was a chopper overhead. Blade heard it hovering above and immediately behind him. Carol, wherever she was at that moment, had seen or heard it as well.

"WAIT."

He did.

"I WARNED YOU, BLADE."

"For Christ's sake, Angel, this has nothing to do with me. I don't know who the fuck it is. They're probably checking the surroundings for the president."

"WELL, WHOEVER IT IS, GET RID OF HIM. I MEAN IT, BLADE. IF THAT HELICOPTER ISN'T GONE WITHIN THE NEXT FIVE MINUTES, THERE'S GOING TO BE BLOOD ON THE STREETS AGAIN. I'M HANGING UP NOW. YOU MAKE SURE THAT THING IS GONE BY THE TIME I RING BACK."

Blade made the call. The garda manning the switchboard at Harcourt Square was as mystified as Macken. It was not a police chopper.

"Find out who it is," Blade ordered. "Find out fast. And tell the cunt to get the fuck out of here. He can fly into the Liffey for all I care."

"This could take time, Detective Superintendent."

"We haven't got any."

"It might help if I had a reg."

"I'll have a look."

Blade got out of the car and glanced at his watch. The helicopter had remained hovering above him. Who the fuck was it? The CIA? No, Redfern wouldn't be that stupid. Then he saw the markings: the familiar, yellow-and-black livery of the Automobile Association. The Sky Patrol provided radio updates on Dublin's traffic.

Blade gave details.

"I'll get on to them, Detective Superintendent. They'll be out of there before you know it."

The operator was as good as his word. Blade saw two faces staring down at him with what might have been curiosity, shortly before the helicopter wheeled and soared out in a northerly direction. He looked at his watch again. Those had been the longest four minutes of his life.

His phone rang.

"NOW THAT WE'VE GOT THAT OUT OF THE WAY, WE CAN GET DOWN TO BUSINESS AGAIN." Angel was no longer in a frivolous mood.

"I'm listening."

"CROSS THE RIVER AND KEEP STRAIGHT ON INTO MOSS STREET. TURN LEFT AT TOWNSEND STREET. HAVE YOU GOT THAT?"

"Yes."

"AND LEAVE THE LINE OPEN."

So Redfern had been mistaken: The rendezvous was to take place south of the river. Blade wondered about that. If Carol's plan was to flee the country with the money, then she'd two possibilities. The ferry terminal was in Dún Laoghaire, a twenty-minute drive to the south; or she could continue on down to Rosslare in County Wexford and take the boat to France. On the other hand, if Carol had decided on escaping by air, then she was close to the East Link causeway that would take her to Fairview, which would provide her with a convenient route to the airport. Better than the regular route—that was being used this morning by the U.S. president.

But she wouldn't take it, would she? She'd never get through the checks at the airport and ferry terminals—not today at any rate.

A chilling thought crossed his mind: Did the bitch want to escape at all? Was the business with the $25 million no more than a pantomime? Perhaps she'd demanded the money simply in order to put the cat among the pigeons, have two governments running about at her whim. A nice revenge when you thought about it. And the more Blade thought about it the more he was convinced that the money was a sham, a front to conceal Carol Merrigan's real motive—that of wreaking vengeance on Blade Macken.

And Blade himself: What was he doing here? There must be, he mused, a side to us all that pushes us to the limits. We want to know. We want to expose ourselves to acute danger. We want to look death in the face. We want to know. Our egos push us there, to the brink. So determined are we to impress upon others our need for the truth, that we will hazard our lives, that we might confront others with the truth, even if the baring of the truth leads to our downfall. We want to know— and we want others to know, too.

As he turned right, Blade glanced at the glass towers of Dublin's financial district. He thought of the deals that would be done there this morning. To be sure, some of them might rival his and Angel's, might exceed their deal. Yet those transactions would involve virtual money, existing on computer screens, as it was shunted back and forth across the world, growing or dwindling as markets fluctuated. Blade and Angel were doing it the old-fashioned way: wads of tactile, folding money stashed in a car trunk.

"WHERE ARE YOU NOW?" she asked abruptly.

Well, thank the living fuck for that, Blade thought. She isn't all-seeing, after all. He'd begun to think that Angel had eyes everywhere.

"Coming up to the junction with Westland Row."

"OK. GO THROUGH THE LIGHTS AND BEAR LEFT AT THE TRAF-FIC ISLAND. THIS IS FUN, ISN'T IT, BLADE?"

"Oh, great *craic* altogether. And to think I could be doing something really boring now, like waiting for the parade."

"THAT'S THE SPIRIT. TAKE THE FIRST TURNING ON THE LEFT."

Blade obeyed. He'd been glancing every few seconds in his mirror. So far as he could make out, Redfern's men were nowhere to be seen. He hoped to blazes they'd kept their word. If not, there'd be hell to pay. Hell, and fire, and brimstone.

Yet another thought struck him. When had he last charged the phone battery? Christ, wouldn't that be something: the president of the United States losing his life and fuck-knows-what-else happening, and all because of a run-down phone battery.

Blade drove slowly past the entrance to Windmill Lane, the graffiti shrine to U2, Ireland's greatest rock band. *"God Save Bono!"* he read. *"I'll see you again when the stars fall from the sky and the moon turns red."*

"TURN RIGHT AT THE END OF THE STREET, DRIVE TWO HUNDRED YARDS, UNTIL YOU SEE A SIGN SAYING 'DONNELLY'S COAL,' AND STOP."

He did as directed. There were not many people on foot in this part of Docklands. As Blade turned the corner, he cast an eye over a group of youths with shaved heads. They were drinking cans of strong cider, at eight-thirty in the morning.

He also noticed a beggar-woman shuffling along the sidewalk, a baby at her breast.

Two hundred yards down the litter- and glass-strewn street, an ancient metal signboard on a gable testified to the fact that a coal merchant's business had once flourished here. Blade stopped the car and killed the engine. In his door mirror he saw the beggar-woman approaching. She wore a plaid shawl that covered her from head to hip, a floral print dress and battered shoes. She had her head down, so it was hard to make out her features. Her hair looked as though it hadn't been washed in months and her face was streaked with grime. Blade had to concede that the disguise was near-perfect.

Fuck her. She'd been so bloody clever, each step of the way. He was damned if he was going to let her believe that she'd won *every* round. This round was his—a part of it, at least, the part where you take the enemy by surprise.

Blade had his pride, too.

He opened the car door and stepped out. "Hello, Angel," he said evenly. "Or would you prefer it if I called you Carol?"

She stopped dead in her tracks and her mouth flew open. Blade had to suppress a grin, a grin of triumph. Know thine enemy—wasn't that half the battle won; wasn't that what the martial master Von Clausewitz taught in chapter one of his primer, the book that was the bible of all fighting men?

They stared at each other, the adversaries face to face at last. He saw that, beneath the grime and the unwashed hair, she was almost pretty: a grown-up version of the little girl he'd dandled on his knee, had bought birthday and Christmas gifts for, who'd called him Unca Bwade when her teeth had been in braces.

She would have been pretty, were it not for the lines etched deep in her face. They were the antithesis of laugh lines; years of insane hatred had put them there. Her eyes no longer resembled those in Rob McGrath's simulacrum. They were wild—the eyes of a mad, feral beast.

But if Blade had surprised Carol Merrigan, then she quickly turned the tables. She reached into a fold of her shawl and when her hand reappeared, it held a small but deadly accurate handgun.

For the second time in less than twenty-four hours, Macken looked death in the face. And Carol frightened him more than Paddy Price had done. He sensed that a woman with eyes as wild as hers was totally unpredictable. He could be dead within seconds.

"You bastard!" she said. "You unscrupulous *fuck*." The gun was pointed unwaveringly at his forehead.

"Carol . . . you be careful with that thing now."

She laughed—and it was a laugh that caused the follicles all over his body to attempt to grow a protective coat of fur.

"Ah no, I'm not going to shoot you, Blade. Not yet. Sure I'd be an eejit to do that. I *need* you, Blade."

His look was inquiring.

"I need your strength," She told him. "Your brawn. Heh heh heh."

He didn't like her laugh; he hadn't liked it when it had been cloaked by electronically generated magic. Reality did nothing to improve it.

Then Carol came nearer—and both she and Blade stiffened as a thin, high-pitched whine emanated from the folds of her shawl. She closed the distance and the whining increased. Carol's left hand sped to her breast; Blade saw it fumble. The whining stopped.

Then she laughed again.

"You fucking amateurs!" She raised her voice. "Yes, Duffy, you! You and the rest of them—whoever's listening. Do you hear me, Duffy? You're an *amateur*. You're out of your fucking league. This is Angel you're dealing with."

She stepped two paces back and pointed the gun once more at Macken's skull. "Take it off, Blade. The wire. Take it off."

He'd known from the start that it was a mistake. And yes, it had been Duffy's idea; Duffy, backed up by some of the others. Stupid. Blade had guessed that Carol, of all people, wouldn't be taken in by such a primitive ruse as a concealed microphone. Any hopes he'd cherished of winning her confidence were fading now.

"Do it slowly, Blade," she said. Holding the gun aimed in his direction, she looked around quickly. The street was deserted; the cider-swilling youths were gone. "Keep your hands where I can see them."

Blade began to unzip his trousers.

"Oh, that's *good*, Blade. Full marks, Mr. Duffy. Did they think I wouldn't search your crotch, Blade? Me, a woman? Or was it your pet psychologist? Was it her idea?"

Blade said nothing. He carefully removed the little microphone and its wiring from the place of concealment and let them fall to the ground.

"Anything else I should know about, Blade? Or is that bulge in your trousers all your own?"

"That's all. And you're right: it wasn't my idea. It's not my style."

Her eyes narrowed. "Oh, I know. I know your style, Blade. Believe me, I know it only too well." She gestured with the gun. "Get in the car."

He obeyed, and Carol Merrigan slid into the passenger seat. The morning sun caught the weapon, a chromium-plated Beretta, lethal at this range. He wondered where she'd got it.

"Where are we going?"

"Just shut the fuck up and drive, Blade. We're going to have a little chat. We're going to talk about, you might say, old times."

Forty

Mr. Sachs had had the embassy radio room evacuated. Nobody had protested; Sachs was Redfern's man and it was understood that you didn't get on the wrong side of Redfern. Now Sachs and Roe had the little windowless room to themselves. Roe had a direct link with Langley, Virginia; Sachs maintained radio contact with the six embassy cars that conveyed the other dark-suited men to the center of Dublin.

"We have a bird," Roe said.

"Good."

"Fifty-three, twenty, thirty-seven-point-five north; zero six, fourteen, thirty-six-point-one east," Roe said, tilting up one half of his headphones.

"I copy," Sachs answered.

He punched in the coordinates on his keyboard and was almost instantly rewarded with a full-color map of a section of Dublin city. A red light pulsed brightly on a narrow street. Sachs spoke into a microphone attached to his own headset.

Unseen from the earth, a satellite with the designation of KH-12 followed an orbit high in the ionosphere. The youngest generation of the Key Hole family of space spies, it carried an impressive panoply of sophisticated equipment. It had multispectral and infrared sensors, and radar that could penetrate clouds. The technician from Dublin Corporation had boasted that his surveillance cameras could pick up two flies "shagging each other on a wall." He'd have been astounded by the reconnaissance capabilities of this silver bird.

At that moment, its sensors were utilizing their fluoroscopic menus. Superman-like, they peeked clean through the thick metal of Blade's car trunk, through the hides of two big travel cases—and registered the presence of certain invisible chemicals with which $25 million in used bills had been treated.

The onboard navigation facility continuously updated the location of these chemicals, via the Navstar Global Positioning System. Encrypted, this information was relayed almost simultaneously to the headquarters of the Central Intelligence Agency, with which Mr. Roe had an open connection.

At separate locations in the heart of the city of Dublin, the drivers of six cars responded to the electronic directive.

"Turn left at Pearse Street," Carol Merrigan ordered. Presently they were passing Macken Street. Macken Street! Then Charlotte Quay. The still water reflected the massive bulk of Boland's Mills, the building occupied in Easter Week, 1916, by militiamen under the command of a young schoolteacher named Eamon de Valera. Luxury apartments overlooked the harbor on their left. A breeze sped over the water, splintering the sunlight.

Carol was adjusting the rearview mirror, angling it toward her. She did it with the hand that held the gun; the other was concealed within her shawl. She nodded, satisfied; she saw no signs of pursuit.

"Keep going," she said, as they passed over the canal and alongside the little mission church.

I was right, Blade thought: We're heading for the East Link; she's planning on making her getaway by air after all.

But he was mistaken; Carol was having him make a diversion. After a bewildering series of turns, they'd recrossed the canal and were heading back toward the city center. She peered every few seconds in the mirror.

"There was no need for the bombs," Blade said. "No need at all."

She laughed. "Yes there was, Blade. I got you here, didn't I?"

He looked at her strangely. "For fuck's sake, Carol. You killed six innocent people—just to talk to *me*?"

"Would you have talked to me otherwise?"

"Yes."

"You know what you did, Blade Macken? You know what

you did? You murdered my parents, that's what you did."
Her voice had risen, out of control.

"I'd nothing to do with it," he said. "Your father was the
closest thing I ever had to a real friend. You know that. You
must remember that."

"Oh, I remember, Blade. And that's what makes it all so
fucking painful. My father trusted you and you betrayed him.
Turn right here."

"I didn't. It wasn't like that at all."

"Liar! You made him go into that bank in Donnybrook.
You didn't want to go yourself, 'cause you were out of your
mind with drink."

"That's not true. That's not the way it happened."

"Oh, so Charlie Nolan is a liar then?"

"Among other things, yes."

"And I suppose he lied about the burglary as well? When
they killed my father?"

Jesus Christ. What had Nolan been doing? Blade was beginning to regret helping the man. To hell with it. No more
Robin fucking Hood.

"You were up to your neck in it, Macken. Admit it."

Blade knew better than to argue. This was not a rational
person.

"Look on the backseat," he said. "The paper."

She glanced back, saw the folded copy of the *Irish Independent*. "Don't try anything."

"I won't. Bottom half of page one."

Carol reached back and took the newspaper. She leaned
against the car door, holding the gun on Blade, and read the
headline above the news item, halfway down the front page.

Two Men Held for 1989 Double Slaying

"I got them, Carol. The men who killed your father. I *got*
them."

She scanned the lines. Blade glanced at her and saw her

265

wince. She held the paper up and shook it contemptuously.

"How do I know this is genuine? Eh? How do I know you didn't have this printed up, like the ones they do in the novelty shops, with your own name? 'Blade Macken for President!' 'Macken Declares War on Saddam Hussein!' Do you take me for a fool?!"

"For fuck's sake, Carol. It's the real thing. If you don't believe me, ring the bloody paper. Here, use my phone."

He saw her lips curl in a menacing smile.

"Ah, that's what you want, isn't it? That's part of the plan, too. Have me ring them up, after you've filled them all in on your little scheme. Well, I won't play along, Blade." She tossed the paper back in the rear of the car and leveled the gun again. "What other dirty little tricks have you got up your sleeve? I *warned* you. . . . "

"Jesus, I nearly got myself killed arresting those two. Fuck it. I'm on your side."

"Sure."

"Will you listen to me? Gerry—your da—was a good friend of mine. I was—"

"Don't even mention his name! I don't want to hear it coming from your dirty mouth." Her voice had risen to a screech, making him afraid. "You're a liar, Macken. Your whole life has been one, dirty great lie. You lied then and you're lying now. Nine years. Nine fucking years. Ah, how very convenient that the great Blade Macken manages to solve a murder at this very time. What took you so long, Blade, eh? Nine years?"

"It just happened that way, Carol. It seems hard to believe, I know, but it was coincidence. Things just worked out that way. Believe me."

"I'd rot in hell before I believed you! Coincidence my arse. You knew all along, didn't you? You knew who did it. I heard. Mammy told me."

He glanced at her sharply. He didn't know what was real and what was delusion as far as Carol Merrigan was concerned. Did she know herself? Dr. Earley thought not.

"You were covering up, Blade. Why? What did my father ever do to you? No, don't tell me. I don't want to hear any more lies. Turn left here."

They were back where they'd started, almost. Sir John Rogerson's Quay.

"Stop here. The red door."

Blade obeyed. He cut the engine.

The building looked derelict. It was wedged between a tall house with bricked-up windows and what had once been the Catholic Seamen's Institute. A faded sign, almost indecipherable, read LUNCHEONS AND TEAS. It might have been a cafeteria at one time.

There were two single-story warehouses on the quayside opposite, and beyond the far bank of the Liffey, the top floors of Jurys Hotel were visible. Blade saw the offices of the British and Irish Steam Packet Company and, farther west, those of the Custom House Dock Development Authority. And, farther still, the Custom House itself. From the third or fourth floor of Angel's lair it would be plainly visible. He'd guessed correctly: She'd had him in her sights until he'd crossed the river.

"Nice little setup you've got yourself," he said. "Very neat."

She ignored the compliment. "Out of the car. Do it slowly, and keep your hands where I can see them."

"There's still time to change your mind, Carol," he said. "Nobody'll convict you if I plead in your defense. We'll tell them the whole story. You won't have to go to prison; you can do time in an institution. It'll be—"

"Bastard!" she screamed. "So I'm cracked now, am I? Fuck you, Blade Macken; nobody's putting *me* in a looney bin!"

"I didn't mean it that way, Carol."

"Like hell you didn't! Now get out of the car and open the boot."

Blade was very conscious of the pressure of his .22 against the base of his spine. Was this the time to reach for it? He could do it easily, have Carol covered before she could discharge her own weapon. Or before she could activate whatever it was she held in her left hand, hidden in the folds of her shawl.

But what if the device she was holding was the equivalent of a hand grenade with the firing pin removed, as used by the suicide bombers of Lebanon? What then? What if her hand held down a lever of some kind that, if released, would send a signal to an underground bomb somewhere in the city? Perhaps only a few hundred yards away. Or was the insane bitch a human bomb herself? If he made a wrong move would the pair of them go up like a powder keg? The Kevlar vest felt sodden against his chest.

And there was something else he'd forgotten. An old soldier like him should have thought of it, but he was out of practice with firearms. Had he checked the safety on the gun? No. There was no point in going for a gun that couldn't be brought into instant play. Shite.

He opened the trunk. The sight of the two suitcases brought a smile to the woman's face. The presence of vast wealth close at hand affects the sane and the crazed in like manner. Carol licked her lips.

"Put them to the left of the red door."

He obeyed. Then she kicked the door at a certain point and it flew inward, giving Blade a view of a dark and filthy interior.

"In there, just inside the door, there's a car cover. Bring it out."

He had to admit that she'd thought of everything, right down to the cover. When he'd unfolded it on the sidewalk he saw it was just the right size for his car: not too big, not too small. Perfect. Once covered by the plastic, his car would be invisible; no one would know he was in the building. It wouldn't survive a night in this part of town but, Blade thought, he might not survive either.

"Hurry up, Blade," she said. "Get that thing on. And be sure to do the cords up tight."

He'd let her go as far as he was intending to. Once inside that building he'd be at her mercy. Once the suitcases were where Carol wanted them Blade was expendable. He saw no reason why she'd spare his life now.

It took Blade no more than a minute to cover the car in its waterproof coat and pull taut the nylon cords that would make it windproof. The final knot had to be tied. It meant that Blade had to crouch down under the rear bumper. He did so, causing his right hand to be momentarily hidden from Carol.

Yes, safety off. He brought the gun out into view.

"Drop it!" he shouted. "Drop the gun. Now!"

"Bastard!" Her face was ugly with hate.

"Yeah, yeah, I know. Let it drop, Carol."

Had it been the movies, Blade considered afterward, then they might have engaged in a stand off. He'd have persuaded her that the game was up, that it was senseless to keep the gun trained on him. Blade would have reasoned with her, showed her "the error of her ways." Then she'd have lowered her shooting arm and done one of two things: either meekly allowed him to take the gun from her limp grasp, or let it fall on the cobbled roadway with a clatter.

But this wasn't Hollywood; this was real life.

Carol shot him.

Forty-one

The impact of the bullet was like a kick in the chest by a mule. Blade, still crouched at the rear of the car, was knocked off balance and sent sprawling backward. He felt as though his heart had stopped. The roar of the gun seemed to come one or two seconds later. There was no pain yet where the bullet had struck, only a numbness that was spreading rapidly. There was an ache in his head where it had hit the stones. He couldn't breathe. From his supine position he saw her move into his field of vision and point the Beretta again, this time at his head.

"Don't, Carol. Please."

Car engines suddenly whined. Tires screeched, as six big vehicles, driven at speed, came to a standstill, blocking the street. Blade and Carol turned their heads as one.

"Back off!" Lawrence Redfern barked.

Two-dozen men had emerged from the cars; they held high-caliber handguns, each trained on the woman in the shawl.

"Back off, Carol!" Redfern shouted again. "Put the gun down."

Instead, she ducked behind Blade's camouflaged car.

"You fuckers!" she screamed. "I'll blow us all sky-high if you come any nearer. Don't make me."

Blade was struggling to his feet. The numbness had gone; fire shot through his chest. He nearly fainted from the agony.

"Hold your fire, Redfern," he managed to blurt out. "For Jesus' sake don't shoot her. She means it."

Carol was moving slowly toward the red, open door, left hand still inside the shawl.

"Devils!" she bawled. "To hell with you all. To hell with your fucking president."

The slug took her full in the left shoulder, spun her around, and sent her tottering through the doorway. Something pink fell on the sidewalk and bounced twice. Blade looked aghast to where the shot had come from and saw a heavily built man holding a gun in both hands, smoke issuing from the barrel. The sound of the shot echoed back from the warehouses, then more faintly from the wharf on the other side of the river. Hands were helping Macken to his feet.

"You okay?" It was Redfern.

" 'No' is the simple answer to that. How did you find us?"

"Magic. You're white as a sheet. Nothing broken?"

"Don't think so. Where is she?"

"Ran into the house. We're going in after her."

"Has she still got the gun?"

"Yes." To an associate he said: "Good work, Mr. Coburn. A nice clean shot."

"Ahm, I was aiming for the heart, Mr. Redfern. She moved."

They operated like army men. They split up: six went swiftly to check any rear or side exits; four went to redirect traffic; the rest took up positions on both sides of the red door. At a signal from Redfern, two men ran inside at a crouch. Gunfire sounded and Blade heard curses. The two came out almost as quickly as they'd gone in. One was holding his arm and swearing loudly.

"Bitch got me in the arm," he said unnecessarily.

Blade had to think for a moment about what he'd have done in a situation like this. Hailed Carol through a bullhorn, ordering her to give herself up? Radioed for reinforcements?

Redfern was more pragmatic. He jabbed a finger at two of his men and pointed to the doorway. The two sprang into position, legs apart, weapons aimed high. Two Colt-Magnums thundered in rapid fire. Then the men pulled back and allowed their comrades to run through. Blade heard heavy feet pounding up the stairs and voices raised. Then he was inside, too.

The banister moved dangerously when he placed a hand on it. He'd no weapon; it lay where he'd dropped it on the street. But Redfern's men had enough firepower. Blade's aching chest slowed him down and he was panting when he reached the first landing. He found two CIA men stationed there.

"Where is she?" he gasped.

"Next floor."

He clambered up the second flight of stairs. Incongruously, a naked light bulb burned on the third floor. Carol—or some other squatter—had evidently found an illicit power source; Blade didn't think that the derelict building was still supplied by the electric company. The yellow light illuminated the faces of Redfern and six of his men, deployed on either side of a paneled door. The walls had once been painted a light green; now their color was indefinable. Redfern saw Macken.

"She's locked herself in there," he told him. "We're going to rush it. Better stand way back. You never know."

"I'll try and talk to her."

"I think," Redfern said evenly, "the time for talking is over, Blade."

"Just let me try. Just this one last time. It's important to me."

Redfern thought about this, nodded and stood aside, gun held at the ready. Macken went to the door.

"Carol?"

No reply. He put an ear against one of the panels. He thought he heard somebody moving around.

"Carol, it's Blade. This is senseless. There's no way out. Look, I can help you. I really can."

He put his ear to the panel again. More muffled sounds came from within.

Then he stiffened and caught his breath. Because of his position—ear against the door, eyes cast downward—Blade was able to see something the Americans could not. There was a contoured molding that ran along the walls about three feet above the floor. Dry rot had set in at a point close by the door and part of the top had crumbled away. Through the break, lighted by the weak bulb in the ceiling, something was reflecting light.

A semitransparent strand.

Blade ducked down and looked beneath the upper rim of the molding.

"Redfern!" he hissed urgently. "Get out. Get out *now!*"

"What?"

"Don't argue, Redfern. Get your men out of here right this minute."

Blade ran a finger along the telltale wire. It felt like a silk thread.

"She's got the whole fucking shebang booby-trapped. It could go any second."

Redfern squatted beside Macken. He needed little convincing. The Iraqis had used it, too—or something so much like it as to make little difference. He holstered his gun, turned, and bawled.

"Everybody! Leave! Right now. We're abandoning the building. Let's *go* now. Everybody out!"

There was the rattle of a bolt being drawn aside. The door opened.

Carol Merrigan's face possessed the serenity of an angel's. The lines were softer, as though she was at peace with herself. The plaid shawl was gone, as was the grubby, floral-patterned dress. Now the woman was clad in a white nightgown that reached to her ankles. Its silky material shimmered when she walked. Blade thought suddenly of a Pre-Raphaelite oil painting that hung in his mother's living room.

The smooth sheer line of the nightgown was interrupted by a bulge at the left shoulder and Blade saw a small red stain there, one that grew with each second. Yet if Carol was in pain she didn't show it; she carried a lighted candle in her left hand. The other was raised to eye level, and made a sign recognizable to Christians for more than a millennium: two fingers rested on the palm; two were held aloft; the thumb was splayed. The sign of benediction.

But the two raised fingers had been taped together. Where they joined, Blade saw an electrode. A strip of tape secured another to Carol's thumb. Twin strands of wire ran behind her hand and trailed behind her as she advanced.

"Christ," someone whispered.

"Go!" Redfern said again. This time his voice was hoarse.

Macken had seldom seen men of their bulk move so quickly. It certainly sharpens the senses, he decided: The prospect of impending death sharpens the senses like nothing else imaginable.

The stairs had been hard to take coming up, Blade thought; but, by Jesus, they were no trouble at all on the return journey. Sixteen burly CIA operatives fairly flew down them. Blade heard the sharp report of timber cracking. He followed, heart pounding, the pain in his chest forgotten. He took the stairs two at a time.

That was a mistake.

His right foot came down heavily on a step near the top. What had cracked under the weight of one of Redfern's men now gave way. Macken's foot drove down through the rotten timber. He cried out as he was thrown sideways against the banister. Something in his right calf tore.

Blade lay sprawled awkwardly on the stairs. His leg was imprisoned to above the knee. He leaned his weight against a step and pulled. The pain was excruciating. He beat the timber with his fist. It wouldn't budge.

Carol Merrigan now stood close to the edge of the landing. The candlelight flickered over her face. She was smiling, a travesty of the sweet child he'd once known.

"It's time, Blade," she said. "Mammy and Daddy are waiting for us."

"No, Carol, don't."

"But I must, Blade. Don't you see? It's what my mammy wanted. It's the power that I got from my mammy. 'You'll only have to click your fingers, Angel,' she used to say, 'and you'll have any man you want.' She was a lovely woman, Blade. She told me I looked just like her when she was a girl."

Macken struggled with the step, pushing, pulling. He heard

a nail starting to come loose with a groan. Somebody was coming back up the stairs. Quietly.

"You do," he said. "You're beautiful, Carol. Really."

"Then you want me, Blade? I know I want you. I told you that already. Now I have you all to myself."

Blade's gaze was fastened to her upraised hand. The deadly electrodes sparkled in the light of the candle. He tugged again furiously and frantically and heard another nail wrench itself loose. He had his knee free. There was no feeling in his calf.

"It doesn't have to be like this, Carol," he gasped. "We can work something out. There's always hope." His calf was halfway out.

"Yes, Blade," she said slowly. "There's hope for us. But not here. Angels have the power of life and death, you know. All an angel has to do is click her fingers. Watch."

"No!"

Strong hands gripped Blade's arms. Pain shot through his leg as he was yanked free. Then he was tumbling head over heels down the stairs, falling over another body. They came to rest in a tangle of limbs on the lower landing. Redfern. They were on their feet faster than the speed of conscious thought, half-running, half-falling down the last flight of stairs.

Daylight.

Then the third floor of the building detached itself from the rest with a roar.

She'd rigged it, Blade discovered later, so that a series of minor charges, strung together and snaking around all four walls of the third story, would detonate simultaneously. Captain Tom Fitzpatrick said—later still, when inspecting the rubble—that he'd seldom seen such expert workmanship.

The masonry, windows, and timber surrounds blown horizontally outward. The debris arced above the heads of Blade and the agency men, coming to earth harmlessly on the other side of the street in the space between the warehouses. The fourth story descended upon the second—and settled there, as though they'd always belonged together. It was like the collapsing of a giant soufflé.

"Jesus H. Christ!"

It was Redfern. His dark suit was powdered with masonry dust. He looked up at the transmogrified building with something resembling awe.

"She didn't miss a goddamn trick. That's the damnedest thing I ever saw."

He turned to his men. "Everybody all right?"

There were mutterings of affirmation, accompanied by curses; heads were shaken in disbelief.

"You okay, Blade?"

"I think so." He could walk—after a fashion. "Thanks again, Redfern. That's two I owe you."

Blade dusted himself off, got out his telephone. He asked to be put through to his assistant.

"Sweetman? You can come on in now. It's over."

"We heard an explosion. Where *are* you?"

He told her.

"And Angel?"

"Hoist with her own petard. Literally."

"*What?*"

"She blew herself up, the poor, twisted bitch."

"My God. We're on our way. Duffy's here, too."

Blade broke the connection, was just about to put the phone away when his glance fell on something on the sidewalk, something that Carol Merrigan had let fall when Mr. Coburn's bullet had smacked into her shoulder. He limped over, bent down, and picked it up.

The doll, no longer wrapped in the discarded plaid shawl, was crudely made by modern standards and had a distinct Southeast Asian slant to the eyes. It was about the size of a six-week-old infant. Blade turned it upside down and, as he did so, a metallic sound came from a hidden speaker. It was a grotesque parody of a baby's voice.

"Mommy!" cried the doll. "Daddy!"

How fucking touching, thought Blade in disgust, remembering Angel's young victims of eleven days before.

276

But there was more. There was a hinged plate in the doll's abdomen; Blade flipped it open. He caught his breath and heard Redfern whistle at the same time.

The doll's body was hollow and contained a phalanx of state-of-the-art electronic equipment, all beautifully designed so as to fit perfectly into the diminutive, rubber torso. Among the items of cutting-edge technology, Macken identified a telephone, an infrared scanner, and a microwave radio transmitter. This last had a button that was ominously labeled ARM.

The breeze was increasing. On its rise and fall, Blade heard the first blaring of car horns from the direction of Parnell Square. The presidential motorcade was making its slow and stately journey through the center of Dublin.

"Your president doesn't know how lucky he is," Macken said. "I think she might have triggered a third bomb just for the sheer bloody hell of it. You were close to her—as close as I was. You saw her, Redfern, heard her. Her fucking mind was completely gone. She was capable of anything."

Redfern looked up as a police helicopter soared over the Liffey, heading their way; sirens wailed in the distance, drawing closer. From a point due north came another chopper and they watched as it grew in size. It was bigger than the police helicopter and painted a dull, olive green; it bore no official markings.

"You're wrong about one thing, Blade," Redfern said. "The president *does* know how lucky he is. Not that luck was ever part of the equation."

The unmarked chopper passed almost directly overhead. Redfern saluted it.

Blade's jaw dropped. "Was that the president?"

"That was the president. God bless him."

"You secretive cunt!"

"Thanks." Redfern was grinning.

The klaxons grew louder. A pipe band struck up—somewhat incongruously, Blade thought—"Scotland the Brave."

The garda helicopter landed a few feet from them, swirling up a cloud of masonry and mortar dust.

Duffy and Sweetman emerged from it, looked about them in bemusement.

Blade jerked a thumb in the direction of O'Connell Street. "Then who in the name of Christ is—"

"An actor, Blade," Redfern said. "A ringer. Oh, he's good; we've used him plenty of times. Everybody does it: the Russians, the French, the Iraqis; it's regular practice. Okay, when you get up *real* close, you see he's not the president, but from a couple of yards away, he's perfect. And that's all we needed for the drive to Leinster House. The crowd won't see through it, nor will the news cameras."

"Christ, just like in *The Eagle Has Landed.*"

"Beg pardon?"

"No, no. Nothing. Just thinking out loud. So the president went along with it. I thought he'd more guts."

"Oh, come *on,* Blade. Put yourself in his position. If you'd heard about the bomb and you knew that the bomber was still out there, with more bombs, would *you* put your neck on the line? He's not a fool."

"No, I suppose I wouldn't."

A phone rang. It was Redfern's. The words he spoke into it were calm and reassuring, each sentence punctuated with at least one "sir."

"That was Bill Seaborg," he told Blade. "Wondering what the hell's going on. He heard about the blast."

Redfern returned the phone to his pocket. "He's the real hero, Blade. He's riding in the president's limo. He knew the risks. Knew 'em better than anybody else. He's one helluva guy."

A fresh thought occurred to Macken.

"But what about the bombs that are still down there? What'll happen to them now?"

"Frankly, Blade, I'd say there's a chance in a million that one of them could explode accidentally. If she used the same explosive, then it's safe to say it won't blow up by itself. But the world is growing more complex and there's so much going on in the ether that it's possible—I'm not saying it's likely, I'm saying it's possible—that some time in the future some kid will be fooling around with his birthday gift—and boom!"

"You mean another radio transmitter could set them off?"

"It doesn't have to be a transmitter. It could be anything—any electronic gizmo, maybe something we haven't got right now but will be invented in a couple of years' time. Look how Angel managed to scan your cellular phone signal and emulate it. Like I say, the air around us is full of all kinds of signals, and it's becoming more crowded out there. All it needs is somebody to send out the right signal: The one that can trigger one of the bombs."

"Jesus."

"However, it's my guess it'll never happen. You see, those buried detonators require power. Not much, just enough to keep them ticking over, and that power has to be supplied by a battery. Fact is, batteries have a limited life span, so even on standby the bombs will drain that power—given time."

"So how long have we got?"

Redfern shrugged. "Who knows? Two, three years more? Five or six? It's impossible to say. And don't forget there's corrosion, too. It's *wet* under the street. Could be the batteries are already dead. Or that the gelignite has 'sweated' and is useless by this time."

Blade fingered the transmitter in the doll's belly. He pulled out the antenna and flipped the toggle switch. Below the little label that read ARM, an LED began blinking rapidly. His finger hovered above the SEND button.

Some distance away across the river the pipe band was playing "Hail to the Chief," and it was plain that they hadn't put in too much practice on it; a growing cacophony of car horns marked the steady progress of the motorcade.

Christ almighty and his blessed mother tonight, Blade thought: It was too, too bloody easy altogether.

He flipped the toggle and retracted the antenna, wrapped the doll again in Angel's plaid shawl.

The clock in O'Connell Bridge registered 47,147,658 seconds before the start of the new millennium.

Elsewhere in this ancient city, founded more than a thousand years before by Viking invaders, *other* sunken devices were quietly registering the slow passage of time.

And waiting.

"Come on, Redfern," Blade said. "I'll buy you a pint."